A NEW HAPPY PLACE

RUTH HANNA

Print ISBN 978-1-913419-67-7

For Matthew, Noah and Seth - My happy place xx

1

Happy place! It's such a warm and comforting notion, isn't it? Everyone's happy place is different, unique to themselves. For some it's being home with family, the curtains closed and a roaring fire, the front door locked for the night, shutting away the rest of the world. For some it's sat on a beach in the sun looking out at a deep blue sparkling ocean, the smell of salt in the air. Others love being sat around a dining-room table surrounded by good friends playing games, drinking and laughing.

A happy place for some could even be work, feeling fulfilled in the day's accomplishments. It could be in the pages of a good book or out experiencing something new. While some people seek the simplicity in life, others look for the more elaborate. A happy place can even change depending on what stage of life you're at. One moment it's wild nights out dancing with friends, stumbling home at three in the morning and before you know it your happy place turns into quiet nights in, curled up watching your children playing together, glass of wine in hand and bed by ten. The majority of happy places do, however, have one thing in common and it's usually a particular feeling. That warm, fuzzy feeling of contentment and satisfaction. The place where your heart is joyful and... happy. But what happens when you lose your happy place? What do you do when you have to start all over again...?

2

2014

The weekend is finally here. I have been waiting and planning for this for what feels like months. The wine is open, my skin has been buffed and polished, and my Spanx are pulled up to my bra – I am officially hen-party ready.

'What time are we meeting everyone, Violet?' Hettie asks me excitedly as she sits on the edge of the bed while I finish her make-up. She's bouncing up and down with such enthusiasm that she might actually fall off the bed if she's not careful. That probably wouldn't be the best start to her hen night.

'Ten minutes in the lobby, let me just finish your make-up,' I answer as I apply a smooth layer of nude gloss to her lips. Hettie looks stunning; her fiery red hair has big bouncy curls through it and her smoky eye make-up looks impeccable even if I do say so myself. 'There, you look gorgeous, although the look isn't finished yet.' Safiyah catches my eye from across the room and gives me a wink. Hettie is possibly going to hate us for this and quite rightly too.

'What do you mean?' she asks me suspiciously.

'Well, no bride-to-be is complete without the compulsory

hen-do attire,' Safiyah teases as she stands next to me with the bag of tricks we've been hiding in the hotel room all day.

'Oh God, please tell me there isn't what I think there is in there,' Hettie says with a look of unease creeping across her face as she eyes the bag nervously. 'I said keep it classy, no hen-party crap.'

Classy is not the route Safiyah and I have gone down. Come on, in all honesty who really wants to have a classy hen do. These parties are the last hurrah of singledom and have hardly been made popular for being sophisticated refined affairs. Nine times out of ten it is alcohol-fuelled carnage with the bride-to-be hugging a toilet seat by about midnight! I really am trying not to laugh as I open the bag.

'Just go with it, Hettie. How often does a person get married, twice... three times maybe?'

'I only plan on doing this the once,' Hettie says with a gooey gushy smile. I can tell she is suddenly lost in all thoughts of her fiancé, Jack, which would be utterly sickening if I wasn't so damn happy for the two of them.

'More of a reason to go all out tonight then,' Safiyah says, pulling Hettie to her feet.

'So firstly, your sash, my lady,' I say regally as I place the gaudy gold bride-to-be sash over Hettie's sixties-inspired blue dress.

'Secondly, your very trashy, very plastic tiara,' Safiyah adds, fixing it to Hettie's head. When I bought it, it looked so tacky but somehow Hettie manages to make it look half decent.

'Ah, how classy,' Hettie says, laughing at herself in the mirror. I think she secretly likes all this crap even though she was so insistent when we were planning the night that she didn't want any of the normal hen regalia you so often see at these events.

'Next, what do we have here?' I say incredulously. 'Ah, of course, your willy straw necklace.'

'My *what?*'

'You heard me,' I cackle as I hang it around her neck. I really can't help laughing out loud this time. She's going to be sucking on a bright pink flashing penis all night – it's completely immature I know but bloody hilarious. Safiyah must agree because she's snorting with laughter next to me. We are bad friends!

'Oh, you look like an angel, if only your future mother-in-law could see you now.'

'She would be so happy her boy is marrying such an elegant lady,' Hettie says sarcastically. She must be very relieved that she hasn't invited her mother and mother-in-law to such a debauched night and instead opted to have a rather more serene afternoon tea with them next week.

'And last of all...' Safiyah says, grabbing the final item out of the bag, 'learner plates!'

'No, I draw the line there, I'm not going out with learner plates on me,' Hettie strictly informs us with her face scrunched up. What, so a flashing willy straw is fine, but learner plates is too far?

'Oh yes you are,' Safiyah hoots loudly, pinning them to the back of Hettie's dress. We are getting far too much delight out of this.

'I hate you,' Hettie says, trying not to smirk as she looks at us both.

'No you don't, you love us... and we love you,' I say back as the words catch in my throat. Christ, now I'm feeling all emotional, I knew this would happen. Quick, where is my glass of wine? I take a gulp and steady my emotions. I watch as Hettie straightens her tiara, she's such a good sport for wearing all this rubbish. I so want her to have a brilliant night. My best friend is getting married, Hettie and Jack have found their happy place in each other, and it warms my heart to see her so giddy with excitement for the night ahead... for her life ahead.

I pull myself together and top up our glasses with the last of the wine. I spill my next words out quickly before I become a blubbering mess. 'To the future Mrs Braithwaite. I'm so happy for you and Jack and I can't wait to see you walk down the aisle next month. I wish you a lifetime of happiness together. You are one of the kindest, funniest, sweetest people I know and you deserve all the love in the world. Jack's a lucky man. So, here's to a fabulous night out to see you off into married life in style... and get you blindingly drunk in the process.'

The three of us chink our glasses together and I blink back my tears. I'll have mascara running down my cheeks before we even get out of the hotel room at this rate. I'm a sucker for the mushy stuff.

'Right, come on, everyone will be there already and we can't keep that stripper waiting,' Safiyah says as she picks up her bag and opens the hotel room door. She looks effortlessly breathtaking as always. Her long black hair hangs down to her lower back and her bright blue eyes sparkle. There is something about Safiyah that is magnetic and alluring, men have literally fallen at her feet ever since we were at school together. I don't know how she does it.

'A stripper! You better be bloody joking,' Hettie warns.

'Yes, I'm joking,' Safiyah says as Hettie walks past her and out of the hotel room. I give myself one last look in the mirror and step into my black court shoes. I don't feel too shabby in my home-made little black dress, with lace detail across the bust and flared skirt. Every woman should own a little black dress!

'When are you going to tell her that you're not joking?' I whisper to Safiyah.

'Oh, she'll figure it out when a half-naked fireman asks if she wants to slide down his pole.'

Ooh, Hettie really is going to kill us. Leaving Safiyah in charge of the night's entertainment probably wasn't the best idea I've ever had. Safiyah notices the look on my face. 'What? She said she likes a man in uniform.'

Who doesn't!

We make our way to the lift to meet the rest of Hettie's friends. The lift door pings open into the large and very fancy lobby. A group of glammed-up girls with whistles and pink balloons suddenly cheer very enthusiastically as we come into view. It's going to be a very loud night.

3

I feel blissfully happy to be out with my girls. I haven't had a proper night out in ages, and I love Manchester. I fully intend to find a dance floor and pull out some serious moves – Manchester, here we come... Wait, my purse, did I put it in my bag? I'm sure I did... did I? Crap, I've doubted myself now so I'm going to have to check.

'Girls, I think I might have left my purse in the room, I'll catch up with you both in a second,' I say as I stop at a little table in the lobby. Bloody hell, why do I have so much stuff in this bag? How does it even all fit? Make-up, mints, hairbrush and... a purse, phew. I quickly stuff everything back in my bag and stupidly run across the lobby to catch up with everyone. I say stupidly because it's a very shiny, very slippery floor and I'm wearing heels – big mistake!

'FUUUCCCKKKKK,' I hear myself yell as I slide across the lobby as if I'm skating on ice. As I try to steady myself, I overcompensate and fall face first towards the floor at speed. I see it coming and there is nothing I can do to stop it. I brace myself and the sound of a thud ricochets through my ears as my head meets the floor. 'Ouch.'

. . .

Am I dead? Nope, I'm pretty sure if I was dead and in the afterlife, then I wouldn't be feeling this searing pain in my forehead. I don't move for a second, leaving my face pressed against the cold tiled floor. Did that really just happen? And why the hell can I feel a cold draft around the top of my legs? Ah, of course, that would be the cool air nipping around my arse as my dress has flipped up, leaving me with no decorum at all. I feel heat flush my entire body with humiliation as I realise I am at this moment flashing my underwear to the entire hotel. Probably not the best moment to be wearing massive knickers that have *SPANK ME* sprawled across the bottom, a hen-party joke literally coming back to bite me on my bum!

'Shit, shit, shit,' I say as I haul myself onto my back pulling my dress down to cover my modesty even though it is entirely too late for that now. The throbbing pain in my head and the sheer embarrassment of what has just happened ravages my face to the point where everything begins to go a bit fuzzy. Please God, I hope no one saw that.

'Wow, are you okay?' I hear a deep voice say. I feel someone kneel down next to me, touch my arm and gently pull me into a sitting position. I'm pretty sure the first rule when someone is injured is don't move them. What if my neck is broken? Clearly this person is not a medical professional but as I blink the fuzzy haze clears and a very handsome, very cute face slowly filters into view. Phwoar.

'Erm, yes I'm fine, just a little fall.' I casually try to brush off my near-death experience. Okay so near-death experience is a little dramatic, but it did flipping hurt, and typically the first person on the scene had to be this beautiful man with a dashing smile. His eyes are blue and remind me of a sparkling ocean from some distant paradise island and his short light-brown hair is slightly messy like he has just stepped out of bed; it makes him look cute and sexy.

'That looked painful,' the angel-like man says, concerned, as he helps me to my feet. I have never been so desperate to run away from someone in my life but running across this floor hasn't bode well for me so far and I'm pretty sure my head couldn't take another blow like that. I reach up and touch my forehead and I am not surprised to feel an egg-shaped lump forming.

'You have a bruise coming,' he says, delicately. 'You still look great though.' The comment takes me off guard for a second and I feel a little group of butterflies rumble around my stomach as my face flushes with heat again. Get a hold of yourself, Violet. He is just being nice, a pity compliment probably.

'Violet, are you okay?' Hettie and Safiyah have made their way over to me – not running, I might add, learning from my mistake.

'I'm fine, really I am.'

Please don't make a big deal out of this, it's embarrassing enough.

'You proper decked it,' Safiyah says bluntly as if I didn't know that already.

'Oh look, the taxis are here, let's go.' I pull the girls away towards the door. I need a gin and I need it now. I hope I don't have concussion because that will be a swift end to the alcoholic festivities we have planned. 'Erm, thank you,' I mumble behind me at the very cute stranger who is looking at me open-mouthed, no doubt wondering what train wreck has just stumbled into his path.

'That was quite possibly *the* most embarrassing thing that has ever happened to me.'

I can feel myself wincing as I replay the entire scenario in my head of what just happened. I can still hear the thud ringing in my ears from my head making contact with the floor. 'Did everyone see my knickers?'

'Yes. The knight in shining armour was cute though,' Safiyah teases, which I can't disagree with.

Blimey, I hope I don't see him again. 'Get me to the nearest bar, I need a drink.'

A few hours later we all make it back to our hotel after what has been a raucous night of tequila shots and wine. I feel a little tipsy... or, if I'm honest, very tipsy indeed.

'I have had such a good night,' Hettie declares as she falls into a huge armchair in the hotel bar, which I'm so utterly pleased about. She looked like she was having the time of her life all night, even when the fireman stripper turned up and started grinding up against her, she willingly helped oil up his chest with baby lotion – it was hilarious.

'Me too,' I say with all thoughts of the disastrous start to the evening long forgotten. 'Safiyah, why are you swaying?'

'I'm not, you are. Hey, is that the bloke who rescued you from the floor earlier?' Safiyah slurs, nodding to the other side of the room, leaning on the bar for support.

'It is.' I think all the alcohol that's been consumed has numbed my embarrassment because I have the urge to go over and talk to him.

'I'm going to take Hettie up to the room,' Safiyah informs me. 'Why?'

'Because she's asleep.' I look over to the armchair to see Hettie snoring with her crown slumped down over her face. God, I love that girl.

'She looks like she's had a good night. Do you want some help?'

'Nah I got this, the rest of the girls are getting another round in, I can't take any more booze tonight. Come on, future Mrs Braithwaite, time for bed,' Safiyah coos, lifting Hettie out of the chair.

'Is it bedtime already?' Hettie hiccups. 'Thanks for a great night, girls!' she shouts as Safiyah guides her to the lift. I go over and join the rest of the girls at the bar. I think I can handle just one more drink, it's a party after all. The man who rescued me earlier is stood chatting to his friends and I can't help but look at him. Perhaps I should go over and thank him, he had been kind and all I did was get away from him as quickly as possible. Yes, great idea, I will go over and talk to the delicious man. I down the drink I've just ordered for Dutch courage (which I'm already full of so why I need another is beyond me) and stalk over to him in what I think is a sexy manner but is probably more realistically reminiscent of Bambi on ice as I realise that I am perhaps more pissed than I thought. Definitely did not need that last drink – *please don't vomit on the nice man, Violet.*

'My knight in shining armour!' I cheer as I stop in front of him, wobbling ever so slightly from the wine. Oops, that came out louder than I thought it would.

'Hey there, how's the head?' he asks, placing a steadying hand on my waist which does the trick and actually stops me from falling. Yep, that last drink was a big mistake.

'Still on my shoulders,' I answer, shaking my head comedically. A snort slips out as I laugh at my own joke which I don't think I need to point out, is not funny at all. 'Oh no, I just snorted.' The shame! And now I have just drawn attention to the fact that I snorted. Going over and talking to him is mistake number two of the night. Why didn't I just go to the room with Hettie and Safiyah? I suddenly feel drunk and stupid and completely self-conscious. That's it, I'm becoming teetotal.

'So, did you find any volunteers?'

'Pardon?'

'To spank you?'

'What!' Outrage fills me. What kind of girl does he think I am? I know I'm drunk and I've come over to talk but that doesn't mean... oh wait, my comedy pants. I flashed them to everyone in the lobby before. 'Oh no, you saw them, didn't you? I'm so sorry about that.' Humiliation takes over once again and I feel hot and sweaty.

'Don't be,' he says, laughing cheekily. He has an ease about him and instantly my humiliation subsides and I start to see the funny side of it all. I mean, that's why I wore them in the first place... because I thought it would be funny. Not that I intended for anyone else to see them apart from Hettie and Safiyah. 'I would volunteer myself, but we don't really know each other that well.'

'We know each other well enough for you to have seen my underwear,' I say, hoping it doesn't sound too suggestive because I'm aiming for witty and cool.

He laughs and holds out his hand. 'I'm Philip.'

'Violet,' I say, shaking his hand, and as I look up into his sparkling paradise eyes, I see him looking into mine, his cheeky smile lighting up his face and making my insides go all mushy. It's like a fizz-bang moment. The second our hands touch, I feel this instant connection, one that I haven't felt before. I don't know him at all and yet I find myself wanting to know everything about him.

For the next two hours we sit chatting and laughing in the bar. It's only when the barman comes over to tell us they're shutting that I realise we are the only two people left in the room, everyone else has gone up to bed. I don't want the night to end though; Philip is so easy to talk to. He's funny and interesting which is actually quite refreshing considering some of the characters I have come across recently. I reluctantly get up and we start walking towards our rooms. I sense that Philip doesn't want the night to end either as he walks slowly, asking me more questions until we finally reach the room I'm sharing with the girls.

'It was lovely to meet you,' I say, suddenly feeling a little nervous. I'm obviously not going to invite him in, but I do want to see him again. Maybe I should ask for his number.

'You too. I would like to do it again if I can give you my number?' Yes, yes you most certainly can.

'Erm, yeah sure,' I say. Very good, Violet, play it cool. I hand him my phone and he types his number in.

'Give me a call sometime,' Philip says as that cheeky smile flashes across his face again, which makes my insides do a flip.

'I will,' I say as coolly as possible when in truth I want to do backflips down the corridor. We both go quiet and I wonder if he's going to kiss me. My stomach is twisting nervously with anticipation and I'm pretty sure I must be blushing hard.

'Goodnight, Violet,' Philip says huskily as he leans in and kisses me gently on the cheek. My body bursts with joy.

4

2019

Well that all escalated bloody fast, this was not how I envisaged my day ending. This morning I was blissfully happy, planning a romantic weekend away with Philip, and now here I am sat crying in my car on the side of the road all alone. As days go, this has been a pretty shitty one. I'm back in Elmsbourne-Hollow. Back in the little village I grew up in. Back in my old life – bugger.

The rear seat of my car is filled with pretty much everything I own, which, now I come to think about it, isn't a lot for a thirty-year-old woman. Just a suitcase full of clothes, a sewing machine and bags of material which in itself is an utterly depressing thought. Is that all I have to show for my life? I look up at the *Welcome to Elmsbourne-Hollow* sign on the edge of the village that I've pulled over next to while I collect my thoughts, and the overwhelming desperation to go back to London and pretend this day never happened feels like it's consuming me from the inside. I feel broken and... sad. That seems like such a small word after the day I've had but that's just how I feel, so very sad... and pissed off.

How the hell am I back here again? How has it all gone so wrong, so flipping fast? Five years ago, I left this little town nestled in the heart of the Lancashire countryside to follow the love of my life down to London, to set up home and live happily ever after – I thought that was it, marriage, kids, the whole shebang. Five years on, the fairy tale is over, my happy place is no more. All that time invested in a life that has somehow crumbled beneath me in less than a day. The man of my dreams, whom I love, apparently no longer loves me back and now I'm heading back home broken-hearted, jobless and wondering where the hell it all went wrong.

Shit, Safiyah was right, I should never have gone in the first place. What will she say when she knows I'm back? Hettie too. Oh Christ, I will have to tell everyone. Bloody Philip Miller, I hate him so much right now. And love him. It's true, there really is a fine line between love and hate. How could he have done all this to me? How did I not see it? The whole car journey from London to Lancashire has been a roller coaster of emotions, toing and froing between hysterical crying whilst listening to Celine Dion's 'All by Myself', to singing Destiny's Child's 'Survivor' at the top of my lungs, thinking of all the ways in which I can inflict pain on the bastard of a man who in one day has completely ruined my life.

'Come on, time to face the music,' I whisper to myself as I wipe yet more tears away. You're a strong, independent woman, so what if you're moving home to live with your parents at thirty. Lots of people my age still live at home. Don't they? Oh God! What is it Mum always says? Ah yes, head up, chest out and walk proud. As those words swirl through my mind, a little light breaks through the darkness that has filled me since the events of the day unfolded. I am genuinely excited to see Mum and

Dad, it feels like forever since I have seen them and all I want is a cuddle from my mum.

Thirty years old and I'm still running home to my parents – wow, I really am a complete failure.

I look in the rear-view mirror to check my reflection to make sure I don't look too red and puffy after all the crying – yikes, I look terrible. I wipe the remains of what is left of my mascara from under my eyes and give my hair a quick brush. If I'm having to move back home feeling like a train wreck, I will at least endeavour to not look like one.

I drive into the quaint little village of Elmsbourne-Hollow. It's one of those villages full of community spirit with summer fetes and Christmas fayres, little sewing bees and book clubs and where everyone knows everyone and nothing remains private. There are no secrets in Elmsbourne-Hollow.

I pull up outside Willow Cottage and see the kitchen light is on. It's nine thirty at night and, in late June, only just getting dark. As I get out of the car, I stare up at the white cottage with its thatched roof and sash windows. A bright red front door is placed in the very centre of the house under a little timber porch. A lavender wreath hung proudly on the door, it's idyllic, the cottage could have stepped out of the pages of a fairy tale. The warm breeze sweeps lazily through my hair and with it the nostalgic smell of fresh country air. I really am here!

This little village was my happy place for my entire childhood and now it feels so alien. My heart gives a desperate thud as I open the white gate and step onto the cobbled path that leads right up to the front door that's framed perfectly with beautiful lilac roses. The fragrance of the garden hits me immediately and instantly feels welcoming, the mixed aromas of lavender, gardenias and sweet peas have always reminded me of home. I walk up the stone garden path and the front door is flung open to reveal the effervescent Lilly Brown standing in the doorway, her arms wide open waiting for me to fall into them.

'Hello, Mother.' My voice sounds so despondent and lost, and I fall into Lilly's waiting arms, taking in the familiar strong scent of perfume. If I could cry out *Mummy* I would but I'm a grown-up and that would be absurd. Lilly's embrace is strong and comforting, she squeezes me so tight and it feels good. I wish I was five years old again when her hugs would make everything better.

'Hello, my darling,' Lilly says as she finally releases me from her tight grip. She takes me by the shoulders and searches my eyes, checking if I'm still in there somewhere. I don't know if I am. 'Welcome home tea?' she says brightly. According to Lilly Brown, a cup of tea fixes everything. Break-up with your boyfriend... have a cup of tea. Get publicly humiliated and fired from your job... have a cup of tea.

I follow Lilly in through the hallway and straight into the kitchen. The traditional cottage kitchen hasn't changed since I was a little girl with its rustic wooden cupboards and large Belfast sink. The familiarity of it feels like a sanctuary away from the hideousness of the day. The delicate sweet smell of banana bread and cookies fills the air, Lilly's been baking.

At the centre of the kitchen is a large solid oak table. This table has been in this kitchen for as long as I can remember and it's seen everything. Each scratch and dent is a memory, a tapestry of the Brown family. Lilly taught me how to use a sewing machine at this very table which is where my love for sewing and making clothes began. It's the centre of the house where everyone seems to congregate, usually over a glass of Lilly's very potent home-made wine or Safiyah's family gin. Lots of gin, to be honest (ooh, I could do with a gin right now). I've cried over more boys than I care to admit at this table and here it is again, waiting for me to pour my heart out once more. Anger suddenly floods me but rather than venting my anger, I break down in tears. Lilly pushes a plate of freshly baked cookies my way and gently strokes my hair.

'I can't believe it all, Mum,' I manage to say through my tears. This wasn't how my life was supposed to go. I was so sure I had found my happily ever after which now sounds so ridiculous and childish. I'm an adult, an actual proper adult who should be doing adult stuff like getting excited about new kitchen utensils or paying a stupid amount of money for fancy cheese (is that what adults do? I'll be buggered if I know) not living in some fairy-tale world of happily-ever-afters. It isn't even just Philip; I've lost my home, my job. A wave of fresh despair washes over me as I think of my beloved job at the wedding boutique that I've worked at for the last three years. What a fucking day! Hot shameful tears pour down my cheeks. I want to be standing on my own two feet not running home to my parents to hide from the world.

Lilly walks over to the dresser and lifts two teacups and saucers from a rather large mismatched collection. She makes a pot of tea and sits next to me at the big table. Lilly has what could be described as an eccentric style with her short grey hair, slightly plump frame and colourful wardrobe. She wears multicoloured cardigans and fabulously large and loud earrings with small purple-framed glasses. On anyone else the clashing colours would hurt your eyes, but not on Lilly. She's a vibrant woman with a vibrant personality to match and I feel an overwhelming surge of love for her. I have missed her so much recently.

'We were perfect for each other,' I say defiantly, still trying to get my head around what has happened.

'Were you?' Lilly asks delicately. What the hell is that supposed to mean? Of course we were. Well, until we weren't anymore.

'Yes! What do you mean by that?' I ask, scandalised that she could think otherwise.

'No, nothing, of course you were, dear,' she says quickly but I'm pretty sure she is just trying to appease me. I don't really care though, I'm too tired to question it and we're over it now anyway so evidently, she is right.

'Where's Dad?' I try to take a steadying deep breath. Must compose myself before Fred comes in, I can't let him see me like this. He was pretty vocal about my decision to leave in the first place and has never really liked Philip. In fact, recently he's often referred to him as the snobby prick with overly groomed hair. He's right, about his stupid hair too.

Lilly was a lot more understanding about me leaving, being quite the free spirit herself. Her mantra is *you only live once*. In fact, they were the exact words she used last year when she decided to do a sky dive for her sixty-fifth birthday. And the year before that when she and a couple of her Zumba group friends had somehow wormed their way into an all-night foam party. She raved the night away with a group of questionable students in Lancaster who were high on something I'm pretty sure wasn't legal.

'Just in the greenhouse, he'll be in in a minute.'

'Have you told him?' I ask quietly as I reach for a cookie. I'm not even hungry but I need to do something with my hands. I feel like such a crap daughter, I've let them both down.

'I have, you can't expect him not to work out something went wrong what with you coming home,' she says to me quite bluntly, and I groan. What must he think?

Lilly can sense my shame because she says, 'He's your father, he won't judge. He loves you and just wants you to be happy. He never wanted you living down there anyway, darling. Ever so worried you were going to get murdered in your sleep.'

'It was only London,' I say, rolling my eyes. I must have had this conversation with them a million times. 'Not a war zone.'

'Big city, darling. You know what he's like.'

I certainly do. My dad is the retired headmaster of a local grammar school, he meticulously plans everything and is such a worrier. Probably the result of being in charge of hundreds of children over the course of his working life and having their overbearing parents on his back constantly.

Everything he does is planned down to the minutest detail which is flipping irritating. He's the complete opposite to my mother who I genuinely think is as mad as a box of frogs. She was a hippy in her younger years and is now a retired art teacher. Lilly has pretty much floated through life with the main focus of having fun and experiencing everything. I do often wonder how my parents work so well together. They are the epitome of the phrase opposites attract but still so very madly in love, even after thirty-five years of marriage. They balance each other out perfectly, he is the yin to her yang. They have the exact relationship that I have always aspired to have, one I thought I had found.

At the back of the kitchen the door is open, letting the warm air circulate the room. I can hear the crackle of gravel as footsteps approach the door. I look up and see Fred with his rosy cheeks, silver hair and immaculate short grey beard appear at the door. He takes one look at me, his green eyes sparkling, and a smile spreads across his face. He has one of those warm uplifting smiles that illuminate his whole face and I can't help but smile back.

'Vi,' he cheers, 'welcome home.'

I get up and hug him and a lump forms in my throat as I realise just how much I have missed him too. I want to sob into his shoulder, but I hold it together. Was it really Christmas the last time I visited? I call every few days but that isn't really the same as actually seeing them.

'Good to see you, Dad.'

'So, it's over with the pompous prick then, is it?' he says, looking far too pleased as he sits down and grabs a cookie. Little harsh perhaps.

'Yes, it's over.' I sigh as the stabbing pain in my chest gives an extra vicious poke and I slump back down at the table.

'I'm sorry, love,' he replies, 'but I'm pleased you're home.'

As we sit around the table together, I wish I felt the same. I wish I was pleased to be back but I'm not. I'm happy to see Fred and Lilly, of course, but this isn't just a visit, is it? I won't be leaving in a few days to head back home to Philip and the bridal shop. I'm staying here, and why? Because I have sensationally failed at life.

'So then, Violet, what will you be doing now that you're home? What's the plan?' Fred asks.

Wow, really? Just straight in there, not even any small talk. Is it too much to ask to have a day to gather myself together or at least wallow before I set my life on a new path? I know Fred loves nothing more than a good plan, but I mean, come on. What's the point anyway? I had a plan in London. I would learn all I could from Anna Pemberton of Anna Pemberton House of Brides, get my bridal designs noticed, open my own boutique and marry Philip. Life, however, had other ideas and has flushed those plans unceremoniously down the toilet.

Philip is probably sat there all smug. He kept saying how plans for my own shop weren't particularly realistic. He liked to remind me that making dresses was very different to actually running a business (as if I didn't know that) and that I'm probably aiming a little too high. Perhaps he's right. Oh heck, my confidence really has been shaken, just another thing to thank sodding Philip Miller for. Now a new life plan is needed, but do I really have to figure all this out now? Can't I at least spend the weekend getting absurdly drunk and slag off the utter shit pig to my friends.

I suppose I could try to get a job at a bridal shop in Lancaster, although having been fired on the spot, I very much doubt I can ask Anna for a reference. I could carry on making the casual dresses for my online Etsy shop. The bridal boutique has always kept me so busy I could never take on too many orders, but I don't have that problem anymore. I have plenty of time on my hands now. I sit and think about Hettie and Safiyah who still live here in Elmsbourne-Hollow, both of them have their shit together. What the hell is wrong with me?

'No idea, Dad,' I finally reply, defeated. 'Work the streets perhaps until I find a new job.' God, I hope it doesn't come to that.

'Oh, darling, we're only a small village, you won't make much money around here – you need a big city for that sort of thing.' Lilly smirks as she finishes her cup of tea.

An hour later I find myself sat on the edge of the bed in the middle of my old bedroom, staring gloomily at the wooden floor. A pang in my stomach lies heavily, weighing me down as I realise that I have to accept that my old life is over, in the past, back in London. Philip gone, job gone... I'm going to have to find a new happy place... Shit.

5

SIXTEEN HOURS EARLIER

The sun is streaming through the chic white bedroom window shutters of the Notting Hill apartment I share with Philip and it looks like another glorious summer's day outside. I hit my alarm clock to off and reach over to the other side of the bed, only to be disappointed to find it cold and empty as Philip isn't here. I sit up, rub my eyes and pull my bed hair out of my face. I must look like I've been dragged through a hedge backwards. I have never understood how some people wake up looking like they have stepped out of a magazine cover. When I wake up, I resemble some sort of mad scarecrow with drool down my face and my hair pointing in all directions – Worzel Gummidge comes to mind. I read the note Philip has left on his pillow.

Gone to the office early – Love you x

I sigh and look back at the empty spot where Philip should be sleeping; this has become a regular occurrence recently. Philip works for a big corporate London law firm and he's up for a huge promotion, so he's really been putting the hours in over the last few months. I shouldn't complain though when I know he's working so hard for us.

Our home is a traditional Victorian town house that has been made into beautiful apartments. Philip bought it a year ago for us and has insisted on paying for it himself. It's an expensive part of London, very expensive in fact, but Philip's on a good wage at the law firm and inherited a ridiculously large sum of money when his grandfather passed away. I felt really uncomfortable about him paying for it, but he was pretty adamant. He said it's an investment in our future.

Don't get me wrong, I like the apartment and I feel incredibly lucky that Philip has bought it for us, but if I'm honest it doesn't really feel like home. It has beautiful traditional features, a fireplace in each room and a stunning stained-glass window above the front door – but with the high ceilings, all these neutral colours and Philip's sudden minimalist taste, it does sometimes feel empty and soulless. There's no personality. I've tried to include my handmade pillows and blankets to ease colour and comfort into each room, but Philip isn't keen. Apparently homely and comfortable isn't what we're trying to achieve, modern and bare is. I don't particularly feel I can push the subject, seeing as technically it is his apartment, but nevertheless, home is where the heart is, right?

And my heart certainly is here with Philip. He had been happy for me to adorn our old apartment that we rented before this with all my crafty makes and vintage finds from markets and charity shops, but when we moved here, Philip made a comment about wanting it to look a little classier. More modern in case people from work ever visit. Apparently patchwork throws don't fit the bill. I'm sorry but if handmade appliqué bird pillows are wrong, then I don't want to be right. His tastes have really changed over the last couple of years. I wanted to go halves on a much smaller apartment in a cheaper area so we could create a home together, but he insisted, so... Still, this is very much a happy place for me, a home with the man I love. I'll grow to love it... I hope.

I climb out of bed, shower and slip into my favourite home-made green wrap-around dress that compliments my curvy figure and makes the deep green of my eyes really pop. I hope it does anyway. It's a go-to outfit when I need to feel good, and today I'm in need of it as I'm a bit out of sorts. Philip's affections towards me have been dwindling lately. I'm sure it's nothing but then there was the little snide comment he made two days ago.

I had been down to the lovely little bakery at the end of our road and bought myself a piece of carrot cake. This cake is orgasmic! Perfectly spiced and fluffy, teamed flawlessly with a smooth, cool cream cheese frosting. Quite frankly, I have no idea how anyone could resist such a delight. I offered to share half with Philip, secretly hoping he would say no, but his answer was rude and damn right nasty.

'Just because it's got carrot in it doesn't mean it's healthy, you know. You might want to watch the waistline.'

I was fuming and hurt. Who the hell does he think he is? Just because he has turned into a gym-obsessed, carb-fearing maniac over the last year doesn't mean I have to, and was he trying to say I'm fat? I didn't speak to him for the rest of the day. That night he was extremely apologetic. He said he hadn't meant it the way it came out and of course he didn't think I was fat, he was just tired and moody and it all came out wrong. I put him being a total idiot down to tiredness and stress from the pressure of the upcoming promotion and after some well-deserved silent treatment, forgave him. I was tired too, I didn't want to argue.

Still, the thought has niggled at me, what with that and the lack of affection I'm starting to feel concerned that I'm not as attractive to him as I used to be. I've never been fat but, from fifteen, have been pretty well-endowed in the breast department, which at that age can make you very self-conscious. I also have what my mother calls child-bearing hips. Philip used to be so complimentary about the way I looked, he would call me sexy, his own Jessica Rabbit.

When we first met five years ago, we were all over each other, we didn't even need a bedroom for things to get frisky. The relationship moved quickly and within six months he asked me to move to London. Philip was fun, loving and carefree, we travelled and had so many adventures together, constantly laughing; we were happy. But over the last eighteen months there has been a change. He works more and more and is always on the phone when he's home. It's like there's a sudden invisible pressure on him, he's so distant. On the very rare occasion when we go to social events through his work, he and his work buddies are so arrogant, constantly trying to impress and outdo each other. Honestly, I almost suggested that they all just get a ruler out and measure their bits there and then the last time we went out with them, perhaps it would have put a stop to the alpha mentality they were all displaying. It's a side to Philip I don't really like.

He's joined a gym and has become obsessed with his body and how he looks. His once thick, slightly scruffy hair which I loved, and made him look cute and sexy, is now immaculately combed and gelled into place. He could walk through a tornado and there wouldn't be a misplaced hair. He's very different nowadays. I am trying to be understanding, I know how desperate he is for this promotion and the stress it's causing. We just need to work together to get through it, soon enough it will be over with and things will calm down. He will go back to being the fun-loving Philip that I love oh so much. We can get engaged and get married – he always says that is where we are heading. Life will be perfect! Right?

.   .   .

I look at Philip's handwritten note again and feel a bubble of something in the pit of my stomach that I can't put my finger on, unease perhaps or worry. I check the time and down my coffee. I'd better get a move on if I want to be early for work. Francesca has been especially moody recently, so I want to get in early to make sure that she has no ammunition to throw at me. I work for the Anna Pemberton House of Brides boutique. It's situated in Notting Hill and helps the rich and sometimes famous pick out bridal gowns and occasion wear. I love my job, being in the boutique is another happy place for me.

I'm a trained seamstress and not only help customers pick their perfect gowns but also do any alterations and embellishments that are needed. I've always loved designing and making clothes, I definitely inherited Lilly's creative flair. It fascinates me how just a roll of fabric can be transformed into something that has the ability to completely change someone's mood. I'm a firm believer in you are what you wear. I don't mean designer labels or price, in fact I couldn't really give a toss about designer clothes, it's about how they make you feel. A power suit can give the impression of confidence and control, you could walk into an interview or meeting and command the room. On days when you're feeling bloated and down, a big cuddly jumper and a pair of jogging bottoms can make you feel all snuggly, swaddling you in a warm hug. A pair of jeans that make your legs look great gives you an extra spring in your step, a certain style of dress that hides areas you don't like while accentuating areas that you do makes all the difference to your confidence.

The one thing that I always notice is that if you are confident in what you're wearing you emanate that; it glows out of you. No not everything suits all shapes and I'm careful to help people with that but what I always want to get across to my customers and friends is that no matter what shape or size you are, if you love something, wear it. If it feels good, wear it, because the majority of the time if you're confident in an outfit, it will suit you one hundred per cent more.

I see it all the time in the bridal shop. Customers come in shy and nervous about finding the perfect dress and then they put something on that makes them feel unbelievably special, suddenly they stand a little taller, head higher. It's cheesy, I know, but I love helping people see the beauty in themselves. It makes me all warm and gooey inside knowing I've helped someone.

Lilly first taught me to use a sewing machine when I was eight. I would make dresses for my dolls and my love for sewing was sealed. I was so self-conscious as a girl, I hit puberty early and my body changed quicker than my friends. I was slim but had big boobs and hips and it made me feel different. I would hide behind baggy jumpers until one day Lilly sat me down and told me that it was okay to be different, that I should celebrate my shape. So, I have always tried to do that and to get others to do the same.

As well as working for Anna Pemberton, I have my own little Etsy shop online. I sell seasonal casual dresses and I'm saving hard so that one day I can have my own bridal shop where I can design and make my own gowns. Be my own boss. Anna has actually shown an interest in some of my bridal designs recently, which I'm thrilled about. To think *my* designs could one day be housed by Anna Pemberton is just mind-blowing. I love her, she's a remarkable woman that has worked hard her whole life to get to where she is and has cultivated an impeccable reputation. She is a goddess!

I leave the house and walk the fifteen-minute journey to work. It's such a beautiful day; the sky is blue and the air warm even at quarter to eight in the morning. I call Philip's phone, I really missed him this morning and I still have that ball of unease in my stomach which I just can't explain. Perhaps talking to him will make me feel better but there's no answer. I hope he finds out soon about this promotion, I can't cope with any more mood swings. I'm sure he will get it. I could take him away for the weekend to celebrate, a spa weekend maybe. Relaxation to get us both back on track and out of this rut we seem to be in. I'll scout the internet for somewhere this evening. I might even treat myself to some sexy new undies that Philip can rip off me!

A tingle of excitement and downright lust ripples through my stomach at that thought and I feel a smile pull at the corners of my mouth. Our sex life has been non-existent of late and even when we do it's perfunctory, like we're just going through the motions. In the beginning of our relationship we couldn't keep our hands off each other, it was wild and passionate, we were at it like rabbits. I know that changes when you have been together a while, but I didn't think it would dissipate completely. The sex is... to put it bluntly, basic and boring. I'm pretty sure the last time we did it I was making a mental shopping list for the following day – not exactly fireworks. But not anymore, I'm going to make extra effort to spice things up. I don't mean any weird sex toys or swingers clubs, just putting more time and passion into things. Philip is going to get quite the treat. I do a little skip down the road; things are going to change for the better.

6

I arrive at work and switch on the lights. The shop instantly illuminates as the light bounces off the large crystal chandelier and rails of beautiful white and ivory gowns. Little rainbows of colour spring around the room as the light catches the jewellery displays and tiaras. The boutique is beautiful with crisp white walls and huge porcelain vases filled with fresh cream and pale pink roses everywhere. The room oozes class and smells glorious. The changing rooms are on one side of the large ground floor next to the stage area with a huge ornate silver mirror. Brides can walk out and admire themselves in front of it, while family and friends sit on a dusky pink chaise longue sipping champagne.

The other side of the shop showcases rails of beautiful gowns. The second floor keeps even more dresses and the third floor is occupied by the office and alterations room. I walk through the shop to the staffroom at the back, and my heart sinks as I notice Francesca's coat and bag on the table. Shit, she must be in early as well. We don't officially open for an hour, but I want to change a few of the dresses in the reception area to create a new display. I had hoped it would be finished before she arrived.

Francesca Delmont is the assistant manager, not a seamstress herself but she deals with all the office-based duties and enjoys bossing all her little minions around. I have no idea why, but I get the distinct impression that she despises me. It's a mutual feeling.

Francesca is beautiful, tall and slim with thick blonde hair always pulled up into a sleek bun. She has beautifully plumped bow-shaped lips, high cheekbones with bright blue eyes. When I first met her, I was in awe of her. She looked so stylish and sophisticated. She had this bright smile that was cheery and welcoming, and she seemed incredibly sweet and kind. I hoped we would become fast friends.

Oh, how wrong I got that first impression; her facade dropped pretty quickly and it didn't take long for her personality to shine through. Snobby and rude is an understatement. She has this air of self-importance about her and speaks to us all like we are dirt on the bottom of her shoe. I can never do anything right in her eyes, no matter how much effort I put in. What's even more annoying is that Philip can't see it; everyone else bloody does.

'She's not that bad,' he says when I come home complaining about her. He even had the audacity to suggest that perhaps I'm jealous of her which I absolutely am not. She may be beautiful, but I would much rather be a decent human being. Surely the boyfriend rules state that he should categorically be on my side anyway. He's only met Francesca a handful of times when he meets me from work to walk home together. It's been a long time since he's done that. Sodding men... sodding Francesca, for that matter. She makes my life hell at work and even manages to cause friction for me at home.

. . .

I look at the time and I'm relieved to see that Sarah and Imogen, the two other seamstresses, will be in soon so at least I won't have to be alone with Francesca for long. I hang my bag and coat up on the hooks in the staffroom, Francesca must be upstairs in the office. I go up to the first floor to retrieve the two dresses I've had my eye on for the display when I hear a bang from the office above me. God knows what she's doing up there. I suppose I should go and put my head around the door to check she's okay, make sure a cabinet hasn't fallen on her or something. No such luck though, I imagine. I reach the top of the stairs and go over to the office where the door is slightly ajar. I push it open further but I'm not prepared for the scene that I'm suddenly confronted with. In one single life changing moment, my world has come crashing down over me.

I stand there stunned; this surely can't be happening. The blood drains from my face and I'm sure I feel my heart miss a beat. I freeze, unable to avert my eyes from the horror in front of me. I want to look away, but I can't. I want to cry, no I want to scream but nothing is coming out, so I just stand there motionless and silent. My legs feel heavy, like they're not going to hold me up anymore and it takes everything I have to keep myself from falling as I cling desperately on to the door handle. There in front of me is Philip, his shirt and tie on the floor, Francesca sat on the desk with her red dress hitched up and legs flung around his waist. My Philip, with her! He looks to the door and sees me.

'Violet!' he puffs, pushing himself away from Francesca. He tries to step towards me, but his trousers are undone and drop to his ankles, and he trips and falls to the floor. My eyes settle on Francesca as she jumps from the table, pulling her dress down. She looks straight at me and I expect to see shame staring back but there isn't any. She isn't horrified at being caught. She actually looks smug.

'Violet, I-I didn't mean for you to find out this way,' Philip stutters, trying to get himself to his feet with his trousers still tangled around his ankles. His face is pallid.

I need to get out of here. The room is closing in around me and I can't breathe, I need air. Surely it's a nightmare and I'm going to wake up any second. I'm still not sure my legs will work but I try anyway. I turn from them both with tears stinging my eyes and run down the stairs. I fly across the shop to the door just as Imogen is walking in.

'Hey, Vi... Wow, are you okay? What's happened?' But I don't stop, I can hear footsteps running down the stairs with Philip shouting at me. He has managed to get his trousers up then! That's good of him. I push past Imogen and run into the street; I keep going as fast as I can. I'm not really sure how I'm managing it because my legs still feel so weak, but I keep going until I get to a little café a few roads away from the boutique. I'm out of breath and boiling hot from the bright sun beating down on me.

I check no one has followed and then duck inside the café. My heart is pounding so hard I can feel it vibrating around my head which is surprising since I'm pretty sure I actually felt it shatter into tiny pieces the second I saw Philip and that bitch together. What the hell am I going to do? How could he have cheated on me? And with Francesca... Francesca of all people. Suddenly the late nights and early mornings in the office make sense. The constant phone calls, it was to her. But what about going for the promotion, was that a lie? Just an excuse? No wonder the sex has disappeared from our love life, he's been getting it from her. How could I have been so stupid? It's so obvious now. Going to the gym, getting buff, that was all for Francesca too. I've been busy planning our future together and he's been shagging my boss. What am I going to do about work now? I can't go back there; I can't work with that woman ever again.

The table nearest to me is empty. I fall into the chair and put my head in my hands, the knot in my stomach twists so hard that I think I might be sick. Tears spill down my face and my body starts trembling from the shock. I now realise that the feeling I couldn't put my finger on this morning, well for the last few weeks actually, was my intuition screaming at me to notice what was happening around me. I knew something wasn't right. I knew, and I tried to ignore it, fearing what it might mean. I hate myself for not listening to my instincts.

'Are you okay, love?' A hand touches my shoulder and my head bolts up in panic. A concerned little old lady with grey curly hair is staring back at me. She's petite, extremely well dressed and has a green polka dot handbag perched on her arm.

'No, I'm not,' I say, the disbelief pouring out of my voice. 'I've just walked into work to find my half-naked boyfriend cheating on me with my bitch of a boss.'

'Oh crikey.' The lady lifts her hand to the waitress behind the counter. 'Pot of tea, please.' The lady looks back at me, her eyes full of warmth, which for some reason makes me want to cry even more. 'I expect we might need something a little stronger though. I'm Molly.'

I have no idea who this woman in front of me is, but I proceed to tell her all the sordid details of what has just happened. Molly listens intently and hands me tissues to dry my eyes.

'It sounds to me that you're much better off without this young man. He's a scoundrel and not worth your tears.' Molly looks at me and I can see the pity in her face for the broken girl in front of her. 'What will you do now?' she asks tentatively.

'I don't know, I haven't thought. Go back to my parents, I guess, while I try to figure something out.' I feel overwhelmed at the thought of having to explain this whole ordeal over and over again. I have plenty of friends I can stay with in London, but I only came here for Philip. It somehow doesn't feel right to stay without him. Plus, what if he and Francesca are an actual thing, I can't bear to see them about together.

Molly and I talk for quite a while. She reminds me a little bit of my grandmother and I end up telling her my life story. It isn't even that interesting. The poor woman only came in for a quiet cup of tea and has just put up with me bending her ear for I don't know how long. 'I should go, I need to pack my stuff up before Philip comes home, I can't look at him and hear his pitiful excuses.' I reach for my bag. I need to be out of the apartment as soon as possible. Shit, my bag. 'I left my bag at work; I ran out without thinking.'

Panic is rising in my chest, and I go a bit fuzzy. I'll have to go back; I'll have to face Francesca. 'The tea, I'm so sorry I don't have anything to pay for it.'

'Now don't you worry about that, love, I will sort it.'

'You have been so kind; how can I ever thank you?' I feel awful and embarrassed. Wonderful Molly has sat and listened as I've cried on her and now, I can't even offer to pay for her drink.

'Honestly, don't you worry. Just remember you have done nothing wrong. It's quite scandalous really isn't it, her doing that at work. She's the one who should be ashamed of herself,' says Molly sternly.

Somehow, I have a feeling Francesca will not be feeling that way at all.

7

I'm standing across the road from the bridal boutique; it's such a beautiful building. It's eighteenth century and has a dramatic romance to it that's perfect for an exclusive designer bridal shop. I always get a sense of excitement as I turn the corner and see its imposing structure at the end of the road... but not today. My heart is pounding. After leaving the café and thanking Molly, I trudged back up to the boutique to retrieve my bag but now I'm here I don't think I can do it.

Then Molly's words whiz around my head – she's right. I haven't done anything wrong; I can go in there with my head held high, it's Francesca who's up shit creek without a paddle. Why should I lose my job over this? She's the one who should leave. I'm pretty sure that shagging someone on the office desk is classed as gross misconduct in the workplace. I just need to explain to Anna what's happened. I will go in there, be grace and dignity personified and not allow that posh bitch to get the better of me. I lift my head up and puff my chest out, a sudden steely resolve is ranging in my stomach and I march across the road and into the shop.

'Violet, oh my God, are you okay?' Imogen asks as she strides to me and throws her arms around my shoulders. Two middle-aged, well-to-do women are sat on the chaise longue sipping champagne and chatting excitably.

'I'm fine.' My voice sounds strong and confident which is unexpected as my insides feel like they are twisting so much that I'm going to throw up. I scout the room looking for Francesca. Phew, she isn't here. I'm desperately trying to grip hold of the steely resolve I felt two minutes previously, but it quickly vanished the moment I stepped over the threshold. 'Where is she?'

'Upstairs in the office.'

'Do you know what happened?' I ask, the tremble in my voice usurping the confidence I'm trying to portray. *Don't cry, don't cry.* Just then Sarah emerges from the changing rooms with a beaming bride-to-be wearing a gorgeous simple ivory satin A-line gown with a sweetheart neckline. There are titters of approval from the two women who are waiting for her. Sarah spots me and Imogen and gives a little wave but looks utterly confused – I know the feeling!

'I can guess,' says Imogen. 'Philip ran down with no shirt on. He was about to run into the street after you but Francesca stopped him and said he couldn't go outside half dressed. They went back upstairs and I could hear them arguing. Sarah came in and I was telling her what I'd seen when Philip appeared again. He could barely look me in the eye. He mumbled an apology at us and left. Francesca hasn't been down since and we've had appointments all morning. Were they... together?' Imogen whispers dubiously.

With the two ladies distracted by the bride, Sarah hurries over to us without them noticing. 'What happened, what's going on?' she asks eagerly.

'They were having sex... I got in early and caught them at it upstairs.' Oh my God, this is a sodding nightmare. The twist in my stomach is getting worse and now I have a headache. I need to call Anna.

'What!' Imogen and Sarah shout in unison. The three customers jump at the sudden outburst and look over at us huddled together.

'Sorry about that, ladies.' Sarah flashes them a smile. 'So what are your thoughts on the dress? Stunning, isn't it?' She walks back over to coo over the bride.

'How has that even started?' Imogen whispers in disbelief as she ushers me further away from the customers.

'I don't know, I didn't think they really knew each other. Christ, Imogen, I have no idea how long it's been going on. Tell me the truth, did you know?' I scan her face for any trace of dishonesty. I loathe asking her because she's my friend but if Philip could fool me for so long then who else can. What if everyone knows?

'No, Violet. I'm stunned. You have to tell Anna, she'll be in soon, and you can stay at mine. We will sort all this out,' Imogen says with a reassuring smile and I'm so grateful, she's sweet and kind-hearted. We've been firm friends from the moment I first started here. Imogen's warmth and gentle personality put me at ease instantly on my first day at such a prestigious place. Her petite frame and long black hair reminded me so much of Safiyah, I'm sure that's why I gravitated towards her in the first place.

'Thank you,' I reply, forcing a smile. Something suddenly catches my eye and as I look towards the stairs, a hot flush ravishes my face, my stomach lurches as if the floor has fallen from beneath me. Francesca! She takes one look at me and halts. The air in the room suddenly fills with an icy tension and my body bubbles with a fury I've never felt before. Sarah has taken the bride back into the changing rooms to try on another dress, but the two older women remain shifting uncomfortably on the chaise longue, sensing the atmosphere.

'Oh, you're back. Well I didn't expect to see you again today,' Francesca says with ease, taking a few steps towards me. You wouldn't have guessed from her tone that she's been caught bonking my boyfriend upstairs. There isn't a hint of remorse, she's just looking me up and down with distaste. What did I ever do to her?

'How could you?' I ask, my hands trembling. *Keep calm, Violet, just keep calm.*

'Perhaps you two should take this into the staffroom, or upstairs,' Imogen pleads through the corner of her mouth as she looks at the customers. 'Another drink, ladies?' she says, feigning cheerfulness, trying to cover the animosity between myself and this... woman.

Francesca walks over to me, out of earshot of the others, a sly smile creeping across her face.

'Come on, Violet, did you really expect a man like Philip to end up with someone like you? He's gorgeous, successful, intelligent... wealthy,' she hisses. 'You were fun for a few years, but he was never going to settle down with you. He needs someone like me, sophisticated and a more intellectual match.'

I'm speechless. Is this actually happening? She's banged my boyfriend and is now calling me stupid. I've never liked Francesca but hadn't until today realised what a spiteful snake she actually is.

'A man of his eligibility doesn't want to be married to a frumpy shop girl who plays around with a sewing machine all the time with delusions of becoming a designer. So why don't you do us all a favour, don't make a fuss and just leave. There is nothing left for you here,' she scoffs.

Don't make a fuss! Don't make a fuss! Francesca has swooped in, stolen my man, and is now asking for me to walk away. What?

Am I supposed to leave quietly like some meek little shrinking violet doing as I'm told? I don't think so!

'Look, I did you a favour,' she continues in a sickeningly sweet voice as if she really does think she's doing me a favour. 'It's better you found out now than further down the line that he cheated on you. And boy did he cheat a lot.'

Realisation hits as I remember that Francesca had been milling around outside the staffroom yesterday when I told Imogen I would be coming in early.

'Wait, you knew I was going to be in early today, didn't you? You wanted me to find you like that?' I'm seething, a red mist has started to descend. Francesca doesn't answer but her arrogant smirk confirms what I already know. She wants it in the open, she wants to push me out and claim my man. I can't take any more as visions of what I witnessed earlier today cloud my thoughts and the words she has so spitefully hissed merge together.

'You bitch!' I scream and before I can stop myself, I've full-on slapped Francesca hard across the face. I'm not an aggressive person, I've never hit anyone before but I'm ashamed to say it feels good as the adrenalin pumps my body. The shop falls silent, Imogen and the two guests of the bride stop and stare open-mouthed. The blood is streaming through my veins, my heart is beating so loudly I'm sure everyone in the shop can hear it. Francesca stands there holding her face, she looks momentarily flummoxed but is quick to regain composure.

'Perhaps if you had shown that kind of passion with Philip he wouldn't have so easily jumped in my bed.'

I'm crushed, it's like another stab to the heart. Had Philip really been so easy to sway? Had he talked about me to Francesca? Have they laid in bed together, laughing at my expense?

'This is it, this is the dress.' The young bride walks out of the changing room in a lovely antique ivory trumpet gown with a lace bodice and a dropped-waist tulle skirt, tears of happiness streaming down her cheeks. Her smile falls when she notices all eyes are not on her. Francesca turns and walks towards the bride like nothing has happened. But something has happened; she has ruined my life and is so nonchalantly walking away like it all means nothing, like my relationship with Philip has been nothing but a passing fling for five years and she can so easily swipe it from beneath me.

And then before I know it, I'm running forward and ploughing myself into Francesca, rugby tackling her to the floor. I don't mean to but in the process, we have hit the poor unsuspecting bride in her beautiful gown. A loud rip ricochets around the shop as the bride crashes to the floor.

I'm on top of Francesca, my arms flailing around the air manically, because I want to hurt her. Hurt her like she has hurt me. I feel hands tugging at my arms, pulling me away from the fray. It's Sarah and Imogen trying to break us apart. The taller of the two guests drops her champagne on the floor with a smash and runs to her hysterically screaming daughter, lifting her from the ground in her ripped dress.

'Mummy, my dress,' the bride weeps.

'Violet, stop!' Imogen begs, as she continues to pull me away.

'What in God's name is going on here?' An angry voice booms across the shop and everybody freezes. Anna Pemberton is stood in the doorway, taking in the scene. Me being dragged off Francesca, a customer in a ripped dress, crying, and Francesca with a bloodied nose. Oh shit! Not quite the grace and dignity I had planned.

Fifteen minutes later the customers have left the shop, furiously vowing never to return. The spilt champagne and broken glass have been mopped up off the floor and I'm silently sat opposite Francesca in the staffroom. She's holding a tissue to her bloodied nose – oh if looks could kill. When Anna finally comes in followed by a bewildered Imogen and Sarah, the look on Anna's face kills me. I'm so disappointed in myself. How could I have let my anger take over in that way. I've never had a scrap in my life, I hate confrontation. I can't deny it felt good though. Oh no, I'm turning into one of those people you see on social media videos who shout and brawl in the street.

'Anna, I'm so sorry,' I say, tears filling my eyes. As much as I wanted to punish Francesca, I never meant to hurt Anna. Anna has always been so kind to me. She's a tall, slender woman but very imposing with a great mind for business. She always looks like she's just stepped off a film set in an oversized coat and sunglasses. Over the last fifteen years she has cultivated her small wedding dress shop into a powerhouse where so many leading designers are happy for her to showcase their designs. Having only worked in small bridal shops, Anna took a chance on me. She said she saw something promising. I imagine she is regretting that decision now. I know how much the shop means to her and the guilt rips through me. How could I have been so reckless?

'So, it was you who started it then?' Anna answers with a look of betrayal.

'It's not that simple, please let me explain,' I plead. 'I caught her this morning with Philip... together... on your desk.' Crap, that sounds so far-fetched, what if Anna doesn't believe me. Hell, I witnessed it and I'm still struggling to believe it.

'Erm... is that true?' Anna looks to Francesca aghast.

'No not at all, more like the other way around,' Francesca replies so brazenly. 'I got in early and when I went upstairs they were at it like animals. Violet left the shop looking very sheepish and when she returned, I told her that I would be informing you and that I imagine she won't have a job by the end of the day and well, you saw the rest. Look at my nose, it's bleeding, she's crazy.'

'No. No that's not true,' I say, shaking. 'Anna you have to believe me.'

'What do you make of this?' a baffled Anna asks Imogen.

'Yes, Imogen tell her what you saw,' Francesca says, eyeing Imogen, and I can see a hint of a smile curl at the corners of Francesca's lips. Oh, she's good, she knows Imogen hadn't seen the events that unfolded upstairs; Imogen can't confirm anything either way.

'I saw Violet running out of the shop and Philip running after her. Vi was crying and looked devastate–'

'Yes, devastated that I had caught her,' Francesca interrupts.

'What, no,' Imogen chimes back desperately and I'm grateful to her for trying but I can already see where this conversation is going.

'So, you didn't see who was caught doing what upstairs?' Anna asks, looking increasingly aggravated.

'Well no, but I believe that Violet is telling the truth.'

'She would say that, they're friends. I hardly even know Philip.' Crikey, Francesca is a good actress. Hand the woman an Oscar.

Anna looks at me, her eyes full of confusion and anger and I know what's coming. 'Violet, I can't prove either way what happened upstairs, I'm astounded to even be having this conversation quite frankly. But I know what I saw when I came in the shop, you hit another employee and that's a sackable offence and not only that but all of this in front of customers. Gossip like that spreads, which can ruin reputations. I have no choice.' Anna's eyes turn sad. 'I'm so disappointed in you, you had so much potential here but you're not the girl I thought you were.'

Boom, another knife is slammed into my chest. I adore Anna and not only have I upset her, but I've potentially dented the reputation of her beloved shop. A reputation that Anna has worked so hard to forge. Any chances of showcasing my own designs have been well and truly smashed to smithereens. How could I have let Francesca get in my head? I haven't just let her win, I've pushed her first over the finish line.

8

I leave the shop broken-hearted; I didn't think the day could get any worse after catching Philip, but it has. Imogen and Sarah try to console me but there isn't anything they can do. I'm single, jobless and will be homeless by the end of the day. There is nothing else to do but go back to Elmsbourne-Hollow. I check my mobile. I have three missed calls from Philip but no messages.

I get back to the apartment and close the front door behind me. I think I'm having an out of body experience, I can see myself just standing here, life crumbling around me with no control over it. The air seems thin and I'm struggling to catch my breath. I pace up and down because I'm furious. Furious at him for doing this to me and furious at myself for allowing Francesca to get under my skin. I need to call home but can't in this state. I go to the kitchen and pull a bottle of water from the fridge, sipping at it in between taking deep breaths. If I didn't have such a long drive in front of me, this would most definitely be vodka and not water. I manage to call Lilly and as calmly as I can I tell her what's happened but as soon as I hang up, I succumb to the sheer sadness that has surrounded me since this morning, and I sob into the sofa. My heart aches. I feel so worthless.

After what feels like hours have passed, I feel a heavy pang set up home in my stomach, weighing me down. I have a headache and my eyes are red raw from crying over that utter shit pig of a boyfriend... ex-boyfriend. I genuinely don't think it's possible for me to cry any more tears, there can't be any left. I resolve to pack my belongings which takes no time at all. Philip's bought everything for the apartment, there are a few items from our old home that I kept but the majority was donated to charity. I long to be back in our old home – we were happy there, weren't we? Well I was. We would spend evenings curled up under a blanket on the sofa watching box sets wrapped in each other's arms. Cooking together in our little kitchen, lazy Sunday mornings in bed. How has it all gone so wrong?

The wretchedness of the situation threatens to engulf me again, but I pull myself back from the brink. When I first caught Philip and Francesca this morning, I never wanted to see his lying, cheating face again. Was that really this morning? So much has happened it feels like days ago. Now I long to see him, I want answers. I want him to walk in through the door and tell me what an awful mistake he's made and that he loves me and only me. I want to curl up in his arms and pretend it never happened and wake up tomorrow from this awful nightmare. I'm angry because I still love him.

I put my bags down at the front door and walk back into the living room. I've never loved this apartment yet now I don't want to leave. It doesn't matter where we are; just being here with Philip was my happy place, sat at the table sewing while he was on the sofa chatting about his day.

What is suddenly very blindingly obvious as I look around is that even though I have packed my things away, the place still looks the same. I had no imprint in here whatsoever. There was no trace of me, of any part of me. He's been slowly pushing me out and I never even noticed. I feel ashamed and insignificant that I could mean so little to someone.

I hear the front door open and my heart jumps. Philip walks into the room wearing the suit that had been so casually flung on the floor back at the boutique and I feel the tug between love and hate. I'm not sure if I want to cuddle him or strangle him so I think it's best to keep my distance just in case. A murder charge would really top this bloody day off.

'I tried to call you,' he says nervously, putting his hands in his pockets and shuffling his feet. I don't answer, I just stand there looking at a man I don't know anymore. My Philip never would have taken someone's heart and used it as a piñata.

'I'm so sorry, Vi, I never meant for it to end this way.'

Hearing Philip use the word 'end' makes my insides writhe and squirm. Of course, I know it's over but hearing him say it makes the pain crash down all over again, another wave battering me. And how dare he say it, I should be the one who gets to say it's over, not him.

'How did you expect it to end?' I sound so calm. 'You cheated on me with my boss. Where I work.'

'It was so stupid of me, I don't know why I did that. Francesca said you wouldn't be in yet and I thought I would be gone before you got there.'

'That makes it all right then,' I shoot back sarcastically. Yep, definitely want to strangle him. We're both silent for a moment. He, unlike Francesca, at least has the decency to look ashamed of himself. I can't believe what I'm about to ask. 'Do you love her?'

I need to know. As much as I don't want to hear the answer, I need to hear the words to believe it all.

'Yes.'

Fuck, he loves her. He loves her and not me. I hear a sob and it sounds painful, did that come out of me?

'I was going to tell you, I just–'

'Never had the guts,' I interrupt, the anger seeping into my voice. 'What about going for the promotion, I assume that was a lie to create an excuse to keep seeing... HER.'

I can't bring myself to say Francesca's name out loud. What the hell does he see in such an awful human being? With anyone this would have been bad but with Francesca, it makes the injustice of it all even harder to swallow. The mere thought of her makes me want to pull the whole room apart. Philip turns his back to me and looks out of the window, he's such a coward.

'I, err, I got the promotion eight months ago.'

'Are you kidding me?' I whisper. 'Eight months? How could you not tell me that?' I've been so supportive. Justified everything, his behaviour, his treatment of me, thinking it was because he was working so hard. The pressure of his job, but he had the promotion this whole time. I feel so foolish.

The lies, all the deception, no wonder he hasn't invited me out with work friends for so long, he was afraid they would talk about work. All those times I thought he was in the office when really, he was with her. Francesca is right, I am stupid. Five years together, all gone in a puff of smoke. It's too much, I fall back on the sofa.

Philip's phone starts ringing, and I see him check the name. His face turns a rather unflattering shade of pink as he ends the call and stuffs his phone back in his pocket.

'It's her, isn't it?' I declare without even looking up. How dare she phone! 'Argh, I hate her... and I hate you,' I shriek, getting to my feet. 'You told me you wanted to marry me, have a family with me.'

'I know, and I did, but things change.'

'I loved you, I did everything for you, all to make you happy and you have screwed me over and broken my heart. What did I ever do to deserve this?'

'You didn't do anything, I'm sorry, it just fizzled out.'

Fizzled out! That's what the breakdown of our relationship comes back too... a fizzle out, like a crappy little firework where there's no bang. It just fizzes around and then... stops... how anti-climactic. He is an absolute shit pig!

'Fizzled out, that's all I get?' I ask, dumbfounded.

His phone rings again, and I feel like I'm about to explode. I want to smash his phone on the floor. He looks at it and then back to me.

'Don't you dare answer that in front of me.' My voice is low and menacing like a growl, it even frightens me. Bloody hell, perhaps I have some dormant anger issues. Philip puts his phone slowly on the table.

'How long has it been going on? Actually no, don't answer that.' I don't want to know. I don't need to know how long I've been duped by someone who I thought loved me. I just need to leave. I need to get away from him and from our boring cold apartment. I need to get away from London. I walk across the room to the door.

'Violet,' Philip calls, and he sounds fraught.

I turn round and look at him as I fight back the tears, refusing to let the last image of me to him be my tear-soaked face, instead it will be my utter disappointment in him.

I pick up my bags, place the key on the table at the front door and walk out.

Elmsbourne-Hollow is calling me home.

9

I'm sat outside in the garden, mindlessly stirring a bowl of fruit and yogurt for breakfast, I'm not really very hungry though. I look at my phone, there's still nothing.

'A watched pot never boils,' Lilly calls as she comes over with a fresh pot of tea and a jug of ice-cold orange juice. Lilly's wearing a bright pink scarf tied around her hair and has a large blue shirt covered in paint over her floral sundress. 'Or should I say a watched phone never rings.'

She sits down on the empty chair next to me and pours us both a cup of tea. She is eyeing me curiously. 'What is it you hope he says?'

'Who?' I reply, although I know full well who she means.

'The scoundrel, the scallywag,' Lilly says playfully. 'The little plonker who broke my baby's heart.'

The truth is I don't know. I don't want him back after what he's done but I miss him terribly. I want to hear his voice, but I know I wouldn't believe anything he says. I'm this weird paradox of wanting him but not, loving him but hating him. My mind is just a fuzzy mess.

'I actually don't know. I think I keep looking out of habit. I hate him, but I do miss him,' I finally say as I look out at the garden. It looks glorious. Fred has worked his little socks off. Luscious green grass surrounded by flower beds full of colour. At the end of the garden there's a greenhouse and to the side of that a vegetable patch full of lettuce, tomatoes and lots of other fresh goodies. Fred's crouched down busily working away. The roses and peonies are in full bloom and the smell on this clear summer morning is so beautiful and fresh.

At the edge of the large garden are two huge willow trees that the cottage is named after. The drooping branches gently swaying in the breeze; it's quite hypnotic. I lift my face up to the clear blue sky and I can feel the warmth penetrate my skin as I soak up all the vitamin D. It actually feels really good after being cooped up for three weeks – gosh, have I been home three weeks?

That first night, I unpacked my car and made my way up to my old bedroom that hasn't been redecorated since I was fourteen. Pink walls with butterflies on and matching bedding and curtains. Could that be any more depressing for a thirty-year-old singleton? There's still a poster of NSYNC on the side of my wardrobe which I actually secretly still love but will never admit to.

I opened up my sewing machine and set it up on the desk in the corner of the room, pushed the bags of material under the bed, and put my clothes away. I sat looking at the large A3 art pad packed full of my wedding gown designs, tormenting myself with what could have been. I finally shoved it back under the bed and vowed never to open it again. What's the point? After falling face first onto the mattress, I buried my head in the pillow and drifted into a deep dreamless slumber.

The first week was just a blur of pyjamas, eating chocolate and crying in bed while watching films. I tortured myself looking at pictures on my phone of happier times with Philip. Searching his face for any signs of his indiscretions or unhappiness. He must be a bloody brilliant liar because I can't see any. I've become a Facebook stalker, searching through his feed, looking for any sign that he might be with her but again nothing. Lilly and Fred have had to coerce me into getting dressed or at least showering most days.

The last two weeks have been a slight improvement in that I haven't actually wanted to wallow in my own filth. I showered without any prompt and ventured downstairs. I refused to see anyone when Fred dared to suggest calling Hettie and Safiyah. I knew I needed to call them at some point but kept putting off the humiliation. I didn't want to admit to them that my life is a complete failure.

Each morning I've woken and for a few blissful seconds all is well, I'm back in London with Philip. Then the crushing memory of Francesca and Philip romping away energetically on the desk hits me and the heavy stomach pang appears, tugging at my insides like a little monster rearing up its ugly head.

Lilly finally decided that tough love was the only way to go and practically man-handled me into the garden for some fresh air and sunshine.

She told me to start sorting my life out. That's when reality hit me. If Lilly Brown is telling me to make a plan, then something definitely needs to be done. This is coming from a woman who, in her early twenties, decided on a whim to move to France for a year to paint with hardly any money in her purse, no accommodation organised and no idea what she was doing. So... pity party is officially over, it's time to get back out into the world.

'So how are you feeling today?' Lilly asks me, much more seriously this time.

'I'm okay, just tired.' I look at my mother. 'And a bit lost. I'm still so bloody angry. Not only at losing him but my job, I loved it there. But I do need to move on.' Fred comes over to the table to join us and pours himself a glass of juice. 'It looks great, Dad.' I point to the garden.

'Thank you. It's not too shabby, is it?' he replies proudly as he surveys his hard work. 'So, what are you up to today?'

'Seeing Hettie and Safiyah in a bit. I called them this morning.' I'm not going to lie, I was dreading telling them both the news. I know it's silly, we've been best friends since before primary school. Our mothers have been friends for years, so we've grown up together. Of course they will be there for me. It's just so demoralising being the jobless single friend who's back living with her parents.

And it's even more humiliating that soon everyone will know that I wasn't good enough, that someone like Francesca, an awful excuse for a human being, was a better option than me. Oh God, the last time I visited I said that I thought our engagement wouldn't be far off. Oh the shame. Tears threaten to spill again and my eyes prick. I swig my tea, desperately wishing it was gin.

Lilly and Fred give each other a nod. I can tell they think it's a promising step forward. 'I figured it was time to stop all this wallowing.'

'I know, darling, why don't you join me for my Zumba class this afternoon?' Lilly asks me eagerly. 'Me and the ladies would love for you to join us. It's a senior group but we can make an exception.'

'Ha ha. Oh, er, you're being serious!' I choke on my tea. Hell no. 'No offence, Mum, but I'm not really sure an over-fifties Zumba club is really for me.' First reason being, I'm twenty years too young!

'Why not? Roberto, the instructor, is so much fun.' Lilly says his name with a roll of her tongue. 'You'll enjoy it. Better than moping round the house.'

I suppose it might be a laugh, and my mother's friends are actually as crazy as she is – it could be quite entertaining. Crikey, am I actually considering this? I look at Fred who gives a slight guffaw and I question what I will be letting myself in for. Lilly looks so hopeful though.

'I'll let you know,' I groan. 'Right, I'm going to get ready, see you both later.'

'Say hi to Hettie and Safiyah for me,' Lilly says as she walks towards the little annex situated at the side of the house which is her art studio. 'I'm going to go finish a masterpiece,' she says enthusiastically, swinging her arms above her head and twirling around.

I watch her dance her way across the lawn and a wave of love flows over me. Lilly is so wonderfully mad.

10

I slip into my home-made ditsy print tea dress; it's one of my favourite patterns to make and I can whip it up in just a few short hours. I brush my hair, which I haven't done in weeks and apply a little bit of make-up. I look in the full-length mirror. My God, I'm pale. That's going to have to do. As I put on my brown sandals, I see the sewing machine sat in the corner of my room. I've always worked through my problems sat at that machine. It seems to clear my mind pouring some creativity into something. This is the first time I've had no urge whatsoever to sit and make anything, the machine is just taunting me. So instead, I pick up my bag and leave the security of the house.

I'm meeting the girls at the village tearoom in the centre of Elmsbourne-Hollow. I walk down the road and past four more cottages like ours as I head to the main high street which is only a five-minute walk away. The village is such a picturesque place. Lots of little side streets darting off in all directions, and the river which runs through Elmsbourne Woods sits on the edge of the village. It's so quiet compared to London. There you are surrounded by people, a constant hum of noise and yet no one really looks up and speaks.

In a strange way it's quite isolating. But here in Elmsbourne-Hollow it's the complete opposite. It's calm and relaxed, there is actual space to breathe and yet everyone knows you and your business, and that can be suffocating.

The main high street comprises of a line of beautiful stone shops on either side of the road with baskets full of brightly coloured flowers hanging off the walls and large iron old-fashioned street lamps dotted outside every other shop. There's the florist, the butchers, Hettie's bakery, the hairdressers, a post office, a local spirits and ales shop, and a delightful antiques store filled with lots of little treasures, as well as the tearoom. The village green stands proud at the end of the road with the church tall behind it, like a beacon.

'Hello, Violet. I didn't know you were visiting,' Paul, the butcher, a plump man with a rather bushy moustache says to me as he stands outside his shop. 'Your dad never mentioned it.'

'Hi, Paul, erm, last-minute decision.'

'Good to see you.'

'Yes, you too.' I smile but quicken my pace past the shop. I hate the smell. I would always stand outside the shop when I was little, waiting for Lilly to go in and pick up her order. Paul would come out every time and hand me a lollipop. Should I wait and see if he brings me one now – no, of course not! Ivy, the florist, is across the road, watering plants outside her shop. She gives me a wave when she sees me. Ivy is so nice, a similar age to me but keeps herself to herself. She is one of the few villagers who doesn't try to delve into your personal life constantly.

'Vi, is that you?' Oh heck, Linda! Linda is the local hairdresser and she's walking towards me in a bright-orange pencil pleat dress, tottering on her matching orange kitten heels, blonde hair bouncing behind her. She's locked her eyes on me and is approaching stealthily like a tiger targeting its prey.

There's nowhere to run. 'Lilly didn't say you were visiting, are you staying long? Is that handsome chap with you?'

'Hi, Linda, sorry can't stop, meeting the girls and I'm running late.'

Bloody hell, this is the problem in a small place, everyone knows everyone. News that I'm back will be around the village quicker than a toupee in a hurricane now the village gossip has seen me. Linda was in the year above me at school and even then, showcased her uncanny ability at being a blabbermouth. She told everyone when she caught me and Oliver Hutchenson kissing behind the bike sheds on lunch break. It had spread around the whole school before the last bell of the day had rung. If there's any information on anyone that you need, make an appointment at the Serenity Lounge. I swear special forces could use her for extracting information. I do manage to sidestep around her though and finally make it to the tearoom.

The quaint little tearoom is the same as always, with patchwork bunting hung on the walls and pink and green gingham tablecloths. The crockery is chintzy chic with little pink roses printed in the middle of them. I love it here. It's owned by Ethel, a fabulous baker who is quite famous around Lancashire. People come from all around the county to taste her afternoon teas. Buttery scones, rich smooth chocolate cake and delicate sandwiches made with her own home-made breads and chutneys, and that's just a sample of the delicious treats on offer. Ethel is a culinary genius. She's training her granddaughter, Tessa, to take over the tearoom when she finally retires which I'm pretty sure will never happen; Ethel enjoys it far too much.

Hettie and Safiyah are already here and are sitting together at a table in the corner. I can feel my emotions teetering on the edge already with one look at them. I'm so happy to see them. I know in an instant I should have called them sooner. I just wasn't ready to discuss it all. I suppose talking to them about it means accepting it really did all happen. Denial is so much easier.

'I'm so glad you're back.' Safiyah jumps from her chair the moment she sees me and squeezes me hard, giving me a mouthful of her long black hair. Safiyah is gorgeous, she has gentle features and a beautiful English rose complexion which gives her an almost angelic Snow White quality. Don't be fooled though, she has a wickedly naughty sense of humour and a sharp tongue but a wonderful heart. Her family own the farm at the top end of Elmsbourne-Hollow. The farm still grazes a few animals, but the main source of income is the gin distillery that her father, Dave Winters, opened ten years ago. The Winters Gin distillery is thriving and winning all sorts of awards. It sells a variety of different flavoured gins and runs tours every other weekend. Her parents have both taken a back seat so Safiyah and her brother, Josh, run it together.

I look at my friends who I know will cheer me up. 'So good to see you both.'

'How are you?' Hettie asks hesitantly as we sit back down.

'I'm good, still a bit shocked, I think.' Yeah, I'm not convincing anyone. 'Oh, who am I kidding? I feel bloody awful. I can't believe it's happened. I feel stupid for not seeing it coming and for trusting him when all the signs were there. I thought he was my happily ever after, my happy place. I'm embarrassed and humiliated, everyone here will know soon enough, and I don't know what I'm going to do for work. I have that horrible heavy pang all the time and everything is just totally shit.' I so don't want to cry but the tears appear anyway. I put my head on the table to hide my face. Hettie places a sympathetic arm on my shoulder. They don't say anything, just sit and let me get it all out. I finally pull myself upright and Hettie hands me a tissue. I must look like crap. 'What am I going to do now?'

'You're going to get through this, that's what you're going to do,' Hettie says sternly, 'and we're going to help you, you're not alone.'

Wonderful Hettie is so fiercely loyal, she always seems to take control and knows exactly what to do. She's the quietest of the three of us but so self-assured. Her fiery red hair falls to her shoulders, she has plump lips and wears black-framed glasses that her husband, Jack, says make her look like a sexy secretary. She owns the village bakery and her wedding cakes are spectacular, often appearing in wedding magazines. I sit and tell them everything and they listen intently.

'He's a shit!' Safiyah exclaims.

'Massive shit!' Hettie agrees. Oh, it's good to be back with them. It feels like it always does when we're together. I can be away from them for months at a time but as soon as we're together, we pick right up from where we left off, like no time has passed at all. 'Have you heard from him?'

'No, nothing. I can't believe he picked her; she wasn't even sorry. I think she actually took some enjoyment out of what happened.' I think back to that horrendous day and it makes the pang in my stomach give a violent prod. 'I should have known when he turned into a gym buff, he was trying to impress someone. It clearly wasn't me. I could barely get him to look at me in bed let alone get frisky somewhere else and they were at it in the shop.'

'I know it's not what you want to hear but you can have a fresh start now. I know you loved the bridal shop but maybe you can concentrate on your own designs. You are so talented, so many people asked me who designed my wedding dress. You could open your own shop... here,' Hettie suggests.

'I'm not sure I have enough money for that yet.'

I do actually have savings; the one positive Philip left me with is that I was able to save some money this past year. He was so adamant about paying for the apartment that it gave me the chance to put a sum of money away each month for my own business venture. Not loads because I paid the household bills but enough to have a little nest egg. At the time I thought how wonderful it was that he wanted to help me save for a shop but now I know it was because he didn't want me to have any rights to the apartment. He knew he would be moving me out and probably Francesca in.

'You could get a business loan.'

'I don't know, I can't think straight at the moment. It's all a bit overwhelming.' Bloody hell, when did I turn into such a mardy arse? I mean, I've always had a flair for the dramatics, but this is ridiculous. I've never been the type to wallow in self-pity and yet that's all I've done for three weeks straight. What has gotten into me? 'I haven't looked at my emails since I've been here, I don't even know if I have any orders.'

Although I don't promote my Etsy shop, I do have a steady stream of orders from friends and friends of friends.

'Well then, that's the place to start. Check as soon as you get home,' Safiyah suggests.

'Anyway, enough about me, tell me what's happening with you both,' I say, trying to muster a grin. We sit and talk. Hettie updates me on Jack and her recent wedding cakes that have made it into the prestigious *Brides* magazine and Safiyah tells me about a new summer fruits gin they are releasing and how Theo has asked her to move in with him. I'm truly happy for my friends, they deserve all the happiness in the world, but this just makes it painfully obvious that as their lives are pushing forwards, mine has taken an almighty step back. I'm being left behind. I need cake!

'These cakes smell amazing, do you both want anything?' I

ask, going over to the counter to look at the choices. It all looks so appetising, I decide on a lemon and poppy seed muffin, some white chocolate rocky road and a chocolate sponge cake for us to share. Calories don't count when you're heartbroken, it's a scientific fact! 'These look delicious, Ethel.'

'Thank you,' Ethel replies as she places the cakes onto plates. 'So, where is that man of yours? Philip, isn't it? Or are you visiting on your own?'

'On my own, Ethel, and we broke up. Unfortunately he couldn't keep his hands off other women so I'm back here... for good,' I blurt out. It was going to come out at some point, might as well put it out there myself. This is the start of me taking back control and not being the victim to Philip's philandering ways. One good thing is I will only have to say it once. In this village it will spread like wildfire.

I pay for the cakes and take the first two over to our table. I go back to the counter for the last plate and oh my goodness, the chocolate cake smells divine. I can't wait to try it so take a bite. Wow, it's smooth and heavenly with a very subtle tang of orange. Basically, I now want to marry the cake. Unfortunately, I'm so consumed with the chocolatey goodness I fail to notice the customer that has walked in and is standing behind me. I walk smack straight into him, stepping on his feet. The shock of him standing so close makes me jump and my arms shoot up, the cake slides off the plate and falls towards the stranger's crisp blue T-shirt. I do try to catch the plate but it's too late. The plate hits the stranger's chest, smearing the fondant down his top. Oops!

'Oh my God, I'm so sorry,' I say with a mouth full of cake. Crumbs fly at the astonished man's face. I can feel the heat rising in my cheeks. *Shit, shit, shit.* Not only have I walked into him, stepped on his feet and thrown cake at him, I've now spat it in his face. I choke down what remains in my mouth and hastily wipe the crumbs off my lips. 'Here, let me help.'

I grab some napkins from the counter to help clear the mess, but instead all I do is proceed to rub the smeared chocolate fondant further into his top. Crap, that's just making it worse. I look up at the stranger feeling panicked and a bolt shoots through my stomach. He's utterly gorgeous. Why oh why does this have to happen to me? I'm still frantically trying to clean his top. Wow, he has some toned abs underneath there. His chest is rock hard. Oh Christ, why am I still rubbing his chest, I look like some creepy sex pest! *Violet, stop touching him – STOP!*

'I think you're making that worse,' he says, looking down at the mess.

Yep I most certainly am. I do manage to stop rubbing his lovely chest though!

'I'm so, so sorry, I didn't see you behind me.'

'Clearly,' he says, wiping a bit of the cake off his T-shirt. He doesn't sound angry though, just amused if anything. 'Good cake though at least,' he says, licking the cake off his finger. Now, I'm pretty sure this wasn't supposed to be an act of seduction but as I watch this gorgeous stranger lick his fingers, my stomach flutters – very pleasantly. It has been ages since I've had any sort of intimacy and it sends shivers to places I thought were long dead. Holy smokes, he's hot. He's taller than me with big brown soul-searching eyes and very inviting lips, his short black hair is thick and wavy, and I want to run my fingers through it. He has a strong jawline with just a hint of stubble, he's... ruggedly handsome. Who is he? I thought I knew everyone in this village. Nothing is kept quiet here and yet no one has mentioned the tall dark handsome stranger that's rocked up.

'Are you all right, Ben?' Ethel comes running around the counter. 'Ooh, that's not going to wipe off.'

'Erm, I think you're right there, Ethel,' he says. 'Can I just get a coffee to go?'

'Please let me pay for it. I insist.' I must do something to make up for this mess.

'No really it's fine, partly my fault, I shouldn't have stood so close behind you.'

He's looking at me, his eyes seem to be searching my face and I feel myself blush. Could it be he likes what he sees? It's far too soon for anything like that, I'm in the midst of heartbreak and... 'You have something on your face,' he says, pointing to my cheek. Of course I do. Obviously he's not captivated by me at all and has just noticed the clumsy streak of chocolate across my cheek. I try to rub it off and push down the growing self-flagellation.

'Here, let me.' He takes a step closer, leans past with one arm and reaches for a napkin. In doing so, his face comes disarmingly close to mine and I lose all train of thought. My heartbeat quickens as the heat in my face reaches dangerous levels. He cups my chin in his hand and wipes the cake from my cheek. His aftershave fills my senses, it's fresh and woody.

'There, all gone,' he says with a smile.

I think I might be dazzled, that hasn't happened to me before. Must form words... 'Thank you and again, I'm so sorry.'

'No worries, perhaps I'll see you around.'

He takes his coffee from Ethel and spins around, only then noticing Hettie and Safiyah with large grins, trying their best not to laugh and failing miserably. 'Oh, hi, girls,' he says and I notice he has gone a little red himself.

'Hi, Ben!' they say in chorus, waving as he leaves the shop.

The girls are looking at me, waiting for some sort of reaction, but all I can do is swallow hard as I try to formulate a sentence.

'You make quite an impression, don't you?' Safiyah laughs.

'Who the hell was that?'

'That's Ben Matthews, he's an architect. He moved here about eight months ago from Lancaster. He plays rugby with Jack. Nice guy, bloody gorgeous as well,' Hettie tells me.

'Hey, you're a married woman,' Safiyah says playfully.

'I can still appreciate a good-looking fella.'

'If I was thirty years younger,' Ethel chimes in as she walks over to the table to move the empty cups.

'Ethel, you naughty thing,' Safiyah says. 'He is single though.' And they all look at me very pointedly.

'Too soon, guys, too soon.' With that, all thoughts of Philip return and the stomach pang prevails, reminding me it is still there. As if I even need reminding – bleugh.

'I'm off to go and get ready for Zumba with my mother and the rest of the Golden Girls because that's how rock and roll my life is now,' I say with a mix of desperation and gloom. 'I'm single, jobless and in a fifties-plus Zumba group. Wish me luck.'

11

I walk into the village hall with, let's say, a large amount of trepidation. What am I doing? I had walked home after the incident in the café with every intention of getting in my pyjamas, putting on an old movie and hiding from the world. That was until I found a note from Lilly on the kitchen fridge: *See you at the hall, 1.30pm. Excited to Zumba with you x*

'She told me to tell you, you have to go,' Fred told me when he caught me reading it in the kitchen. 'It would make her so happy if you went, love, she's been so worried about you.'

Slight emotional blackmail but I really didn't want to let Lilly down, so with a sense of foreboding dread I stuffed my hair up into a messy bun, put on a black baggy vest and matching cropped leggings and... here I am.

'Darling, you made it,' Lilly shrills, running over to me in bright pink trainers, purple leggings and a grey top that says *Zumba now, wine later*. The look is topped off with a green sweatband fixed around her head. She looks like she has stepped out of an eighties fitness video – only Lilly could pull off this attire. That is until I look around and see nine more women in the room wearing similar outfits.

I know most of the ladies here and I do a little wave as they all give me big welcoming smiles. Maggie and Jane are Lilly's closest friends, they are just as loud and as mental as Lilly but brilliant fun. Jenny, Bonnie and Verity are stretching in the centre of the hall, they've lived in the village for as long as I can remember. They are active members of the local WI, book club, and on the village council. Olivia and Rosalind Kimberley are chatting by the benches, sisters who even now in their seventies still bicker like they're teenagers. They are what are described these days as cougars! They still wear push-up bras and flirt outrageously with the local rugby team, and are very nimble for their age.

Finally, Mary, my old primary school teacher who's now retired, is sat on a bench next to Winnie. I don't know a lot about Winnie. She moved here about eight years ago after retirement with her husband but was sadly widowed not long after they arrived. She's a quiet soul but very friendly. Like the rest of the ladies she seems to join in a lot of the groups around the village, always contributes a cake to the bake sale and shows up to every village event.

'Sorry to hear about your boyfriend,' Jane says. Bloody hell, they all know then! There is certainly no mistaking whose mother she is. Jane and Safiyah share the same English rose complexion and thick dark hair and it's certainly her mother who Safiyah gets her straight-talking attitude and great sense of humour from.

'He sounds like a complete waste of space, we always said it would end in tears, didn't we, Lilly?' Maggie chirps up.

'Did you?' I say, widening my eyes as I look from Maggie to my mother. That's news to me, Lilly's kept that one quiet. I thought she liked him. Maggie is Hettie's mum. However, looks wise, they are polar opposites. Hettie gets her striking red hair from her father, Maggie on the other hand has a short grey pixie style haircut and small hazel eyes.

'Never mind that now, dear,' says Lilly, casually brushing off Maggie's comment. 'Roberto's here.' Suddenly all the ladies are fluffing their hair into place and getting in a line with huge cheesy smiles on their faces. I'm pretty sure I've just seen one of the Kimberley sisters plump her breasts up even higher.

'Ladies, are you ready?' I jump a mile as a man in his late thirties sashays into the room and produces the highest leg kick I have ever seen. He makes his way over to the speakers and attaches his phone. He's wearing tiny blue shorts and a black vest, his thick honey mane flicking around gloriously like there is a wind machine in front of him. 'You are all looking fabulous.' The group swoons. 'I see we have a new member today. What's your name and where do you come from?' he calls, a little too reminiscent of a nineties game show host.

'Oh, Roberto, this is my daughter, Violet.'

'Get away, Lilly, you're not old enough to be her mother, surely you're sisters.'

What! Sisters! Cheeky bugger.

'Oh, you are bad.' Lilly giggles, tapping his arm. 'She's moved back from London. Been dumped, haven't you, darling, so I thought she could join us and Zumba her problems away.'

'Oh no, you poor thing. Well, you have come to the right place, love. We will work that man right out of your hair,' Roberto says with an encouraging smile. Damn it, he is lovely, and I can't help but smile back, he's totally endearing. He jumps over to his phone and presses play. All of a sudden the Spice Girls' 'Spice Up Your Life' booms out of the speakers. What the frigging hell have I let myself in for?

'Okay, ladies, let's warm those bodies up,' Roberto shouts over the top of the music as he flicks his blond hair from side to side while running on the spot.

. . .

After a five-minute warm-up, I spend the next forty-five minutes doing the salsa, swinging my hips and arms and pumping my chest as best I can with my two left feet. All the ladies have the routines nailed and I'm desperately trying to keep up.

'Step to the left one, two. Step to the right one and two. Don't forget to swing those hips,' Roberto sings.

For a bunch of pensioners, they can certainly move. At the beginning of the class I felt so self-conscious, I kept checking to see if anyone was laughing at me swaying nervously from side to side and shuffling my feet to the music but as I watched the class it soon became obvious that no one was taking any notice of me at all. I mean why would they? They are all here to have fun and get some exercise, so slowly I loosen up.

I watch Lilly dance around, laughing with her friends, being the free spirit that she is. Lilly doesn't care what other people think. I wish I could be more like her. I used to be. When did I start worrying so much about other people's opinions of me? I think it was when Philip went on and on about giving the right impression, I wondered if perhaps I was giving the wrong one. The house had to look a certain way, he had to look a certain way, perhaps I had to as well. Lilly brought me up to be myself, to bask in my own individuality, to be assured in who I am. I told people every day in the shop to have confidence and yet somewhere along the way, I stopped taking my own advice! I've lost my way.

I begin to get swept along with the Latin beats, all the tension and drama of the last few weeks that has built up inside me is coming to the forefront and I plunge it into the workout, dancing around energetically, shimmying my heart out and I have to say, I'm loving it.

'To the left and two and three. To the right and two and three. What are we not to forget?' Roberto bellows.

'To swing your hips,' the ladies call back in chorus.

I'm not exactly following the moves well but I am trying. I laugh when I jump in the wrong direction or trip over my own feet. I can't remember the last time I have really laughed. You know, those deep belly laughs that reach right down to your toes. It's been weeks, no that's not right, it's been months! How odd. Perhaps I've been unhappy for longer than I've realised.

'NOW SHAKE IT, SHAKE IT,' Roberto roars. 'Shake what your mama gave you.'

Yes, yes, I will shake it. I am fully absorbed in the party vibe music and going off-piste from the routines that I don't know anyway. I place both hands on my thighs, bend forward slightly and thrust out my bottom, twerking away to the music. I'm not sure if it's a Zumba move but I don't care, the music is calling for it and who am I to say no. Mid twerk though, my eyes fall to the window and I freeze.

Oh no... no, no, no. Is that gorgeous Ben from the tearoom at the window? It is and he is looking straight at me, while I'm thrusting my arse backwards and forwards, with the biggest grin on his face. Please, world, swallow me up, this is mortifying. I'm sweaty and hot and now turning beetroot. I feel myself shrivel down, hoping he hasn't recognised me. How has it happened that twice in one day I have seen Ben Matthews and twice, I have done something to look completely ridiculous.

'Oh, look, everyone, it's Ben!' Lilly shouts. 'Everybody wave.'

Everyone waves and I want to run away and hide. I can see him looking straight at me and he's doing his best to suppress a laugh, but it isn't working. He's cracking up as he walks away from the window. What is he doing here anyway, perving in on the class?

'Must be his turn to set up for rugby practice. He is lovely,'

Jane says as if she's reading my mind. 'Single too, you know, Violet.'

'Oh, don't you start. Safiyah and Hettie have already mentioned it.'

'If it were me who was single, I would give him a go.'

'Give him a go! Maggie, please,' I say stunned.

'I would too,' Jane agrees. Okay this conversation is going down a disturbing route.

'If I were you, Violet, I would stay single and date as much as you can. I wish I had put it about a bit more,' Verity says wistfully. I feel my mouth drop open, horror-struck at the turn in conversation, especially as Verity looks so sweet and innocent. Her petite face and big round glassy eyes remind me of a spritely elf but without the pointy ears. 'I was with my Harold from the age of eighteen, lovely man don't get me wrong, but I don't really have anything to compare it to.'

'Same here,' Winnie surprisingly pipes up.

'That's how I felt with my first husband,' Olivia adds.

'Yes, but you had certainly sampled life by your third one, hadn't you?' Rosalind quips, trying to wind her sister up.

'You've got no room to talk,' Olivia argues back. 'You went through half of the male population of Lancashire before you settled down. She was a right floozy, Violet.'

Flipping heck, I should have stayed at home!

'That was why I made sure I sampled life before I settled down,' Lilly suddenly exclaims to my horror. 'Made sure I found a man who could satisfy me.'

'Mother... please.' I think I might gag. I really don't want to hear that my mother put it about in her younger years. I don't want to even accept that she had sexual relations with my father. I'm more than happy to keep believing I was the result of an immaculate conception.

'Oh, now don't be prudish, darling. We're all adults here.'

'Would you say your Fred is an attentive lover then, Lilly?' Roberto asks as he dabs the sweat on his head with a towel.

'Please don't ans–'

'Ooh, yes he is,' Lilly interrupts me and I really do gag this time. Why are we having this conversation?

'Aww that's lovely. Right, on the floor, ladies, time for the cool down... and thrust!' Roberto shouts.

As I lie down, I'm wondering where I went so wrong in my life to lead me to this moment of having to hear all about my parents' sex life whilst thrusting on the floor with the over-fifties Zumba club – this must be rock bottom, surely?

'So, Violet, will you join us again?' Jane asks me at the end of the cool down.

'Depends, do I have to hear any more sex talk from you randy lot?'

I've actually really enjoyed myself. Until the harrowing moment when I realised that Ben had been watching and the awful conversation which led on from that. I fully expected to hate it, but the class was good fun. The best bit was that I was so completely distracted, I forgot all about my crappy heartbreak.

'Do you know what, I think I will come back.' For twenty glorious minutes there was a break where the Zumba class acted like a drug numbing the pain and I'm desperate to relive it. Who would have thought a senior Zumba class would do that? We all leave the village hall and as Lilly and I walk home I swing my arm around her shoulders.

'Thanks for inviting me, Mum. It was good fun, just what I needed. They're a good bunch, even if they do overshare.'

'My pleasure, darling. I thought it might be a good distraction and it was wonderful spending time with you.'

'I haven't been around much recently, have I?' I feel so guilty.

Over the last few years my visits home have become more and more scarce. What's worse is, I hadn't actually noticed until now. Life in London had been so busy, the weeks flew past. At first, Philip always enjoyed coming to Lancashire with me, but over the last eighteen months or so he never seemed to have the time. Now I think about it, his remarks had been a little scathing too, he called the village quiet and boring. He's clearly forgotten all about the Golden Girls when making that comment, they are most certainly not quiet or boring. When I had mentioned visiting, he would remind me about a show or a meal or a day out somewhere that I had somehow forgotten. It would just appear on the calendar even though I was sure it hadn't been there before. How had I allowed that to happen? Been so easily manipulated by him and not noticed. I feel angry and upset and hot shameful tears flush my eyes. I blink them back, determined not to cry after such a fun hour with Lilly.

'Well no, but that's okay, darling, you were off living your life and that's all I have ever wanted for you. Plus, you're home now, aren't you?'

'Yep, dumped and alone.' I look at Lilly and we burst out laughing at the sheer abruptness of my point. It was one of those moments when you can either laugh or cry, only this time I chose to laugh. My phone beeps, it's Hettie asking me to the pub in the village tonight. My instant reaction is to say no but I promised myself I would start moving forward and it will be good to go for a drink and socialise with friends again.

'Perhaps Ben will be there,' Lilly suggests with a wink.

'God, I hope not. I've embarrassed myself far too much in front of him for one day. He must think I'm a complete nutjob.' I would question his judgement if he thought otherwise after today. It's Saturday night though, the majority of the locals frequent the Chugging Bull on a weekend.

I can't cope with the humiliation of seeing him after such

aggressive twerking! Well if he is there, I will just have to avoid him at all costs. I imagine he will want to avoid me anyway which is good because I'm going to spend time with my friends, drink gin and *not* talk to drop-dead-gorgeous blokes that hide lovely Adonis-like muscly physiques under T-shirts.

12

A few hours later I'm sitting on my bed opening emails on my laptop. I spot one from Imogen and my heart misses a beat. Maybe she's emailing to update me on Francesca and Philip. Perhaps she has seen them about together. Oh God, what if she's trying to let me know that they have eloped and are now blissfully married, rolling around on the bed sheets I bought, having sex all day. I take a deep breath and click it open. Relief washes over me though, there is no mention of either of them.

Imogen is just checking in with me but has kept the email brief. I've had a few messages over the last few weeks mainly from Imogen and Sarah. A few other so-called friends have messaged too but they're mutual acquaintances with Philip and, by the sounds of things, all knew what was happening behind my back. Apparently, they wanted to tell me what was going on... well perhaps they should have bloody tried if they wanted to so badly, but they didn't. They sided with Philip and kept his dirty little secrets for God knows how long. The majority I've ignored because I now know what crappy friends they are, stabbing me in the back, but not Imogen and Sarah. They are decent and lovely so I've made an extra effort to reassure them that all is well.

Amongst the emails is an order for two dresses that only came through yesterday via my Etsy account. They are simple enough designs, both skater dresses, one floral and one plain red. It's one of Imogen's friends and I've made dresses for her previously and have all her measurements. There's no reason for me to say no apart from the complete loss in creativity.

I see my sewing machine sat in the corner of the room like a stranger I no longer know. I think this is the first time in my life where my creativity has abandoned me. Like my love life, it has dried up. Perhaps this will reignite my passion and I can't exactly say no to work. I reply that I will of course make the dresses but will send them out by post as I no longer live in London. Seeing the words written in front of me gives me a lump in my throat. I sit and stare at the computer screen and can't stop my thoughts wondering what Philip might be doing. Is he with her?

It's Saturday night. We used to order a takeaway and snuggle up together to watch a film (although thinking about it, we haven't really snuggled for a while) – is he doing that with her? Francesca always gave the impression that she liked to be wined and dined, quite high-maintenance. Perhaps he's taking her out for a posh dinner with his pompous work buddies and their equally stuck-up girlfriends and then back home to whisk her off to bed. My bed! I feel queasy because now I'm wondering if they used my bed before Philip and I even broke up. I mean they must have been doing it somewhere besides the office desk.

The impulse to check his Facebook page is suddenly too impossible for me to ignore. I haven't been on for over a week because it was driving me crazy, checking his page religiously waiting for something to appear. I click on his name, the profile picture that had been of us both together on top of the Eiffel Tower from New Year's Eve the year before is gone. It's now a picture of Philip with two mates, holding pints up in the air from a recent night out. He's definitely not been missing me then – looks like he's been out with not a care in the world. I scroll down to his posts and there it is, the thing I've been dreading.

The air seems to rush out of the room and I scramble to breathe, my stomach is flipping ferociously as I look at the happy faces smiling back at me. Why do they get to be happy? Francesca has tagged Philip in a photo of them both enjoying a picnic together. They are sat on a tartan rug, Philip's arm hanging lazily around her shoulders and she snuggles happily into him while holding a glass of something bubbly. Francesca looks flawless as per usual, smug bitch.

I slam the computer shut and throw myself backwards on the bed because even though I looked, I don't want to see them together so happy. I want them both to be miserable and perhaps in a small amount of pain – okay, a large amount. I want Philip to be full of regret and dump her. I want him to come running after me and bang on the door declaring his undying love so I can shove it back in his face and dramatically tell him to sod off.

Oh, they deserve each other. He's back in London living his best life while I'm sat here pining for him. Well, not tonight. I'm going out, I'm going to have a great time with friends, drink gin and forget all about Philip Miller.

I look at the time and go over to my wardrobe. I pull out my dark-blue skinny jeans and a red embroidered Bardot top.

After a shower I put a few extra waves in my hair, cover the tired bags under my eyes with industrial-strength concealer and apply some make-up. I pull on my black stiletto heels because they make my legs feel longer and let's be honest, I need all the

tools in my arsenal to make me feel half decent tonight. Okay...
I'm ready.

'Look at you,' Lilly says as I step into the kitchen. Lilly and Fred
are sat at the trusty oak table, sharing a bottle of wine. 'You look
rather sassy, darling.'

'Thanks, I feel it,' I say with a slightly renewed sense of
optimism. 'No more moping for me. I'm going out tonight and
I have two new dress orders which I'll crack on with
tomorrow.'

'Good for you,' Fred says, and I think there is a hint of relief
in his voice.

Lilly gets up from the table, walks over and kisses me on the
cheek. 'That's my girl.'

I walk towards the Chugging Bull. The pub is at the top of the
main high street opposite the village green. It's painted bright
white and covered in hanging baskets filled with bright red
begonias. It's pretty much the heart and soul of the village. The
landlady, Norah Abbots, is so warm and welcoming and the
food is mouth-wateringly good. Norah makes proper hearty pub
food, the best pies you have ever tasted.

I get to the door and pause. What do I say if people ask why
I'm back? What am I thinking? In this place they will already
know why by now. I don't want to go in, I don't want to see the
pitiful stares for the girl who's been dumped and left on the
shelf to rot for all eternity. I want to go home and hide,
preferably with a bottle of wine. I know I'm being dramatic
(again), no one probably even cares I'm back. I'm just
overthinking. I do, however, need to make a decision one way or

another though because I can't stand here all night holding on to the door handle.

'Are you going in?' The voice startles me and I spin round. Typical, of course Ben would catch me stood here, clinging on to a door handle for dear life like some weirdo. He's smiling so at least, if anything, I'm entertaining. He looks good this evening; he's wearing jeans and a fitted black T-shirt which compliments his broad shoulders that I want to run my hands over. He has the same aftershave on as this morning, musk and citrus, it's heavenly. I realise that I haven't actually answered him, I'm just stood here... staring.

'Yes, yes, I am. Sorry, again.'

'Violet, right?'

'Yes.' Oh heck, he knows my name, how does he know my name? I must look confused because he answers my question without me having to say it out loud. For some reason he renders me speechless.

'I put two and two together when I saw you in the tearoom earlier. I assumed you were with Hettie and Safiyah, they've spoken about you before and then I bumped into Fred earlier at the post office, he was telling Mr Thompson that his daughter's come home.'

'You know my dad?' This doesn't actually surprise me; everyone knows everyone here.

'Yeah of course, he always comes to watch the rugby when we play. I saw you with Lilly at the village hall earlier too.' A smile spreads across his face and he does a little cough to quash a laugh.

'Oh God, you did see.' A hot flush ravishes me once again.

'Don't be embarrassed, you look good for fifty plus,' he says with a chuckle, and I don't know why but I feel irritated. Actually, I do know why. I'm frustrated because I don't want to feel foolish and worthless because that's all I've felt for the last few weeks. I know he's only joking but I don't want to be the butt of the joke. Weeks of feeling shitty and then seeing the photo of Philip and Francesca combine together in my head. All I want is a night out with my friends, to have fun and laugh and not think about my heartbreak and not feel like... a total shit tip!

'Funny,' I say indignantly, and I can tell my tone has surprised him. 'For your information, my mum invited me, so we could spend a little time together. And actually, the class was good fun. They're a great bunch.' I don't mean for the outburst to be quite so snippy, but I just want to get away from him. 'Excuse me but my friends are waiting.'

He tries to say something, but I walk off in a huff before he can even open his mouth.

'Hey, you look great. Now do my eyes deceive me or did you just walk in with Ben?' Safiyah asks with a suspicious grin, giving me a kiss on the cheek.

'I bumped into him outside, that's all,' I say, but it seems to fall on deaf ears as Safiyah and Hettie are both giving me goofy grins. I think I should put a stop to this before they both try to play cupid. 'Look, I'm not interested in Ben Matthews so don't go looking for something that isn't there. In fact, I'm swearing off men completely. Now, who's for gin?'

Two strong arms suddenly wrap themselves around me from behind and squeeze.

'That's a bit excessive isn't it, we're not all bad?'

'Hello, you,' I reply, instantly recognising the dulcet tones of Jack Braithwaite. He engulfs me into a bone crushing hug followed quickly by Theo, Safiyah's boyfriend. Safiyah and Theo have been together for about a year. He works for the advertising team that was hired to promote Winters Gin and it was love at first sight.

'Good to see you,' Jack says to me as he walks over to Hettie and puts an arm around her waist. He's tall, dark and burly but his face is soft and cheeky. I adore how in love he is with Hettie; he gives her this look of utter adoration whenever he sees her. They've been together since we were fourteen – love's young dream and the most perfect couple. They had a rough old time of it last year, Hettie suffered a miscarriage early in her pregnancy and they were both understandably devastated. They got through it though together, they were each other's rock. I rushed back home when I got the call from Hettie and hated having to leave her again but knowing Jack was there by her side supporting her made it a little easier.

'So how are you?' he asks me kindly.

'Not too bad, I'm getting there.'

'Good to hear it. Who's for a drink then? Norah, gins all round please,' he calls. Now that's more like it. Is it appropriate to get so drunk I forget my own name as well as Philip's?

'Coming right up,' Norah calls as she pours the drinks. 'Linda said she saw you, Vi. Good to see you, love.' Bloody blabbermouth Linda! Norah hands me my drink and I take a huge gulp.

The pub is bustling and lively, a local band is setting up in the corner and I feel myself slowly relax. It's a traditional country pub with an open inglenook fire at one side, a dark wood bar, low ceiling and lots of little nooks with tables and chairs that you can huddle into and enjoy a drink. There are so many familiar faces and dare I say it, I'm actually having a good time. No one is looking at me with pity and I haven't heard the word 'spinster' aimed in my direction so I will take this as a win.

'Violet!' Josh, Safiyah's brother, comes flying towards me, picks me up and swings me round. 'You're a sight for sore eyes.'

'God, am I pleased to see you,' I say, squeezing him tight. 'It's been way too long.' Josh is two years older than me and I had such a crush on him all the way through school. His dark hair, the same colour as Safiyah's, with piercing blue eyes made him the target of interest for all the girls. He was always so cool and captivating.

When I was eighteen, we finally got together and ended up dating for two years much to Safiyah's dismay. He was my first love, my first everything really but we eventually broke up when Josh decided to go away to university to study business. I knew if I asked him to stay, he would have but he needed to see a little of the world outside the village. Long distance would never have worked so we went our separate ways. After quite a few more girlfriends, Josh finally settled down and married Ayda after the birth of their son, Hector.

'You look great,' I say fondly. 'Fatherhood clearly suits you.' He's the only ex-boyfriend I've ever managed to stay friends with, clearly my choice in men went severely downhill after him.

'When are you coming over to the farm?'

'Soon, I promise. I want one of these distillery tours Safiyah's been telling me about. Where's Ayda?'

'Over there, we're having a rare night out. Mum and Dad have Hector.' He points in Ayda's direction and I see her waving frantically from the other side of the pub.

'Let me just get another drink and I'll be over to you both,' I say as I down the last of my gin and then push my way over to the bar.

'Sorry to hear about you and Philip,' Josh calls after me. Hearing the dreaded name throws me off balance for a second. 'You were way too good for him anyway.' He says it with such a heartening tone that it makes me feel weepy. I muster a *yeah, you're right I'm much better off without him* look and get myself another *large* gin.

. . .

I'm paying for my drink when I am suddenly accosted by Hettie who has charged over to the bar with Collette in her wake. I don't really know Collette too well. She was a couple of years younger than me at school. I'm sure she moved away to college and never moved back but her parents still live here.

'Violet, do you remember Collette?' Hettie asks.

'Yes, sort of. Hi, how are you?'

'I'm good thanks, just back visiting my parents.'

'Collette's getting married and we were just talking. She mentioned how she was struggling to find the perfect dress. I suggested perhaps having one made,' Hettie says, widening her eyes purposefully at me. 'I mentioned your experience in bridal wear and showed her a picture of my wedding dress you made; I thought you could help her.'

I'm stunned and I don't know what to say. I thought all chances of designing wedding dresses would be out of reach now so I'm a little taken back, plus the added issue of my creative mojo doing a runner.

'Hettie's dress is stunning. Is that something you would be interested in helping me with?' Collette asks, full of hope.

Something in her voice calls out to me and I'm finding it impossible to say no. 'Yes, I can help.' What am I saying? I can't help.

'You will be in great hands with Violet, she's so talented.' Good old Hettie having so much faith in me.

Hettie's dress was a triumph if I do say so myself. An elegant sleeved satin gown with a bateau neckline, a scooped back and finished with delicate crystal buttons and a small train. As I think of the dress a trickle of excitement runs down my spine. Designing a wedding dress would be a perfect distraction, and the money would be great. I have a sudden urge to hop back behind my sewing machine. The feeling is only fleeting, but it was definitely there so maybe my creativity hasn't upped and left me completely. It just needs a spark to set it alight. I feel so happy at that thought, I could jump on the bar and do a tap dance. 'Perhaps we could meet up tomorrow and talk through some ideas and I could draw up some designs, see if it really is something you want to go ahead with?'

'That sounds great.' Collette takes my number and leaves looking thrilled. I throw my arms around Hettie's neck, practically strangling her with joy.

'Thank you so much, you're wonderful. This could be just what I need.' Exhilaration is coursing through me. If Collette likes my designs and decides to go ahead then someone else could see Collette's gown and it could lead to more orders. Perhaps the art pad under my bed will have some use after all. I join the rest of the group feeling buoyed by my conversation with Collette and start chatting cheerfully to everyone. The drinks are flowing, the band begins their set and the dancing soon commences with everyone in high spirits.

I don't know why but my eyes keep wandering in the direction of Ben and I see him look over at me. He's probably thinking what a demented cow I am after my outburst before. If our paths ever cross again I should really apologise for being so rude.

13

Theo has been whirling me around the dance floor for the past twenty minutes, my feet are throbbing so hard I think they're going to drop off and I've drunk way too much gin because my head is spinning – I need some fresh air. I stumble into the beer garden and after the heat from the pub, the cool air feels glorious as it tickles my skin. A few people are milling about as I sit down at an empty picnic bench and slip my feet out of the *shoes of death*. Oh my God that feels better, stupid bloody shoes, why didn't I wear slippers out? I could say it's a new cool trend that everyone in London is doing.

The evening is warm, it's nearly eleven o'clock, and the sky is dark but so clear. With just the light from inside the pub shining through the windows, I can see all the stars twinkling about the hills in the distance. It's so beautiful. I forgot how incredible it is to look up and actually see the stars. For the first time since I returned, I'm appreciating how good it is to actually be back here, to be home.

'Need any company?' I recognise his voice and my stomach gives a little buzz of butterflies. I look over my shoulder and see

Ben strolling towards me with two glasses in his hand. He holds one out to me. 'Peace offering.'

Oh balls, I feel bad. Why did I get so defensive before when he was only joking? I cringe when I think of how I snapped at him.

'No peace offering needed,' I reply sheepishly. Ben sits next to me and hands me the drink anyway. 'In hindsight, I think it's me who should be apologising. I'm sorry I was so... frosty before.'

'It's okay, I'll let you buy me a drink later then.' He smiles and it's completely dashing. 'Caught you at a bad moment earlier?'

'Something like that, yes,' I say as I look at the drink he's given me. A quick sniff tells me it's rhubarb gin – good choice.

'Winters Gin. The best gin around, according to Safiyah.'

'It is,' I agree. 'Although my dad did always say I should never take a drink from a stranger.'

'He's right, you shouldn't. Although this is the third time we have seen each other today, and I do know your family and friends pretty well, and you have smothered cake all over my body, so can you really call us strangers?' I blush when I think of the cake fiasco, or maybe it's the dazzling smile he's giving me that lights up his face.

'Oh God, don't remind me about the cake.' I lower my head – oh the shame. 'I keep getting flashbacks of it flying at your chest, I'm mortified.' Not to mention how bloody good his chest felt!

'Don't be, it was delicious. Luckily I love Ethel's cakes.' He chuckles. 'Feet sore?' He points to my shoes strewn on the floor.

'Ridiculously, don't know what I was thinking wearing them.'

'Yeah, that's why I chose trainers instead of heels myself.'

'Oh really, do you wear heels often?' I ask, my eyes widening in amusement.

'All the time. Quite partial to a slingback but you know, I figured there may be dancing tonight.' He says this completely deadpan, then his face breaks into that beguiling smile again. He's funny, he doesn't seem to take himself too seriously which makes a nice change. 'So, you lived in London, didn't you. What did you do there?'

'I worked for a bridal house. I'm a seamstress but I hope to one day design my own dresses.' I've done so well all evening limiting my thoughts of Philip but talking about London makes the stomach pang rear up again. No, come on, Violet. You're moving on now. Shit, Ben's looking at me, what was I saying... oh yes. 'I'm hoping to start my business here instead though now. In fact, just this very evening I may have scored an order for a wedding dress.'

'Well done, you. That's great. So what made you leave the big smoke and come back to Elmsbourne-Hollow?'

Had my heart pulverised to smithereens. 'I, erm, I broke up with my boyfriend.' Urgh, this is awkward, please don't ask me what happened.

'Oh, sorry... Are you okay?'

'I'm fine,' I say a little too eagerly. This is not a topic I want to discuss. I need to change the subject. 'So, Hettie tells me you're an architect.'

'Yes, I work in Lancaster. I lived there too but I'm a country boy at heart so when my house came on the market I couldn't resist.'

'Where is it you live?'

'I bought Bracken Lodge.'

I love that place. Bracken Lodge is an old farmhouse just around the corner from Willow's Cottage. It's been empty for years. When the old owner died, it went to relatives in her will, but unfortunately there was an issue with probate that continued for years. The house ended up getting in such a state of disrepair that in the end no one wanted to spend the money getting it back up to scratch, so they just sold it off. I didn't know it was to Ben though.

'I love that place, I'm so glad someone bought it. I was worried it was going to get torn down. It was a beautiful home years ago, needs some work doing to it now though.'

'It needs loads, but I love a renovation. I've seen old photos of it so I'm doing my best to keep as much of the original features as possible. Don't suppose you're handy with a paintbrush, are you?'

Is that an invite? No of course it isn't. An impromptu group of butterflies ripple through my tummy which I hastily try to ignore. 'Sure, I'll give anything a go.' Oh God, that sounded dirtier than I meant it too.

'Good to know,' he says cheekily. Wait, is he flirting? No surely not, although it's been that long since someone flirted with me, I wouldn't know what the signs are. There's an awkward silence between us. Shit, come on, Violet, say something.

'So... do you come here often?' No... not that!

'Is that your chat-up line?' Ben laughs. Oh no, he thinks I'm flirting which I most definitely am not, I just panicked.

'No, not at all, I would never – not that you're not. I just mean... is this your local?' My voice is coming out all high-pitched. Why am I making such a hash of this. Of course, it's his local, it's the only bloody pub in the village.

Ben's smiling though, I think my squirming must be entertaining. 'Yes, it's my local. Norah fed me a lot when I had no kitchen. Luckily the kitchen's all finished now.'

'Great, I would love to see it, not that I'm inviting myself round.' I should really stop talking!

'I would be very happy for you to see it,' he says gently and I feel his eyes connect with mine. There's something about a sky full of stars and a beautiful man that make things flutter that really shouldn't. It's almost romantic. The light and bumbling energy between us is suddenly replaced with an electricity in the air and I feel a little breathless. I can't quite pull my eyes from his, they're magnetic and I feel hypnotised – no, no this is dangerous territory.

'There you are!' Hettie hiccups as she stumbles out of the pub which seems to break the spell that is hanging over us. The interruption forces me to drop my gaze from Ben and as the haze clears, I'm able to think clearly again.

'Oh sorry, am I interrupting something?' she asks optimistically, unable to hide a huge grin.

'No not at all. My feet were hurting so I came out for a breather and Ben bought me a drink.' Even I know I sound like I'm protesting too much.

'Oh, aren't you a good 'un,' Hettie says, smiling at Ben like he's some sort of superhero.

'I try,' Ben replies puffing his chest out valiantly. Hettie tipsily stumbles. Ben jumps around the table and catches her. Maybe he is a superhero after all. 'Too much gin, eh, Hettie? Come on let's find that husband of yours.'

Hettie giggles as she holds on to Ben and allows him to escort her back inside. I step into my hideously painful shoes and hobble in after them.

'I better get you home, love,' Jack says as he takes Hettie from Ben's arms.

'And have your wicked way with me,' she states very loudly and Jack blushes. He is certainly going to have his work cut out for him trying to get a drunken Hettie home.

'Think we will get off too,' Safiyah says, yawning. 'We'll walk you home, Vi.'

'No don't be silly, it's the opposite direction. I'll be fine.'

'I can walk you home,' Ben suggests helpfully, or unhelpfully, depending on which way you're looking at it. I don't trust myself with him, so it has 'bad idea' written all over it. 'I'm going in that direction anyway.'

'No, honestly I'll be fine. You don't have too,' I say, a nervous wave encroaching up my chest. Why does he have such a strange effect on me?

'It's late, you are not walking on your own,' Safiyah interjects firmly. 'Thanks, Ben, great idea.' Safiyah smiles at me smugly.

Oh I could kill her right now. She kisses me on the cheek. 'Don't do anything I wouldn't do.'

I shoot her a warning look. 'Goodnight, Safiyah!'

Why is everyone so eager to try to push me towards Ben, especially when I've only been back for five minutes. Safiyah and Theo leave in the opposite direction, hand in hand, giggling to each other as Ben and I start walking down the high street and towards the other side of the village.

I can sense he is looking at me which does nothing to subdue my nervous energy. Perhaps he's some sort of serial killer. Should I really have been left alone with him? I risk a peek in his direction, only to find him giving me the oddest of looks. It's a mix of confusion and intrigue. Do I have something on my face again?

'What is it? Why are you looking at me like that?' I ask, feeling paranoid.

He pauses for a moment as if he's contemplating his next move. 'Are you really swearing off all men?'

Wow, I was not expecting that – Jack or Theo must have told him what I said earlier. That's quite a bold thing to ask me when we don't even know each other. Ben looks worried, like he might have overstepped the line.

'You've been chatting to Jack and Theo,' I say as more of a statement than a question.

'Jack mentioned it when I asked about you.' I see Ben grimace as he realises he has just openly admitted to asking about me. He looks embarrassed as his cheeks flush pink. It makes a nice change for it to be him and not me.

'So, you asked about me, did you?' I chuckle, nudging his shoulder, enjoying his discomfort.

Ben laughs. 'Maybe, I might have asked about you.' He nervously puts his hands in his pockets and looks straight ahead not making eye contact.

Why would he be asking about me? He probably just wanted to know who I was, a strange face in the village and all that, it can't be anything more. I imagine he fancies leggy supermodel fashionistas, not women who hurl cake at strangers and can't walk in stupid heels. (God, they are killing me. It would be more comfortable to walk across hot coals the whole way home than these frigging things.) Anyway, whatever his motives are, it doesn't matter because I'm not remotely interested in him. 'What did Jack say?'

'Just who you were. You all grew up together and that you had moved back home after a break-up.'

'So, you did know why I was back?' I throw at Ben frostily. If he bloody well knew why I was home why did he ask me earlier. Is nothing private in this sodding place?

'No, he didn't go into any detail. Honestly that was all he said. It's none of my business anyway.'

'Too right it's not,' I snap. Ben looks abashed and I realise I'm being rude and defensive again. 'Sorry, I didn't mean to snap... again. I was cheated on and it's just not something you want to talk about and in a small village like this everyone gossips enough and it all makes me a bit defensive.'

'I get it, people do like to talk here.' Understatement of the century! 'Men like him give us all a bad name. We're not all like that though.'

'True. I guess not all men think it's appropriate to shag their girlfriend's boss.'

'Your boss!' Ben staggers as he stops abruptly. 'Holy crap, and you caught them?'

'Yep, at work on the office desk.'

'What did you do?' he asks, gobsmacked.

'I rugby tackled her to the ground.' A titter slips out and I don't mean it to, it just sounds so ridiculous. 'Not my finest hour, I'll admit.'

'I'm quite impressed actually,' Ben says. 'Well, I guess I can understand your motivation for swearing off men. I think it would be a shame though. Someone might come along that surprises you,' he adds, raising an eyebrow at me. If that's a hint that he might surprise me then he can think again! I've had all the surprises I can take.

'Are your feet still sore?' Ben asks. He must have noticed that my hobble has got increasingly slower and more unstable the further we go.

'Yes, they're killing me, hold on.' I can't pretend any longer, we're only a few minutes from home, but I have to get these things off. I cling on to Ben's shoulder and rip them off. The cold floor brings instant relief to my hot throbbing feet. 'Oh my God that feels so good.' I'm fully aware that I sound aroused at this precise moment, but I don't care, the relief is wondrous.

Ben tries to be gentlemanly and ignores my erotic moans of relief, but I can see him swallow hard and look the other way with a little smirk.

'You can't walk home like that. Here, hop on.' He crouches in front of me so I can jump on his back. Not a bloody chance of that happening.

'You're not giving me a piggyback home!'

'Why not?'

'Because I will break your back.'

'How weak do you think I am?' he replies, pretending to be offended. 'You either hop on or I'll just throw you over my shoulder and fireman's lift you home,' he says, taking a step closer to me. I hear myself take a big gulp of air from his proximity. A warm bolt jolts through my body. I feel all flustered. I really hope my face hasn't let on how appealing that actually sounds.

'Fine,' I groan. He turns round and I climb on his back gently to make myself appear lighter because that sort of thing works. You know, positive thinking defying the laws of gravity and all!

He starts walking like I weigh nothing; he's strong and it's agonising how attractive that makes him to me. My arms are hanging on tight around his neck, his scent dancing under my nose. An image of him in a fireman's uniform ploughs across my mind and it's irrefutably satisfying. No, Violet, stay strong, you're not interested.

'Here we go,' he says, stopping outside the cottage a few minutes later.

'Thanks for the lift,' I say, sliding off his back.

'No worries. I think Lilly is waiting for you.' He doesn't take his eyes off me but nods towards the house. I look to the kitchen window in time to see Lilly quickly duck down out of view. I sigh and shake my head. How long has she been stood there waiting? That woman is so embarrassing. I'm thirty, for Christ's sake. Ben chuckles. 'I think that's my cue to say goodnight.'

'Yes, goodnight, Ben.' I go to open the garden gate but I'm so flustered I fumble, trying to unlock it. Why won't this blasted thing open? I wrestle with it for a few moments until Ben comes to my rescue. He leans his arm over me and in one quick motion, opens the gate effortlessly.

'Thank you,' I say, rolling my eyes at my own incompetence. He doesn't say anything else though, just another dashing smile and starts to walk away. I walk up the path to the front door. I can hear his footsteps moving in the opposite direction so before I go in the house, I find myself giving him one last look. Unfortunately, he catches me doing so – fuck-balls.

14

'Mum, are you in here?' I call, walking into Lilly's art studio that's attached to the side of the house. The room smells of wet paint and there are old jam jars full of brushes lined up on the windowsill. Canvases are scattered all around the room with incredible views from in and around the local woods. The village is holding an art exhibition at the end of the summer and Lilly is so excited to be showcasing her work – *A year in the life of Elmsbourne Woods.*

'Mum, these are wonderful.' Wow, Lilly is so talented. I stop in front of a beautiful scene of rabbits grouped together under a tree. The detail is exceptional, the expression on the rabbits' faces look so lifelike. If I reach out, I'm sure I could step into the painting.

'Do you like them? This is one of my favourites from the spring collection,' Lilly says, gushing at the picture I'm looking at. 'Your father snapped this photo when we were out walking and I just had to paint it.'

'I love it, Mum. You're so talented.' I feel a pang of guilt ricochet in my chest, it's been so long since I've been in Lilly's studio. I should have shown more interest but instead, in the weeks I've been back, I've been too busy feeling sorry for myself. I must be a better daughter, to Fred too. I'll start asking if he wants help in the garden.

'What can I do for you, love?'

'Just wondering if you have a spare art pad, I've left my supplies back in London. I was in such a rush to leave I only picked up my full pad and forgot all the spares.'

'Of course, dear, look in the drawer over there and take what you need. What's it for? Have you finally got your creative mojo back?' Lilly asks hopefully.

'Sort of. Something wonderful happened last night,' I say, bouncing excitedly.

'Oh, with Ben, did you kiss? Did he get your creative juices flowing? Tell me all the gory details,' Lilly replies excitably, sitting on the edge of the desk readying herself for a good story.

'No, Mum!' Lilly isn't great at boundaries when it comes to what conversations mothers and daughters should share. 'Do you remember Collette Fletcher? She was a couple of years below me at school.'

'Oh yes, Bernie and Esme's daughter. I go to book club with Esme. She said Collette was home for the weekend.'

'Yes, well she's interested in me designing and making her wedding dress,' I say proudly as I pick a pad out of the desk drawer. 'Hettie's idea.'

'Violet, that's wonderful,' Lilly screams. 'See, I knew it. Good things are coming, my girl.' I can't help but get caught up in Lilly's excitement. I've woken up today with a buzz of design ideas fizzing around my mind.

'Collette will be here in a minute and Hettie's coming for moral support.'

'You don't need moral support, have confidence in your own abilities. Look at the dress you're wearing now,' she says, pointing to my home-made white strappy summer dress that's covered in red poppies. 'It's beautiful, and just look at the wedding dress you made for Hettie. So many people asked where it was from, it was stunning. I know at least two people who were interested in wedding dresses from you after seeing Hettie in hers.' This was true. Two of Hettie's friends had asked me, but I politely declined. I had just moved to London by then and was so busy with the boutique I didn't have time to keep popping back to Elmsbourne-Hollow for fittings. Such a wasted chance.

'I won't make that mistake again,' I state firmly.

'Good. Now, let me show you my latest picture from art class last week.' Lilly grabs a canvas from the easel and spins it round to show me. 'We had a model in for the afternoon.'

'Oh, holy shit balls!' I shout, scrunching my eyes up and covering my face. But it's too late, my poor eyes have already seen it. Before me is a picture of a man in his late fifties posing with his hands on his hips, one leg up on a step. Oh, and he's naked. His *large* male appendage is there for all to see. It wouldn't be an issue if I didn't recognise the man's face. 'Is that Mr Thompson from the post office?' I say, peeking from behind my hands. Oh my, why did I look again? That will be etched into my memory forever.

'It is, darling. Charlie volunteered to be our muse,' Lilly says cheerfully. 'I must say I found it rather hard to draw, struggled with the proportions if you know what I mean. All I'll say is Caroline's a lucky devil,' Lilly adds with a mischievous snort.

'For the love of God,' I say wearily, that will be in my nightmares. Good on him for having the confidence to pose but that painting should come with a warning – graphic content. 'His thing is like Mona Lisa's eyes, Mum, it follows you around the room. I'll never be able to look at Mr Thompson in the same way again.'

'Me neither, love.'

. . .

After that rather disturbing art show, I go back inside. I've already placed the pad with my designs on the kitchen table. I boil the kettle and retrieve a teapot and three cups from Lilly's collection. I find a packet of biscuits in the cupboard and place them next to the teapot. I thumb through my designs while I wait for Hettie and Collette to arrive but as I get to the last page my heart plummets. I'm looking at the dress I drew one lazy Sunday afternoon for myself, the dress I imagined walking down the aisle to Philip in.

A simple fitted gown with a fishtail silhouette, lace-capped sleeves and pearl buttons up the back. Delicate embroidery around the top of the dress for a vintage vibe. The majority of my designs have a vintage appeal to them. The dress is simple and elegant. I slam the book shut. My emotions over the break-up have moved on from despair to full-on rage over the last day or so which I hope is normal. Whenever I think of the smug shit I want to scream, not just a little scream either. A full-on guttural explosion.

I'm not actually sure designing a dress for such a romantic occasion is really the thing for me at the moment. Perhaps a ritual dress to wear when eliminating ex-lovers by burning photos while dancing around a fire would be more appropriate with my current state. Collette is giving me an amazing opportunity though. I can't ruin it over him. I need to find my new happy place and perhaps my work could be it, this could be the start of something special. I look out of the window and see Collette and Hettie walking down the path, their hands filled with bridal magazines. *You can do this, Violet – come on.* I answer the door feeling ever so slightly anxious, I hope I can hold it together for however long this takes.

15

'Hi, girls,' I say in the brightest voice I can muster. 'Come on through to the kitchen, there's a pot of tea on.'

Collette looks just as nervous as I feel.

'I brought cake with me,' Hettie says, holding up a box, and I feel instantly better knowing that Hettie is here and not just because she has brought cake with her.

'I was hoping you would bring one of your delights with you.' I take the box and give it a good sniff. 'Coffee and walnut?'

'Yep.'

'Yum.' I have an uncanny ability to decipher any cake even with the tin lid firmly in place. Not an ability that will take me far in life but still proud of, nonetheless. I pour us all a cup of tea and sit down opposite Collette and Hettie. 'Right, let's get started, so when's the big day?'

'December the eleventh,' Collette says, and even through her nervousness I can sense the excitement.

'I love a Christmas wedding. Right, that gives us five months. Have you tried many dresses on?'

'Yes, loads,' she says heavily. 'But time's running out and...'

'None of them have felt like *the one*?'

'Yes, exactly. There were a few that came close, but each one didn't quite have everything I wanted. Oh God, does that make me sound like a brat?' she asks me anxiously.

'No, not at all. When you're spending hard earned money not only on a dress but a whole wedding that you've probably been dreaming about since you were a little girl, you want the perfect one. You want to feel the best you've ever felt when you're stood waiting to walk down the aisle.' My heart gives a thud as the last page of my pad screams out at me. I take a sip of tea.

'When I looked in the mirror at each dress, I just wasn't comfortable. I didn't feel like I looked very much like a bride, they didn't suit me. And everyone had an opinion: Mum, my sister, my friends, telling me what I should have.' Collette looks sad as she lets her hair fall in front of her face slightly. I want to make her feel better; I want her to know how beautiful she is, so I reach out and touch her hand.

'Collette, I'm sure you looked amazing in them. It's a very common feeling, I've seen it lots of times. There are so many different dresses, it can be very overwhelming and there's a lot of pressure that brides put on themselves about how they want to look. I promise if there is anything that I think won't suit you I will let you know, and I won't pressurise you into anything that *you* don't want. I can assure you though that no matter what dress you pick, you will be breathtaking and your very lucky husband-to-be will agree.' Collette smiles and I think my little pep talk might have helped.

'There is one thing I was hoping for. My late grandmother left me a beautiful brooch. It's quite delicate and has pearls and diamonds on it, and I was hoping perhaps we could include it somehow on the dress.'

'That's a lovely idea,' Hettie says.

'That is something that we can definitely do, a really lovely personal touch. Now, the good thing is, after trying on lots of dresses you will probably know what you do and don't like which is a great start. Let's go through the magazines and you can show me different elements and styles that you like.'

We spend the next half an hour munching on biscuits and cake, looking through copious amounts of dresses, laughing and chatting. I sketch a couple of different ideas as we talk. I'm starting to get a good idea of the direction Collette wants to go down and she seems to be relaxing more with each passing second.

'So, what I'm thinking is you want to steer away from big princess-type gowns, and you don't want anything strapless?'

'Yes.'

'Nothing too fussy?'

'You seem to like the vintage vibe,' Hettie adds helpfully.

I'm busy sketching a new design onto a fresh piece of paper when the familiarity of the dress suddenly dawns on me, and my eyes begin to prick. I try to clear my throat, I mustn't cry. Oh my God, am I doing this? Am I giving her my dress? The style will suit her shape and she has such an elegant old-fashioned look to her that the vintage style will match in perfect harmony with her. Plus, if I can't wear it, someone else should, it's a beautiful design even if I do say so myself. I open my art pad to the back page that I so desperately didn't want to lay my eyes on ever again. 'How about this?'

'Wow, that's perfect,' Collette declares, pulling the pad closer to her.

Hettie looks at me, sympathy emanating from her eyes. 'It's beautiful, Vi.' Bugger, she knows it's mine.

'We could add a ribbon around the waist, perhaps in a

colour, and attach your grandmother's brooch to it in the centre?' I say, forcing myself to push on.

'Violet, yes. That's it, that's the one.'

'You will look beautiful, Collette, and any changes you want to make, we can do as we go along with regular fittings.' I show Collette a few different colour samples for the satin and lace that I have in my stash upstairs and after picking a rich ivory satin, we finalise a price.

'Right, just some measurements now.' Collette stands as I get out my measuring tape. She seems a little self-conscious letting her strawberry-blonde hair that sits just below her shoulders fall in front of her face again, almost hiding behind it like a shield. She's understatedly pretty, she has delicate features, high cheekbones and a small button nose. She doesn't wear a lot of make-up but doesn't need to, her milky complexion is flawless.

'The dress would look lovely with the front of your hair pulled back so we can see that beautiful face of yours. You have killer cheekbones,' I say, trying to bolster Collette's confidence. 'It would really emphasise the neckline of the dress, and the ribbon around the middle will show off your slim waist too.'

Collette smiles but seems embarrassed about the compliment. However, it must have worked because she pushes the hair away from her face and lifts her head a little higher. 'We have a few months, but it will take time to make so I will go into Lancaster over the next few days and get all the material ordered and we can go from there.'

'Sounds like a plan,' Collette says, beaming. She picks up her bridal magazines and says her goodbyes, leaving Hettie and I to chat.

'Was that the dress that you designed for yourself?' Hettie asks tentatively. She never misses anything.

'How did you know?'

'I could see it on your face. I remembered you saying you'd designed one.'

'Do you think Collette knows?' I ask uneasily.

'No, not at all, but she doesn't know you like I do.' Hettie pauses. 'You know, you will meet someone else. Just because you and Philip have ended doesn't mean that there isn't someone else for you.'

'Maybe. Still, that was the dress I imagined marrying him in. I couldn't wear it for someone else and it would have been a waste not to use it when it was so perfect for her. It's actually quite cathartic in a way. Hopefully I will see it as Collette's dress instead of my own. She seemed so much more confident before she left than when she walked in. I like that I was able to help her feel better about herself.'

Hettie nods at me in agreement. 'You're good at doing that. So how was the walk home last night?'

Wow, she sneaked that question in quickly. Somehow I knew the conversation would steer its way around to Ben at some point.

'Fine, thank you.' A warm buzz fizzes ever so slightly at the thought of him which I immediately try to quell.

'He's nice, isn't he?' Hettie continues, twisting her hair around her finger.

'He seems it. But I don't really know him that well,' I answer, taking our cups over to the sink. I'm trying to hide my face in case the creeping warmth I'm feeling shows, fuelling Hettie's questions further. She gives up quick enough though and sighs when I don't divulge any more information.

'Okay, well, I better get off. Jack said he is taking me to the pub for a roast. Fancy it?'

'Thanks for the offer but no. I have two dresses on order that I want to start.'

'Look at you, Miss Fancy Pants, getting all these orders,'

Hettie says playfully. 'That shop of yours isn't as far away as you think.'

'What's this about a shop?' Fred asks as he walks into the kitchen, catching the end of our conversation.

'I will leave Vi to explain. Here, Fred, you can finish this,' Hettie says, putting the remainders of the cake on a plate and pushing it in front of him.

'Hettie and Fiya think I should open a shop,' I explain to Fred once I've seen Hettie out.

'Here in Elmsbourne-Hollow?' he asks.

'Maybe, yeah. I mean I haven't really looked into it yet but it's a possibility in the future.'

'That sounds like a great idea. You know your mother and I will help you financially to get you started.'

'Thanks, Dad, but no, you have both done so much for me already, I don't want to take your money. I need to do this on my own. I haven't researched anything yet and I know how much you like a plan,' I joke, although there is actually an element of truth there. Fred would want a full business proposal presented to him.

'If you change your mind, you only have to ask.'

I honestly have the world's best parents, I really do, but if I'm doing this, then I'm doing it myself. It's bad enough I'm living with them still let alone taking their money as well.

'I know,' I say, kissing his cheek. 'Thank you.'

16

I spend the next few days completing the Etsy order. Luckily, I have the correct material as they are two of my most popular fabrics. I lay the pattern out on the fabric and carefully cut out each piece and pin them all together. As the dresses take shape my love for sewing is back to full swing. I fire up my sewing machine and the familiar whir of the needle pulsating up and down gives me such a thrill.

Although it hasn't taken me long to rediscover my passion, I'm utterly pissed off at myself for allowing Philip and Francesca to take away something that I love so much, even if it was only temporary. I run all the different pieces together through my sewing machine and lay the two finished dresses on the bed. I flipping love the feeling of accomplishment I get when I see the finished garment in front of me. It's like a little burst of joy.

In between making the two dresses I've spent time with Lilly in the art studio talking about the exhibition that's fast approaching and helping Fred in the garden. It's been years since I've potted plants with him. I had forgotten how enjoyable it is to laugh and chat while getting your hands dirty. Fresh air is certainly food for the soul and I'm actually starting to think that finding my happy place back here isn't beyond the realms of possibility. I love spending time with my parents and it's great to be back with my friends again. I just need to get some direction. Perhaps my own little business venture could be it.

After a few enjoyable hours in the garden with Fred, I box up the dresses ready to take to the post office. I've promised Lilly I will go to Zumba again and as much as I hate to admit it, I'm actually really looking forward to going. I put on my gym gear and grab the parcel. I can post it on the way to class.

'Good morning, Violet,' I hear Charlie Thompson chime across the shop as I walk in.

'Morning,' I reply, and Lilly's painting regrettably pops into my mind. Caroline Thompson walks out from the back room and after saying hello to me, plants a smacker of a kiss on her husband's cheek before filling up the card display. She always has a smile on her face and now I know why! I laugh as I remember Lilly's comment about her being a lucky devil which I subtly turn into a cough.

'First class, please,' I say, passing Mr Thompson the parcel, averting eye contact as naturally as possible. I decide to look extremely interested in the poster advertising the summer festival that is taking place on the village green this coming weekend. Anything to get Mr Thompson's large penis out of my mind would be good right now! (Not something I ever thought I would have to deal with.)

I actually can't remember the last time I went to the summer festival; three years ago perhaps. I did mention it to Philip last year, but he had coincidentally invited a colleague from work and his girlfriend around for dinner. Philip said he really needed my help to try to impress them, that it would be beneficial for his place in the law firm. He flashed those puppy dog eyes at me which made it impossible to say no.

The night was awful. Hugo, Philip's colleague, asked me if being a seamstress was a real career and rudely asked if I made much money. I had contemplated asking him what he earned in retaliation, but he's the type of smarmy git who would have been more than happy to announce what his grotesquely large pay cheque was.

His girlfriend was no better, she called me a shop girl and said I should have got caterers in as she stirred the food around her plate without eating any of it. Philip seemed unaware of my misery or the snide comments and just laughed at Hugo's idiotic jokes. In fact, he pretty much ignored me most of the night. God, what a crappy evening that was. Why didn't I question his behaviour then? Especially his new-found friendship with such, well, shitty people, to put it bluntly. When did I lose complete self-respect to have to put up with all that? I never even noticed I was being walked over and manipulated into staying in London when I wanted to visit home. I hear Mr Thompson talking to me which pulls me out of my reverie.

'Sorry what?' I ask, feeling bad that I wasn't listening.

'Are you going to the summer festival?' he says, nodding towards the poster.

'Oh yes, probably.' I'm still trying to avoid eye contact without offending him, so I pay for the postage and hightail it out of the shop.

As soon as the door closes and I'm out of sight, I burst out laughing.

'You seem happy today.' Ben is walking past with a coffee, looking jaw-droppingly gorgeous – phwoar is a word that comes to mind.

'Hi,' I say, composing myself. Ben's looking at me with anticipation, waiting for me to share the joke which I can't possibly do. 'It's nothing, believe me you don't want to know.' I can't get the image out of my head. I most certainly don't want to impart it on someone else. 'Not working today?'

'No meetings for a few days so thought I would work from home. Just taking a coffee break,' he says, holding up his coffee cup. 'You off for a run?' He's looking me up and down in my gym kit and I suddenly feel very self-conscious in my ultra-skintight leggings. There's nowhere to hide in leggings, is there? All wobbly bits are just there on display!

'No, off to Zumba again.' I give him a menacing look, daring him to laugh. He throws his hands up in the air in surrender, noting my look.

'Hey, I'm not laughing. Perhaps I will join you, I could do with learning a few moves.' I bet he can move quite well already. The fireman uniform vision comes to mind again and it sends a tingle down my legs. Where did that come from? And stop looking at his arms, Violet!

'I think a few of the Golden Girls would be more than willing to teach you a few things, although you may end up giving one of them a heart attack.'

'I don't know about that, they're a feisty bunch.'

I notice the smile on his face drop. He suddenly looks nervous and shuffles his weight from one foot to the other. 'Just wondering, will you be going to the summer festival this weekend?' He nods towards another poster that's on the post office window.

'Yes, probably. It's been a few years since I've been to it but it's always really good fun. Are you going?'

'Yes, definitely. So, I will see you there then? Perhaps we could grab a drink or something?'

I look behind me, surely he is talking to someone else. Nope, nobody there, he must mean me. He wants to get a drink with me, why? Probably just means as friends, nothing to get excited about. I have no idea why the butterflies in my stomach are now doing the conga! 'Erm... yeah sure,' I manage to say while reminding myself to keep it cool. There is nothing in it, just two people grabbing a casual drink.

'Right, well I shall let you get on then.'

'Yeah, cool. See you later, alligator.' I playfully punch his shoulder and then giggle awkwardly. What the hell was that? I have never said that in my life.

'Okay then,' he says, sounding a little confused as he walks away. 'Bye.'

I scrunch up my face and make my way towards the village hall, cringing – *See you later, alligator! Violet, you're an idiot!*

17

I walk into the village hall and I'm surprised to see Winnie is already here. I thought I was early.

'Hi, Winnie.'

'Hello, love,' Winnie replies, her face lighting up as she sees me.

'I thought I'd be the first here.'

'Yes, I'm a little early myself. Always am. Gets a little quiet at home so I like to get out and about.' For some reason that really pulls on my heart strings, I hope she isn't lonely at home.

'Do your children live far, Winnie?'

'My daughter, Keira, lives in Manchester so not too far, we visit as much as we can. My son, Robert, and his girlfriend live in Yorkshire, but both travel a lot with work. He's forever calling and Skyping me though. Isn't modern technology marvellous.'

'It is. You know you should pop in for a brew sometime if you ever feel like you want to get out but have nothing on,' I say with a sudden overwhelming urge to keep Winnie company. Perhaps it's because she's so quiet and gentle; she has an almost venerable quality to her. Just then the door to the village hall flings open and the Kimberley sisters (who do not have a venerable quality to them) walk in squabbling. This time it sounds like it's over who Paul, the butcher, has waved at.

'He was looking right at me,' Olivia says in a discernible tone, as if that should have been obvious to her sister.

'How would you know, you're as blind as a bat,' Rosalind scathes back.

God, do they ever give it a rest. How they haven't killed each other in the last seventy years is beyond me. Lilly and the rest of the Golden Girls follow them in and drop their bags at the bench.

'I thought we had scared you off,' Jane says, coming over to me.

'I won't lie, the sex talk nearly did.' I give Lilly a kiss on the cheek. Today she's sporting the same outfit as the last class only this time her top has the slogan, *Gym? I thought you said gin.*

'So, have you heard from that ex of yours yet? Has he come running back with his tail between his legs?' Olivia asks as she bends over and touches her toes to stretch. Very impressive, I wish I was that flexible, that might have kept Philip interested!

'No, I haven't, and I doubt I will. He seems very happy with the boyfriend-stealing backstabbing cow.' I realise I still sound very bitter, I really need to work on that. I open my phone and show them the most recent picture of the two of them on social media. Honestly, do either of them have no shame? We didn't break-up that long ago.

'It won't last, mark my words. His smile looks strained to me,' Olivia says. All the ladies have a good look and give a disapproving appraisal of them both in solidarity of me. I know they're just trying to be kind as even I have to admit they look good together. Still, I appreciate them trying.

'Sorry I'm late, ladies,' Roberto calls as he comes running into class all flustered, sporting a rather orange shade of fake tan. 'Are we all well?'

'We are,' the group reply in chorus, gazing at the instructor like he's a movie star.

'Good to see you again, Violet. Well, you all look beautiful, so come on, let's get started,' he says, switching on the music and turning the volume up. How does he have so much energy? Salsa music booms from the speakers and I can feel my shoulders bounce in response.

Yes, come on, let's do this. I need to pummel these feelings into something productive.

The class continues very much like last week, full of vigour and fun. I've remembered a few of the dance moves, I don't jump in the wrong direction as many times, although I still seem to trip over my feet a lot. By the end of the class I'm lying on the floor, panting for breath but feel amazing.

'Ladies, you all did fantastically but I think the star of the class is Violet,' Roberto shouts with a clap of his hands. 'You were in the zone, Vi, I've never seen someone shimmy so passionately.'

The whole class gives me a round of applause. I'm not sure a shimmy deserves such an accolade, but I take it anyway. I practically drag myself over to my bag. God, that felt good, absolutely knackering but brilliant. The Golden Girls have so much energy and charisma that it's rubbing off on me. There's no time to feel down when I'm in their company.

'Violet,' Jenny, one of the ladies from the group, comes over. 'I heard you're making a wedding dress for Esme's daughter... I was wondering, is it only bridal you make?'

'Not just bridal, I enjoy making all sorts of clothes,' I say between breaths, patting the sweat off my head.

'We're having a retirement do next month for my husband, Simon, and I want to look special for it. I'm struggling to find something suitable. I keep going shopping and finding nothing. I need help. Would you be interested in making something?'

'Of course I will,' I say, starting to get my breath back. How exciting, another order. I had been thinking about going into Lancaster to start applying for jobs, but with these orders perhaps I could put it off for a bit. I know it's only two but maybe if I advertise there will be potential for more. It's worth a go at least. I can see Lilly listening to the conversation and have the distinct impression she may have had something to do with this proposal. 'Do you have an idea of what you would like?'

'Yes, I think so,' Jenny replies. 'I have some pictures at home. I'm having all the Zumba ladies round in a bit for cake club, why don't you join us and I can show you?'

'Cake club? Okay. I'm going into Lancaster tomorrow to order material for Collette. I could get yours too if we find something you like.'

'Excellent,' Jenny says, picking up her bag.

As she leaves, I turn to Lilly. 'Did you have anything to do with that?' I ask suspiciously.

'Don't know what you're talking about, love.'

I'll take that as a yes then.

We all leave the village hall and I fall into step with Jane.

'You seem to be doing better.'

'Yes, I think I am.' There is something to be said for exercising your heartache away, and it's a hell of a lot more productive than drinking gin and wallowing.

'You know who's single, don't you?' Verity calls loudly from the front. 'Roberto, and he is ever so lovely. Why don't you ask him on a date?' she says in such an innocent manner.

'Don't really think I'm his type,' I laugh – obviously she's joking.

'Now don't be so hard on yourself, you're a bonny-looking girl,' Verity says, her innocent eyes imploring me.

Nope she's not joking! 'You know he's gay, right?'

'Really? Is he? I had no idea. Oh well in that case then, Violet, I wouldn't bother. I don't think he would be interested in you at all,' Verity says, looking perplexed.

The ladies carry on walking in front of me and I shake my head as I hear Verity's mumblings asking everyone else if they knew. Lilly stops so I can catch up with her.

'So, Mum, cake club?'

How many groups is Lilly actually a member of?

'Oh yes, darling, it's wonderful. After all the hard work of Zumba, we eat cake and chat,' she says, looking at me like it's perfectly normal. I don't have the heart to ask what the point of the workout is if you're going to eat a load of cake afterwards. I suppose any excuse for cake is good in my eyes though.

'Right then, show me what it is you want.' The Golden Girls and I have arrived at Jenny's for cake club. We are sat around her large dining-room table, all with different magazines in front of us. There's a large selection of cakes at one end. Ethel from the tearoom has joined us and brought with her a rather indulgent-looking *Sachertorte* which I'm currently eyeing up. Jenny points to a plain navy-blue shift dress with a round neck in the magazine in front of her.

'Okay, that's simple enough to make,' I say gently, not wanting to offend her. 'But it's for a party, isn't it?'

'Yes, Simon's retirement,' she responds despondently.

'It will look lovely, but do you not want something a little fancier, perhaps more colour?' I suggest.

'What Violet is trying to say, rather diplomatically, is that you're not going to work in an office, Jenny. You need something with a little more pizazz,' Jane says emphasising her words with jazz hands.

'Not quite what I meant.' I was trying to say it with a little more tact.

'Jane's right,' Mary agrees. 'You will look like you're going to a funeral not a party.'

Again, not how I would have put it but they do have a point. Jenny looks dejected.

'What about that lovely dress you said you liked when we were looking through magazines?' Lilly suggests helpfully. 'The dusky purple one.'

'Oh no I couldn't, that's not me at all.'

'But you said you loved it,' Lilly pushes.

'Yes, I love the dress but not for me. I'm too old for that and I don't have the right shape,' Jenny protests, abashed.

'Can I see it?' I ask.

Jenny opens the page and points to an A-line chiffon tea-length dress in a dusky purple with white lace detailing and little capped sleeves.

'Oh, Jenny, that's divine,' Lilly says.

'It's really beautiful,' Winnie agrees. 'Much better than the first one.'

Jenny looks up at me, her eyes screaming for help.

'I think it will look stunning on you. I have a pattern already for the shape of the dress and I can make adjustments for the lace sleeves,' I say in my best reassuring voice. Jenny still doesn't look convinced though and I don't want her to feel pushed into a decision she's not comfortable with. 'Jenny, which one do *you* prefer?'

'This one,' she says, pointing to the dusky purple dress. 'I just haven't worn anything like it before.'

'Do you like the colour?'

'Yes, I think so, if you think it will suit me?'

'It will look beautiful.'

Jenny gives me a determined nod as she makes up her mind.

'Okay, why not, let's do it.' She takes a deep breath and looks back at the photo.

'Great, I'll go into town tomorrow and see what I can find, there's a lovely little fabric shop I used to go to ages ago. I googled it and it's still there, so I'll see what I can find. They don't hold a lot of stock, but she can order in if I can't find what I need. Shall we do some measurements?'

The rest of the ladies make their way into the living room through a large double partition door. Jenny hands me her measuring tape and I set to work. 'I hope you don't mind me saying but you look like you have lost weight since the last time I saw you,' I say, slipping my arms around Jenny's waist with the tape.

'I have, three stone. Simon and I went on a health kick twelve months ago. It's been a long slog and cake club has been... difficult,' Jenny says with a wry smile.

'You look fantastic.'

'Thank you. Listen, Violet, be honest with me. This dress, you don't think I'll look like mutton dressed as lamb, do you?'

'Not at all.' I'm shocked it would even cross Jenny's mind. 'I would never agree to make anything that I didn't think was right for someone.'

'I really want to look good at the retirement party. There's going to be lots of people that we've known for years and I haven't seen since my weight loss.'

'Jenny, you don't need to worry. You'll look amazing, it's a gorgeous dress, glamorous yet tasteful.'

'What about my hair?' Jenny says, pulling her fingers through her shoulder length locks as if it were lacklustre and plain.

'What about it?'

'Do you think I need a change? I've had the same style for twenty years. Any suggestions?'

'Your hair is lovely the way it is but if you do fancy a change, a chic bob would look great. It's simple but very classy and you would probably feel like you've had quite a transformation without it being too risky. Especially if you have it angled.'

'And that would suit my age?' Jenny asks me thoughtfully.

'Yes, a bob is timeless. Jenny, age is just a number, you know, try not to worry so much. As my mother would say – you look fabulous, darling.' I do my best impression of Lilly which is scarily quite accurate. It makes me sad to think that Jenny has no confidence in the way she looks. I personally think she looks fantastic, but I guess we all have hang-ups about ourselves.

We finish up and head into the living room to join the others.

'Could I put an order in too?' Jane ambushes me as soon as we walk in.

'Of course,' I say, delighted. Another order – this is great!

'I want this, please,' Jane says, shoving a picture of a beautifully elegant cocktail dress in emerald green under my nose.

'Where on earth would you wear that to?' Maggie asks.

'I don't know, but if I spend money on it then that husband of mine will have to take me somewhere special to wear it,' she says with an impish laugh.

'If you want it, I will make it. Let me get Jenny's finished and then I will make a start on yours.'

18

After indulging in enough cake to render me diabetic at Jenny's, I decide to have a much-needed walk. I have a quick shower and throw on my handmade green sundress with little wooden buttons down the middle and head out into the balmy late afternoon air. I walk down the road in the opposite direction of the village centre towards Elmsbourne Woods.

Within two minutes I'm at the top of a steep path that winds its way down through the trees towards the river. As I carefully walk down the uneven steps, I can hear the trickle of water in the distance. I make it down to the riverbank and gaze out at the view. It's beautiful, the tall trees tower over the river, gently swaying in the breeze, the sunlight dancing merrily off the water. I sit down on the bench and take a few deep breaths allowing the fresh earthy air to fill my lungs. It's so quiet. Nowhere in London feels this tranquil and relaxing.

I love the stillness of it here, just watching the birds flitting about the trees and the odd duck swimming past on the river, it's therapeutic. In the distance I can see someone jogging on the opposite side of the bank. The figure is getting closer and as it crosses the wooden bridge onto my side of the river I can see it's Ben.

The corners of his lips turn upwards slightly as he sees me and waves. He stops and pulls his earphones out of his ears as he reaches me. His thighs look ridiculously pleasing in black shorts and his electric-blue running top clings to his broad chest with sweat – gulp – be still, my beating ovaries.

'Bumping into each other twice in one day, people will start to gossip,' he says through ragged breaths after his run.

'No change there then.'

'So, what are you doing sat here?'

'Just fancied some fresh air. It's so peaceful here,' I say, trying to tear my eyes from his chest that is panting up and down rapidly.

Ben swigs water from his bottle as beads of sweat trickle down his forehead. The old Diet Coke advert springs to mind, the one where the hot workman strips off his top and guzzles Diet Coke down in slow motion. Why does he always look so good? I should really close my mouth because I might actually drool if I'm not careful. I avert my attention to a family of ducks floating by.

'It's so lovely here. Did you miss it living in London?' Ben asks, sitting down next to me.

'Yes, I guess I did.' I'm suddenly annoyed at myself again. The times I thought of coming home to visit and then didn't because Philip needed me. I'm becoming painfully aware of how much I succumbed to his needs. I was so blinded by love. Not again! 'How's your run?'

'I could think of worse places to do it.' He looks out at the river.

I'm losing my train of thought as Ben's knees brush against my bare legs. My nerve endings feel like they're on fire at his touch. I move my legs a little and sit up straighter so our skin is no longer touching.

'How was Zumba?' he asks with a cheeky grin and I can't help but reciprocate. Is it really so strange I go to Zumba with the Golden Girls?

'Pretty good, actually. I got another couple of orders for dresses.'

'A wedding dress?' Ben asks, looking bemused.

'No,' I chuckle. 'An evening dress, although I wouldn't put it past one of the Kimberley sisters to put in an order for a wedding dress. I think they're both on the hunt for their next husband.'

'They get fairly amorous, those two. One of them slapped my arse the other week in the pub.' Not at all surprising, they're man-eaters. The look on Ben's face makes me chuckle.

'Ooh, you could be lucky number four for Olivia.'

'Ah yes, but then what about Rosalind?'

'True, it would cause more arguments. Hey, you can't blame them, they see a hot guy, it's just too tempting for them.' Wait, no, did I just call him hot?

'You think I'm hot, do you?' He nudges my shoulder as a satisfied grin lights up his face.

Oh crap, I did say that. 'I mean you're okay, if you like that ruggedly handsome sort of thing,' I try to say casually. The air seems to have ramped up a few degrees. I think my face might be burning.

'Ruggedly handsome, eh? I'll take that.' He looks very pleased, but his cheeks are a little flushed from my compliment which only endears me to him more. He's confident but not cocky.

'Yeah okay, let's forget I said that.' I get up. I need to put some distance between us. 'Haven't you got a run to finish?'

'Okay, okay, I'll be on my way.' He takes another gulp of water and puts his earphones back in. He gives me one last heart-stopping smile and returns to his run.

I watch him go and my eyes linger for longer than they should on his rather scrumptious bottom.

19

I'm rabid with excitement, I have my shopping list in hand and I'm in Lancaster about to go to the fabric shop. Now I know this is a very niche passion, but I love having a mooch around haberdasheries and craft shops. I love the smell of the fabrics and imagining what I could make with each and every one. It sets my creative juices alight. I'm about to walk into the shop when I hear my phone ringing.

'Hi, Imogen.'

'Violet, hi, how are you?'

It's good to hear her voice. We haven't actually spoken on the phone since I left London, the only communication has been through email. 'I'm doing good, thanks. Sorry I haven't spoken to you much, I just...' Crap, how do I finish the sentence? How do I explain that she reminds me too much of my life before with Philip? A life I'm trying to put behind me, it sounds so lame and pathetic.

'I get it, don't worry,' Imogen replies, relinquishing me from having to find the words. She's so understanding which just makes me feel like an even crappier friend.

'How are you?' I ask.

'I'm good. I miss you though. It isn't the same in the shop without you.'

'Yeah, I miss you too.' I really do. 'Is the shop busy?'

'Very much so. Harriet Sinclair was in the other day,' Imogen tells me excitably. Harriet Sinclair is one of my all-time favourite actresses. Imogen and I have spent many hours talking about her style in the shop and wondering what it would be like if she ever came in.

'No way, that's amazing. What's she like?'

Typical, I leave and she shows up.

'Bit of a bitch, to be honest. You know what they say; never meet your idols. Proper stuck-up. She took an instant dislike to Francesca though, which was brilliant. Really knocked her down a peg or two. You should have seen her face, it was a picture,' Imogen says, shamelessly happy. Hearing Francesca's name is like a punch to the gut, and I feel my body run cold. 'Shit, sorry, I shouldn't have mentioned her.'

'No, it's fine, I'm fine. Just gutted I missed Harriet. I think I like her more now I know she doesn't like Francesca.' It's petty, I know it is, but I feel brighter knowing that having Harriet Sinclair, the famous actress, dislike her would have really narked Francesca off. I know I shouldn't think like that but I'm not quite at the stage yet where I can be impassive about the woman who stole my man.

'Me too. So, come on, tell me what have you been up to?'

'This and that. I've had a few orders for dresses, one of them is a wedding dress actually which is exciting. I'm in Lancaster now, about to order all the material. A few of the ladies from Zumba and cake club have asked me to make some evening gowns for them too.'

'Zumba, cake club, wow, Violet, it sounds like you're busy up there.' Imogen's words spur me on to realise that I am actually making some positive steps forward.

'Yes, well, it helps having distractions.' My thoughts have wandered to Ben offering to throw me over his shoulder again. I try to shake the image out of my mind. That is certainly not a distraction I should be entertaining.

'I'm so pleased for you, Violet, I really am. You sound like you're settling there.'

'I think I am.' We say our goodbyes and hang up. I'm so relieved to have finally spoken to her. A weight has been lifted. She's such a good friend to me and I don't want to let that go. Just because my relationship is over doesn't mean I have to cut all ties to my life before.

I make my way inside the haberdashery and after a long mooch around pulling out rolls and rolls of fabric I find the shop assistant.

Forty-five minutes later I'm leaving with all of the items for the wedding dress on order, and the fabric for Jenny's dress all wrapped up nicely in a bag. Successful shopping trip all round.

I've decided to pop to Hettie's bakery for a quick catch-up on my way home. The thought of one of Hettie's vanilla slices is far too enticing.

'Hettie, are you here?' I call as I enter her shop but find the counter empty.

'I'll be there in a minute!' I hear her shout from the back.

I look around at the selection of home-made cakes for sale, salivating at how delicious they all look. The bakery smells sweet and welcoming, freshly baked bread and cinnamon pastries... delicious. Once you're in the shop the smell is so tantalising you never want to leave – a very clever marketing ploy.

Hettie has wedding cakes made out of polystyrene for display purposes but decorated beautifully in sugar paste scattered all around the countertops, showcasing how talented she really is. My favourite is the 'topsy-turvy' cake. Three intentionally wonky layers made to look like they are only just balanced on top of each other, covered in vibrant icing, each layer is a mismatch of colour and pattern.

'What you can't make out of icing isn't worth knowing. They are all brilliant,' I say, awestruck, as I hear Hettie come into the front of the shop.

Oh no, something's wrong. Hettie's eyes are red and puffy; she's been crying.

'Hettie what's happened?'

'Nothing, I'm fine.'

'No, you're not, you've been crying.' Hettie never cries, it must be serious. She always has such a calm demeanour about her, nothing ever fazes her. Someone has clearly upset my friend. When I find out who it is, oh, they're in for a whole heap of pain.

'Violet, I don't know what to do,' she says wearily, succumbing to tears once more. 'It's Jack.'

'Jack! Is he okay? Has something happened?'

'No, no, nothing like that,' Hettie says, trying to regain her composure. 'He... he wants to try for another baby.'

That's not what I was expecting at all. 'Hettie, that's good, isn't it?' I ask gently. 'I mean you both want children, don't you?' But Hettie doesn't answer me. Hettie has always wanted children, she always talks about baby names and imagines children running around the bakery. I'm so confused but she looks lost and troubled and I want to hug her. I walk over and lock the door, turn the sign around to say closed and take Hettie by the hand.

'Come on, let's sit down.' We walk through the kitchen and into a little office with a desk and two chairs. 'Have you changed your mind?'

'Yes... no, I don't know. Violet, I'm scared.' She looks so helpless, her eyes full of sadness and I suddenly understand, of course she's scared.

'In case it happens again, a miscarriage?'

'I know it happens, Violet, to so many women, and they go on to have children. But I'm frightened of having to go through it again. It's not just the physical pain, that I can almost cope with. It's the feeling of loss and emptiness again that I'm petrified of. And not just mine but Jack's too. What if we do end up pregnant again? What if the worry and panic causes something to go wrong?'

'Have you spoken to Jack about it?'

'No, I don't want to disappoint him.'

My heart breaks for her. How long as she been dealing with this and not telling anyone? I've never seen her look so vulnerable. I wish I could ease her worries.

'Now you listen to me, Hettie Braithwaite, that man loves you more than anything. You could never disappoint him. I'm sure he'll completely understand, and I bet he has the same fears as you. I can't tell you it won't happen again, I wish I could, but what I can say is that whatever happens, you're so strong, and Jack will be by your side the whole time and so will I.'

In this moment I'm so glad to be home, to be here for Hettie. I've spent too long away. She has supported me so much over the last few years and now it's my turn to repay the favour.

'If you're not quite ready yet then that's perfectly fine, don't rush yourself but don't give up either. You've wanted to be a mother for as long as I can remember, you're the most maternal person I know.'

Hettie throws her arms around me and I let her sob into my shoulder. I know this sounds strange, but I suddenly feel like this is where I am supposed to be. I felt so bitter about having to move back home but that doesn't matter anymore. I want to be here.

I decide to stay with Hettie at the shop for a while to make sure she's feeling better. I put on an apron and help serve behind the counter. I spot Caroline Thompson across the road cleaning the post office windows and decide to tell Hettie all about Lilly's painting. It does the trick and Hettie falls about laughing as Mrs Thompson crosses the road and walks towards the shop. 'Shit, Hettie, she's coming in, pull yourself together.' The door pings open. 'Good afternoon, Mrs Thompson,' I exclaim loudly, giving Hettie a few extra seconds to calm down.

'Oh hello, love. Hettie got you working in here then?' Mrs Thompson says brightly.

'Just keeping her company, she doesn't know yet but she's paying me in cake.' I flash Hettie a gleaming smile. 'What can I get you?'

'A pecan muffin for Mr Thompson, please, and I will have a Bakewell slice. Could I have that one, please?' she asks, pointing to a large one at the back. 'I do like a big one.'

Oh, I know you do, you little minx. Unfortunately for Hettie, Mrs Thompson says this just as she's taking a big swig of tea. Hettie snorts into her cup and then coughs as tea comes out of her nose.

'Are you okay?' My voice is cracking because I'm trying to suppress my own giggles that are clawing their way up my throat.

'Yes,' Hettie splutters. 'Went the wrong way.'

'Here you go.' My voice is strained because I'm still trying not to laugh. I hand the cakes over. 'Three pounds please.'

'Thanks, girls. See you both later.' She leaves the shop just in time because we explode with laughter once she's a safe distance away.

'Good for her,' Hettie says, taking a few deep breaths and wiping her eyes that are watering from laughing so much. That has certainly brightened Hettie's mood.

'Hey, can I ask you something?'

'Yes.'

'What's your happy place? Where are you most happy?'

'Hmmm, it probably sounds boring but home, with Jack. Especially when we're cooking together in the kitchen, telling each other about our day. Fairly simple really. Why?'

'No particular reason, just wondering.' That's not entirely true. I guess in my quest to find my happy place I've suddenly become intrigued to see what other people's are. Hettie's is home with her love.

'Cup of tea?' she asks brightly.

'One more then I better be off. I want to make a start on Jenny's dress.'

Hettie heads into the kitchen as the shop door opens, I look up and see Ben. He seems surprised to see me stood behind the counter.

'New job?' he quips.

'Just a helper for a few hours, an excuse to spend time with Hettie really. So, do you actually work or do you just spend most of your days wandering around the village?' I tease back.

'Doing my bit supporting local businesses.' He smiles and it seems to do all sorts of things to my insides that it shouldn't.

'On that note, what can I get you?' I ask as I hold my arms open displaying all the treats on offer. He looks intently at the options, and then with an impish grin, says, 'I think I will go for a piece of chocolate cake, I have good memories of the last one I was *given*.'

The butterflies fly harder and faster.

'And how would you like this one? In a paper bag or smothered all over you?' My imagination suddenly runs wild as I imagine licking cake off his chest! A pleasing tingle ripples through my legs. Where the hell did that come from?

'Now there's an offer,' he says, raising his eyebrows, a playful glint flashing across his eyes. 'Best stick to the paper bag though, can't ruin all my clothes.'

I tip the cake into a plastic case and pop it in a bag. I feel his eyes studying me and I risk a quick look at him. My stomach lurches forwards like I'm on a roller coaster, zooming down the first big drop.

'Two pounds fifty, please.'

He counts out the money and then without dropping his gaze from me, hands me the coins. 'Guess I will see you on Saturday then.'

'You will?' Will he? What? Shit what's happening here?

'Summer festival, you said you're going?'

'Yes of course, the festival.' Bloody hell, Violet, what did you think he meant?

Ben heads to the door. 'See you there then,' he calls in a deep husky tone which sends my ovaries in to overdrive once again.

'Yep, bye,' I say, struggling slightly to form words. Ben turns and leaves the shop and I feel a little fuzzy.

'My God, you could cut the sexual tension with a knife,' Hettie banters as she walks out from the kitchen, smirking, with two steaming mugs of tea in her hands. 'You two are terrible flirts.'

'No we're not, there was no flirting. I told you I'm not ready for anything like that,' I protest defiantly.

'Really?' I can tell by Hettie's tone she doesn't believe me. 'Well, you know what they say, the only way to get over one man is to get under another.'

'Hettie! Bloody hell have you been hanging out with the Golden Girls? You're as bad as them.'

We weren't flirting, were we? Of course not, Hettie's mistaken, that's all. It isn't a completely displeasing thought though. Perhaps a bit of no-strings-attached fun with a gorgeous muscly architect could be just what I need.

20

I work hard over the next two days on Jenny's dress, the pattern has been cut out and I've already started pinning the fabric into shape. I found my old dressmakers mannequin up in the attic. The first apartment in London that Philip and I rented was too small to take it with me, so I stored it up there and forgot all about it until Fred reminded me. I hang my work in progress on it and stand back.

The A-line skirt of Jenny's dress is complete, made from dusky purple satin which starts just above the waist and drops down to the calf. The bodice of the dress is white and strapless with a sweetheart neckline. The dress will eventually have lace gently starting in the middle, opening up over the bodice and spreading across the shoulders to form little capped sleeves but for now everything has been pinned together ready for Jenny to try on. I can't wait to show her but I'll have to do that tomorrow because it's Saturday morning, the day of the summer festival.

I've promised Safiyah that I will go over to Winters Farm and help take some of the gin to the village green for the gin tent. I tuck my sleeveless white shirt into my blue high-waisted denim shorts and slip into my black ballet pumps. I wear my yellow tassel earrings for a slight festival vibe which Fred says look like curtain tie-backs. I step out into the glorious morning sunshine and make my way towards the village green. There's a buzz of activity as busy villagers set up stalls and tents selling food and drink. There are traditional summer fete games, craft stalls selling handmade gifts, and even a little petting zoo for the children. Excitement is in the air.

After a very warm walk (I'm glad I'm in shorts) I've made it to Winters Farm. It's a pretty stunning place. At the end of the long drive is Jane and Dave's farmhouse. I have so many memories of running around that place as a child, lots of rooms for some pretty epic games of hide-and-seek. I even snuck out of the windows a few times when I was dating Josh. To the left of the house, across a courtyard, is a large converted barn where Josh, Ayda and three-year-old Hector live, and next to that another large outbuilding that Safiyah and Theo are hoping to one day convert into a home. Further back is the distillery and the fields that grow all the fruits they use to make and flavour the gin. It's a pretty impressive empire.

Safiyah is walking out of the distillery with two boxes precariously balanced on top of each other clattering the bottles of gin. She's wearing a calf-length fitted short-sleeved dress in bright red that I made her for her birthday last year and she looks effortlessly stunning in it with her hair pulled back into a simple plait.

'Hello, my little worker bee,' I sing as I jog over and grab the top box from her.

'Thank you, that was heavy.' She looks flustered and very grateful for the help. 'We need to take these to the green. Josh roped a few of the rugby lads into helping so they've already set up the tent and tables. We just need to stock the gin and mixers up now,' she tells me as we walk towards the green. 'Thanks so much for the help.'

'My pleasure. Ooh is that mulberry gin?' I ask, peeking inside one of the boxes, it's my favourite.

'Sure is, I'll have one waiting for you behind the bar.'

'My mouth is watering already.'

'So how are you?' Safiyah asks me as we walk.

'I'm doing good.' I'm feeling quite peppy today actually. 'The Golden Girls have been keeping me busy with Zumba and dress orders, and I'm really excited to get cracking on Collette's wedding dress. I still miss Philip... actually I don't, I miss who I thought he was. The longer I'm home, the more I'm starting to see that I put him on a pedestal. I didn't notice the subtle changes in him and in me.'

'I'm pleased that you're feeling better,' Safiyah says with a reassuring smile.

'Can I ask you something?' I ask rather sombrely. There's something that's been playing on my mind. Safiyah has always been honest with me, brutally honest in some cases, so I know she's the right person to ask if I want a straightforward answer. 'When I first met Philip, did you like him?'

'Yeah, he seemed nice. I don't think he ever made a massive effort with us, but I didn't dislike him.'

'But over time he changed?'

'Well yeah, but even you admitted that. Where are you going with this?' Safiyah asks, confused.

'Did I change?' I'm apprehensive to ask but that's the real question I want answering. 'The longer we're apart, the more I'm starting to see that there was so much wrong with our relationship that I thought was a perfect fairy tale. Over the last eighteen months things changed so dramatically. I put up with things that I never would have before without even noticing, or maybe I did notice and was just in denial. The snide comments about the way I look and the things I like. He was controlling, quite manipulative really, guilting me into staying in London all the time so I couldn't visit home. Even the affair, the signs were there and I just ignored them.'

Safiyah sets the heavy box down on the floor very seriously, something bad must be coming. Oh God, perhaps I shouldn't have asked.

'You didn't change, it was more that you started to become the shell of the person you once were.' She says it gently because I know she doesn't want to hurt my feelings. 'Not initially. For the first few years you seemed so happy.'

'We were.'

'But you're right, over the last year or so we noticed little things. You didn't come back as much, when you did he didn't come with you but would constantly call. I didn't think there was necessarily anything wrong, I thought you were just wrapped up in your life there. But when you popped back for those few days before Christmas you seemed sad, like something was weighing you down and then on the phone since then you haven't sounded quite right.'

My eyes fill with tears. I had already started to realise this but hearing Safiyah say it twists a knot of shame through my gut. 'Jesus, what happened to me? I'm so ashamed of myself, Safiyah, for trusting him. I was so weak. Why didn't I do something about it? I was so consumed with him being my happily ever after, forcing it, that I let him walk all over me. I wanted so badly what my parents have and I was prepared to convince myself I had it.'

'Violet, there's nothing to be ashamed of. You didn't do anything wrong,' Safiyah says firmly as she takes me by the shoulders. 'You were in love with someone and you wanted to make it work. Perhaps you were a bit blinded by love, but we are all guilty of that at some point in our lives. But let's remember he did this to you, not the other way around. You're not weak for believing in something. He was just good at being a complete arsehole.'

'I feel so awful that I didn't come back more. On Mum and Dad and you and Hettie.' I can't even look Safiyah in the eye.

'You're here now, and you were always there on the phone. We didn't feel ignored by you, not once. You were here the moment Hettie needed you when she miscarried. Don't be so harsh on yourself. Don't blame yourself for his issues.'

I wipe my eyes. 'Thanks, Fiya.' I think she's possibly being kinder than I deserve.

We spend the next two hours going backwards and forwards, setting up the displays of gins and mixers and making the tent look welcoming with bales of hay covered in tartan blankets for people to sit on. I'm stood on a chair at the front of the tent helping Safiyah hang up some brightly coloured bunting.

'Need any help?' Ben's voice booms. I jump with shock and miss my footing. I can feel myself falling through the air and I brace myself for impact with the floor. This is going to hurt... but instead, two sturdy arms catch me.

'Sorry, didn't mean to startle you,' he says, holding me tightly in his arms.

'Good catch,' I answer breathlessly. He smells good again and my God, those eyes. I think I might actually be swooning, I thought that was just a thing in movies. He's looking at me so intently and I feel a pleasant warmth spread through my whole body. The world seems to have filtered out and it's just Ben and I staring at each other.

He slowly places me back on the floor as Safiyah gives a little cough reminding us both that she is actually still stood there. That seems to do the trick and wakes me from the spell that I seem to fall under far too easily around him. For goodness' sake, what's wrong with me? I need to get a grip. I'm a strong, independent woman. I do not need a man coming to my rescue, no matter how lovely and muscly his arms are.

'Oh yes, hi,' Ben says as if he's just noticed Safiyah. 'Can I do anything?'

'Yes please. The last two boxes of mixers are outside the distillery, could you fetch them over?' Safiyah asks, trying not to laugh.

'Sure.' He looks a little embarrassed and scuttles off across the green in the direction of the distillery. I watch him go as some rather lustful thoughts enter my mind but Safiyah does another little cough which pulls me back to reality again.

'Right, yes, bunting,' I say, reminding myself of the job in hand.

'Are you okay, darling?' Lilly has suddenly appeared hand in hand with Fred. 'We saw your little fall.' Oh great.

'Yes, I'm fine.'

'We would have come over sooner, but you looked like you were in safe hands,' Lilly replies as she gives Safiyah a wink. Oh God, they witnessed me swooning over Ben... bloody marvellous.

21

The fayre is in full swing with children running around in face paints and delicious aromas emanating from the various food stalls. With Safiyah working hard in the gin tent, Hettie and I are walking around the fayre with Fred and Lilly. Fortunately, my fall from the chair and Ben's heroic catch hasn't been mentioned again. I am, however, finding it increasingly hard to keep Ben out of my thoughts. I mean, come on, how can you have a moment like that where a gorgeous specimen of a man catches you from a potentially neck-breaking fall, holds you in his arms and not feel like you want to drag him off to somewhere private and rip his clothes off. Moments like that are what lustful daydreams are made of. Those thoughts are suddenly put on hold though by Hettie.

'We need to go to Dunk the Hunk,' she says eagerly.

'Dunk the what?' Have I heard her correctly?

'Hunk. Come and see,' Hettie says joyfully, dragging us all to the other side of the village green. A crowd has gathered around a small but very deep pool. Dean, one of the biggest and burliest players on the rugby team, is sat on a chair above the water with a target next to him. Three very excitable teenagers are taking it in turns to throw the ball at the target. The tallest of them hits the bullseye and Dean drops, crashing into the water, spraying the crowd in the process. The rest of the team are stood in a line in their kits and cheer as Dean hits the water. Ben is one of them and nervously catches my eye. This will do absolutely nothing to help my X-rated thoughts; he looks mighty fine in a rugby kit.

'It was Olivia and Rosalind's idea,' Lilly says hysterically. 'Anything to see a group of men soaking wet in rugby kits, eh, girls?'

'It's all in the name of charity,' Rosalind says, flashing the team a smile as Olivia eyes up Dean, who has climbed out of the pool and is walking back over to the group, soaking wet.

'I have a towel here, Dean, if you need any help drying off,' she calls flirtishly, holding up a towel.

'You're a bloody minx, Olivia,' Dean retorts, opting for his own towel which is a much safer idea.

'The best part is you can pick the player!' Hettie shouts. 'Jack, you hunk, you're up.' She hands her money to Mark, the team captain. Everyone in the crowd roars as Jack makes his way up the steps and onto the chair.

'Now, Hettie, remember I'm your husband, go gently.' He flutters his eyelashes, I'm assuming so Hettie takes pity on him.

'Not a chance,' she shouts with a wicked glint in her eye. 'You're going down.' She throws the first ball, but it misses, as does the second.

'Come on, Hettie!' I shout getting caught up in the moment. This is so much fun.

'What did I do to you, Brown? I thought we were friends.'

'Sorry, Jack, but when push comes to shove, us girls stick together.' Hettie throws the last ball, it smashes into the centre of the target, sending Jack into the pool with a large splash. Hettie jumps up and down ecstatic as the growing crowd erupts with cheers. Jack climbs out of the pool and walks over to us soaking wet.

'Ooh, I'll get you for that.' He playfully chases Hettie around. She tries to run but he catches her and quickly pulls her into a tight cuddle, getting her stripy summer jumpsuit wet in the process.

'Okay, I deserved that,' she says giving in and lovingly wrapping her arms around his neck. 'Your turn, Vi, who are you picking?'

Oh, I know exactly who I want! 'I think Ben looks far too dry.' Again, the crowd cheers as Ben climbs up onto the chair to take his place. I can hear heckles for me to dunk him, my eyes fix firmly on his. He looks back, nervously laughing but doesn't break eye contact and I can feel the electricity sparking between us.

'What's your aim like?' he shouts casually. I think he's trying to unnerve me, but it won't work.

'You're about to find out.' The first ball misses but only just, dammit. Lots of 'ooh's come from the crowd.

'Not good then!' he jokes, provoking me.

I suddenly feel like I'm in the Olympics going for gold. Adrenalin pumping, I pick up the next ball and aim. I don't see where it lands as I'm watching Ben's face. He scrunches his eyes up, the seat disappears beneath him and he falls into the water. I bloody did it! Everyone cheers as Ben emerges from the pool drenched and I can't stop myself from laughing. He walks towards me with his soaked kit clinging to his body and running his fingers through his wet hair, pushing it back from his face. Wow... the man is sex on legs, my heart gives a thud of appreciation and I have to swallow quickly before I drool.

'You got me,' he says huskily with an undertone that I think is suggesting more than just the dunking.

'Didn't even need all three balls,' I retort, throwing the last one into his hands.

'You do know you owe me a drink though now.'

'You might want to dry off first,' I say with a wink as I walk away. Bloody hell, look at me being all flirty and aloof.

What a brilliant afternoon it's been. Hettie and I decided to regress into giggly schoolgirls after the Dunk the Hunk fun and run around the fayre all afternoon. We've been on the carousel (not once or twice but three times) which I haven't been on in about twenty years and bloody loved. We then decided to have our faces painted too so I'm now sporting a very sparkly blue and pink butterfly design from my cheekbone and up around my left eye.

We queued with a bunch of eight-year-olds for the mini zip wire that has been set up on the far end of the green for children. It seemed like a good idea at the time until I set off and realised I was possibly too big for the ride as my bum dragged across the floor for the latter part of the zip wire journey. I was lucky I didn't end up wearing arse-less shorts. We played Splat the Rat which only as an adult have I realised, is actually quite a violent game for children to play.

Essentially, we are giving them a bat and telling them to pulverise the rat as it comes flying out of a tube. Nevertheless, it was good fun. After attempting a few more of the fayre games, we ended up in the gin tent. Fred and Lilly came to join us just before Hettie left to get some food with Jack after his shift of being a hunk for the day ended. So here I am having a lovely chilled mulberry gin with my parents after a brilliantly fun yet massively childish afternoon.

'So how are you getting on with Ben then?' Fred asks,

coming over with a fresh round of drinks for the three of us. 'You looked close when we first arrived.'

'We weren't close.'

'Violet, you were sat in his arms.' Oh shit. I was, wasn't I?

'I slipped, that's all. We get on fine, nothing to report,' I mutter.

'I detected a spark when you dunked him in the water; he couldn't keep his eyes off you,' Lilly says, her eyes twinkling with curiosity.

'Really, do you think?' Crap that was far too eager.

'So definitely nothing between you then?' Fred adds sarcastically. I pull a face at him. I don't know why I'm being defensive; it's only adding more fuel to the fire. 'Oh look, here he is now.'

'Dad, no!'

'Ben,' Fred calls as Ben enters the tent looking a little dryer in jeans and T-shirt. 'Would you like to join us?'

I shoot Fred a look of betrayal, I expect that sort of behaviour from Lilly but not from him.

'Love to, let me just grab a drink.'

After a quick trip to the bar, Ben sits down next to me on a hay bale. We look at each other awkwardly. The hay bale isn't that big so we are squashed up next to each other.

'Dried off then,' Lilly says cheerfully.

'Yes, no thanks to someone.' He gently nudges my shoulder.

'If you will volunteer for Dunk the Hunk...'

'Don't, it's so embarrassing,' Ben says, flinching. 'I only found out this morning that the team had been put forward for it. The Kimberley sisters are a menace. I love the butterfly, by the way.'

Oh shit, I forgot I had my face painted. 'Oh, err yeah, thanks.' I self-consciously touch the side of my face.

'It's pretty.' He gives me a smile and I feel even more self-conscious now. I don't know where to look. Do I return the compliment and tell him he looks pretty? No of course I bloody don't. Luckily, it's Fred to the rescue who changes the topic of conversation to his favourite subject matter – rugby!

'So, are you playing next week, Ben?' Fred's a very proud supporter of the local team.

'Yep, certainly am, are you coming to watch?'

'Oh, I know, darling, you should go and watch with your father,' Lilly quickly interrupts just as I'm taking a gulp of gin.

I quickly swallow it down. 'Yeah maybe.' Why on earth would I do that, I have no interest in rugby. Why is everyone so determined to play matchmaker? Ben gives me a sneaky wink and I know that he must be thinking the exact same thing. Putting the matchmaking aside though I do feel relaxed in his company.

We continue to all chat happily about rugby, work and the village for the next hour and it all feels very natural. Whenever Philip and I had been with Lilly and Fred, it was uncomfortable and awkward, conversations were forced, but not with Ben. He seems to have a genuine friendship with my parents that was established before I ever returned home. It's... nice.

'Right then, my love...' Fred says, standing up and holding out his hand to Lilly. 'I need to go win you a teddy. Hook a Duck?'

'Oh yes, come on,' Lilly squeals. 'We're going to have a wander and then head home for tea, you two enjoy yourselves.' She raises her eyebrows at Ben and I, then skips off with Fred. All I can do is shake my head at how obvious she is.

'They're the cutest couple ever,' Ben declares as he watches them leave.

'I know, he wins her a teddy every year. He's been doing it since I was little. It's become their tradition. You should see them all in the spare room. Even after all these years she still gets excited about him winning her another one.' Fred and Lilly certainly are relationship goals.

'So do you get the impression from pretty much everyone we know in the village that they want us to get to know each other? Even your parents seem quite keen.'

'Yes, thank God it's not just me then. They are all so bloody embarrassing.'

'I bumped into a few of the ladies from your Zumba class before; they were asking me if I had seen you today.'

'Did they?' I'll be having words with them.

'They were telling me what a lovely girl you are,' he continues, amused.

Sod having words with them, I'll flipping kill them instead. 'They just don't give up, Hettie and Safiyah are even worse.' Despite getting harassed by the Golden Girls, he's still here talking to me. That makes me feel far happier than it should.

'For the sake of keeping the villagers happy, do you fancy a walk?' Ben asks nervously, motioning towards the tent door. He looks so cute when he's nervous.

'Sure, just for the sake of the village though,' I reply with a gallant nod.

'We're such selfless people.' Ben laughs.

22

We leave the gin tent and walk out into the sunshine. We wander around, chatting easily and looking at all the stalls with their local produce and handmade crafts. I didn't actually get the chance to look earlier when Hettie and I were running around like kids hyped up on sugar. We stop at Ivy's flower stall to admire her work. She's the local florist and like most people in Elmsbourne-Hollow, grew up here. Ivy had moved to Cornwall but when her aunt got sick three years ago, she moved back home to look after her and take over the florist. Ivy's wonderfully talented, the table is covered in beautiful summer wreaths and jars filled with lovely bouquets.

'Ivy, all these look amazing, they are so pretty.'

'Thanks, Violet,' Ivy says, busily making another wreath, cleverly entwining some pink peonies into the thick green foliage. 'Don't forget to take one of these.' She points to a large vase filled with vibrant yellow roses. 'They're free but you have to pay it forward. The idea is to spread a little kindness. You take a rose and give it to someone else.'

'What a great idea.' I pick a rose out of the vase; it smells so sweet. Ben follows my lead and takes one too. We step away from Ivy's stall and awkwardly eye up each other's flower. It's such a lovely idea of Ivy's but it has presented me with a dilemma. Do I give mine to Ben or will that be weird? We carry on around the fayre and I feel the tension rising. Is he going to give me his? Do we just do a swap? Do I even want him to give me his rose? No, of course I don't, or do I? Yes, I think I do. Oh God.

'Hello, you two,' Winnie calls, pulling me from my internal struggle.

'Hi, ladies.' Winnie is walking around the fayre with Verity and Mary from the Zumba group.

'Are you having a good day?' Ben asks kindly.

'I am. I do love the hustle and bustle of village occasions,' Winnie says happily. She certainly looks like she's enjoying herself. She has a bag of popcorn in one hand and a little gift bag from the handmade soap stall in the other, her smile beaming from ear to ear.

'Come on, Winnie, let's leave the lovebirds alone,' Verity says with a mischievous and very obvious wink before heading towards the tombola. Seriously, none of these ladies have any sort of filter.

'Winnie, for you,' I say, making a snap decision and swiftly passing her my yellow rose. There, dilemma over and by the look on Winnie's face I have made the right decision.

'Oh, Violet, that's so sweet.' She takes it from me and breathes the scent in deeply. 'Thank you.'

'My pleasure.' I feel such a pull towards her. Winnie waves to us and hurries over to the tombola.

'I think you've made her day,' Ben tells me as we watch her merrily walk away to catch up with the others.

'Just spreading a little kindness.'

'Here, I want to spread some too,' Ben says, stepping closer to me, handing me his rose. I feel something... shit, I think I'm really happy he's given it to me. No, no, no, I don't want to be happy about this. It's not a romantic gesture though, just an act of kindness as Ivy intended it to be. Don't go reading into this, Violet – you are not interested!

'Thank you,' I say shyly, taking it from him. Ben holds my gaze for a moment, and I can feel myself getting all hot and sweaty with nerves which is not a good look. His eyes are catching me off guard, making my head go all hazy, so I force myself to look away. I snap the stem of the rose off and delicately tuck the flower behind my ear. 'What do you think?'

'Beautiful.' His eyes open wider as if he hadn't meant to say that out loud. 'Erm... fancy a burger? I'm starving.'

'Ooh yes.' Yes, sustenance to soak up the gin is definitely needed if I'm going to keep my head straight and my lustful thoughts under control. Must not get drunk and throw myself at the gorgeous architect. Also, mustn't drip ketchup down my white top!

'Come on, Ben, your turn!' Dean shouts across to us as we're finishing up our burgers – white top remaining unscathed. We go over to see what the fuss is about. It's the High Striker game. Dean's name is scribbled at the top of the scoreboard with a score of two hundred and thirty. This doesn't surprise me, Dean's a builder and has arms the size of tree trunks, it would take a lot to beat him. Second place is Jack with a score of two hundred exactly. Ben picks up the hammer. 'You get three goes to try to ring the bell,' Dean tells him.

Ben looks nervous with all eyes on him but confidently lifts the hammer above his head and wallops down three big hits. I'm trying to ignore how sexy he looks wielding the large hammer. On the final bash he hits a whopping two hundred and ten.

'Second place,' Dean cheers, clearly thrilled to be top of the scoreboard still. There's a round of applause and a muttering of appraisal as Ben walks back over to me, beaming.

'That was pretty impressive.'

'And I beat Jack,' Ben says, punching the air. 'Come on, let's go find him so I can rub it in.'

We make our way back over to the gin tent and join Hettie and Jack who are stood at the bar with a few locals. Hettie looks far too pleased to see me with Ben but I'm having far too much fun to try to explain that we're just friends. It falls on deaf ears anyway. Safiyah, Theo and Josh are busy working behind the bar. The atmosphere is fun and relaxed, the warm day is giving a real festival vibe to the small village.

Ben teases Jack about beating him at High Striker and the evening rolls on in good spirits. Lots of acts of kindness have been spread too as so many people are holding Ivy's roses, there are flashes of yellow everywhere you look. A folk band is playing, and dancing spills out of the tent onto the green until it's time for the bar to close. The night seems to have passed by so quickly, it really is true what they say: time flies when you're having fun and drinking the gin bar dry.

Safiyah comes over to me, giving me a huge hug. 'Thanks for your help earlier.'

'My pleasure, I've had a really good day.'

'Not over yet, I think someone is waiting for you.' She looks over my shoulder.

I turn to see Ben approaching with his hands behind his back.

'Do you not want any help taking everything back over to the farm?'

'No, thanks to you lot there's hardly any gin left. We can

carry it between ourselves. Not going to tidy until the morning. Thanks for your help earlier, Ben,' Safiyah says before leaving us both alone.

'So, I checked the High Striker score and it turns out that I kept second place,' Ben tells me, looking a little coy. 'I won this.' He swings his hands from behind his back and I see a little brown fluffy teddy bear. At this point some women would flutter their eyelashes flirtatiously and glow at such a sweet gesture. Not me. The sweats are back and I think I'm turning postbox red. So attractive.

'You get a teddy for the High Striker?' I reply, amused.

'Actually it was a bottle of wine, but I asked if I could swap. There's probably a kid somewhere walking round with a bottle of red.' He hands me the bear and it looks exactly like the ones that Fred wins for Lilly.

'For me?' I ask sceptically. Just my luck it'll be for Lilly.

'Yes, for you.' Ben laughs. I'm touched. I don't know what has come over me, perhaps it's the gin, or perhaps it's this incredibly sweet and kind man in front of me that makes me ignore all the strict instructions I have told myself about not getting involved.

'Fancy walking me home?'

'Would love to.' My heart gives another thud.

We set out across the green and down the high street together. As we walk, Ben's hand gently sweeps past mine. I chance a glance at him, his cheeks are a little flushed from the alcohol and heat from the tent, but he looks relaxed and I like it. I feel very free and unburdened in his company, it's the most welcome feeling after the past few months.

The butterflies haven't stopped dancing since we left the tent and I finally admit to myself that I really do fancy the pants off him. It doesn't have to be anything serious, does it? Just some fun, which I can't deny I'm in need of. As long as I don't overthink it and keep a certain amount of distance then why not enjoy myself.

I don't pull my hand away and instead leave it casually brushing against his. Ben responds by reaching out further and entwining his fingers through mine. I thought it would feel strange, holding a different hand to the one I've been holding for the past few years but it's quite the opposite.

We finally stop outside Willow Cottage and I check to make sure Lilly isn't at the window waiting to be our captive audience. Thankfully there is no sign of her this time.

'Thank you for the teddy.' I feel giddy. Is that the gin or Ben? As I look up at him, I bite my lip. I'm pretty sure I want to kiss him, but I'm genuinely worried I will end up ripping his clothes off right here which would be highly inappropriate.

'I was wondering if you're free tomorrow night?' Ben says, standing enticingly close to me.

'I haven't planned anything.' Oh God, oh God, oh God.

'Would you like dinner at mine? I'll cook.'

'Depends.'

'On what?'

'Can you cook?' I feel my face break into a glowing smile which he reacts to with his own.

He lets out a deep breath. 'I thought you were going to turn me down for a moment there. Yes, I can cook.'

'I guess that's a yes then,' I say. Oh heck, I hope this is a good idea.

Ben leans his face forward and gently kisses me on my cheek. As he moves his lips away, I can feel the trace of his touch burning into my cheek.

'See you tomorrow then. Eight o'clock?' He backs away, smiling.

I'm gripping hold of the teddy as I make my way up the garden path towards the house. It feels like I'm floating on air. Shit, perhaps I should have said no, it's too soon and... oh come on, Violet, pull yourself together, it's only dinner, no big deal – don't overthink it.

I shut the front door and look down at the little teddy bear. I can handle this, just a bit of fun and nothing more.

23

'I hear you have a date with Ben Matthews,' Jane says fervently to me as I walk into the kitchen the following morning. Jenny, Jane and Maggie have come around to see how the dress for Jenny is coming along and are sitting in the kitchen with Lilly putting the world to rights over a pot of tea.

I look at Lilly irritably then look back at Jane and exclaim, 'It's not a date it's just dinner. He probably just wants to show me the work on the house. We were talking about it last week and he knows I'm interested in renovations.'

'Yes of course, dear, because you've always shown such a keen interest in renovations,' Lilly says humorously as the rest of the ladies titter with amusement.

'There is nothing between Ben and I,' I argue but to no avail as their eyes all fall on the little teddy Ben gave me. I stupidly left it on the kitchen table last night. I knew I shouldn't have told Lilly what happened as she has obviously relayed the story to the rest of the group. I grab the teddy and storm towards the stairs. 'Come up when you're ready, Jenny,' I say despairingly.

I don't even know why I'm playing my dinner date down so much. So what if I have a date? So what if I find someone massively attractive? I'm single... and a grown woman. I put the teddy on the desk in my room and realise that I'm unconsciously smiling at it as I think of Ben.

'Can I come in?' Jenny pops her head around the door which startles me, I was lost in thought.

'Yes of course.'

'Oh, Violet, that looks wonderful,' Jenny says, spotting the dress hung on the mannequin.

'I'm so pleased you like it. Now I haven't started the lace yet. I want you to try it on first and I may pin some of the lace into place while you're in it, if you don't mind, so I can check it sits right.' I slip the dress off the mannequin and lay it on the bed. 'There's a zip in the back. There are pins in it still so be careful. I'll leave you to get dressed and then I will come back in and zip you up.' I stand outside my room, waiting for Jenny to put it on.

'How does it feel?' I shout impatiently through the door. I can't stand the suspense any longer as I bounce up and down on the spot. Does it fit?

'So far so good,' Jenny calls back. 'Okay I'm ready to be zipped up.' I bound back in. Jenny is stood in front of the mirror, she looks incredible.

'Jenny you look great,' I say, walking over to zip her up. The fit is perfect. I would so give myself a high five right now if I could. 'How do you feel?'

Jenny's silent for a moment, gazing at herself in the mirror. She looks emotional. Shit, maybe she doesn't like it.

'It feels... wonderful. I can't believe that's me. You can see my waist.' Shock is emanating out of her voice as she runs her hands down the side of the dress over her waistline. 'Even after losing weight, I haven't really worn anything where you can see my shape. I'm just so used to covering up.'

'I don't know why; you've always looked great to me.'

'I know it's been thirty-five years but ever since I had the boys and my figure changed, I lost all confidence. I didn't care at the time, I was just happy being a mum. You sort of forget yourself. But at my age, I got to the point where I never thought I would be happy in the way I looked.' I feel so sad for her. All those years not feeling confident or comfortable in her own skin when she's so beautiful inside and out. 'Thank you, Violet.'

'Hey, I didn't do anything other than make a dress,' I tell her. 'What you're seeing in the mirror is all you. All your hard work.'

'But if I had gone shopping, I never would have had the guts to pick it up and try it on. You making it has made all the difference. Left to me I would have ended up in a funeral dress, as Mary put it,' Jenny quips.

I feel so delighted. After all these years Jenny finally sees the beauty in herself. It's why I fell in love with making clothes in the first place.

'Come on, let's show the others.' We head downstairs and into the living room. It's a cosy room with pale green walls, dark beams and a huge inglenook fireplace. The room has two large sofas and a dresser in the corner adorned with lots of little trinkets and photos that Lilly and Fred have collected over the years. I open the door and Jenny struts into the room, pretending to be on a catwalk.

'Jenny, that's gorgeous,' Maggie gasps. 'My God, look at that waist, where have you been hiding it?'

'I don't think I've ever seen you in anything that isn't loose fitting before,' Lilly says, looking at Jenny in awe. 'My darling, you look sensational.'

'Oh, you're so talented, Violet,' Maggie says, popping on her glasses and taking a closer look at the dress.

'Thank you. I just need to do the sleeves. Are you happy with the length, Jenny?'

'Yes, it's perfect, the material hangs beautifully.'

Everyone sits down and watches me carefully pin lace onto Jenny's dress while she is in it.

'That really finishes it all off,' Jane says as I stand back, checking my work. I've started with a little lace in the centre of the dress and have made it look like it is creeping up as the lace weaves its way over the bodice and into two little capped sleeves. I bring the mirror down to show Jenny the difference.

'I didn't think I could love it more, but I do.'

'The sleeves are a lovely touch. Sometimes a strapless dress can make you feel a little exposed having bare shoulders, so the lace sleeves give you a little security but are really only decorative. Right, carefully take it off. Here, let me undo the zip, you can use my bedroom and leave the dress on my bed.' Jenny does as she's told and when she returns, we all retire to the kitchen for another pot of tea. I hear my phone ringing and see it's Safiyah.

'Hey, Fiya,' I answer brightly. I'm feeling really good after such a successful fitting and can't wait to tell her about my dinner plans later.

'When were you going to tell us about your date?' she practically yells down the phone at me. Looks like someone has managed to spill the beans before me then.

'I can't believe you didn't tell us!' Hettie shouts in the background.

I look at Jane who is suddenly very interested in a crumb on the table.

'I was going to phone; it's just been a busy morning so far.' I leave the kitchen and go to my room for some privacy. 'And it's not a date, it's just dinner.'

'It's a date,' Safiyah says firmly.

'Yes, okay, it's a date.' I'm not convincing anyone anyway, I may as well admit it.

'Are you excited? Are you nervous? What are you going to

wear? Are you going to sleep with him?' Hettie shoots question after question at me.

'No, of course I'm not going to sleep with him,' I reply, although in all honesty the thought has crossed my mind – a lot. 'I don't know him that well.'

'That's certainly one way of getting to know him,' Safiyah chuckles.

'You two are terrible. Do you think he's expecting it?' I ask, feeling rattled. Perhaps that's why he's invited me to his house and not a restaurant.

'What, Ben? God, no. He's not like that, although I don't think he will bat you off if you want to.'

'I'm not sure I remember what to do it's been that long. I can't remember the last time Philip and I had sex.' I vaguely remember a drunken romp in bed a few weeks before things ended, but it most certainly hadn't been fireworks. 'I'm worried moths will fly out as soon as I open my legs.'

'Sounds like you deserve a good–'

'All right, Fiya,' I interrupt, laughing. She might be right though. Perhaps I need a good night of unbridled lust to get it all out of my system. I have been feeling ridiculously horny of late whenever I'm in Ben's vicinity.

'In all seriousness though, Vi, he's a good guy. I know you want to swear off guys and all that but give him a fair chance, we like this one.'

'I agreed to go, didn't I?'

'True, well, have fun. Tell him we say hi.'

'And remember don't do anything we wouldn't do,' Safiyah and Hettie sing in unison down the phone.

'That doesn't leave much, does it, girls,' I retort, laughing.

'Call us tomorrow and tell us everything. Bye.' Safiyah hangs up and I feel even more nervous after that conversation.

. . .

The evening has come around quickly. I've spent the whole day running Jenny's dress through the sewing machine and then hand sewing all the lace into place so that time has completely got away from me. It's six thirty when I hang the finished dress back on the mannequin.

After a shower, I slowly get ready for my date. I look in my underwear drawer and my earlier conversation with Hettie and Safiyah has pretty much left me reeling. If I choose my very best underwear that would be admitting that sex is a possibility which of course it isn't! Then again, I have promised myself that I will have more fun and I'm pretty sure that a rampant night in bed with Ben would blow away the cobwebs.

Okay, I'm overthinking again, who's to say he even wants to have sex with me anyway. I pull out a matching set in purple lace that's the colour of the wrap dress I plan on wearing. Sod it, I will feel good in them whatever happens. I slip into my dress and opt for my nude court shoes. I look in the mirror and notice that all the pottering in the garden with Fred has given me a slight tan and the bags under my eyes are disappearing now I'm sleeping much better. I look so much healthier than when I first arrived back in Elmsbourne-Hollow. I take a deep breath; grab my bag and the bottle of wine I bought earlier and scoot out of the house.

24

Bracken Lodge is only two minutes away, but my heart is thudding so hard, I walk slowly to give myself time to get my heart rate under control. My mouth is so dry, I should have had a glass of Dutch courage before I left. I'm tempted to swig some wine now but I'm guessing it won't look great if I turn up with an open bottle and half the contents gone.

I arrive at Ben's. Wow, he wasn't kidding about how much work he has done to the place. The last time I visited home, Bracken Lodge looked dishevelled and unloved but now the place has a new lease of life. The overgrown weed-filled front garden has all been cut back and fresh turf laid. The old rickety looking window frames have been replaced with fresh new grey ones, and a beautifully crafted large solid oak front door with oversized heavy black hinges stands front and centre. It looks like a modern farmhouse, a perfectly balanced combination of old and new.

I stand at the front door. Oh God, I feel sick I'm so nervous. I fluff up my hair and straighten my dress, making sure it's not tucked into my knickers. The aromas from the house have wafted through, whatever he's cooking smells amazing. The door opens, and Ben is stood there in brown chinos, a light-blue shirt with the arms rolled up and the most disarming smile I have ever seen. All previous notions of keeping it cool have been launched out of the window. I feel like one of those cartoon characters whose eyes pop out of their head when they see someone they fancy.

'You look great,' he says, standing back slightly so I can walk in. I step over the threshold and his familiar scent of aftershave washes over me. I hope he hasn't noticed my hands are trembling. I look around the big open hallway and can smell fresh paint. The white walls and beautiful light oak staircase make the house feel bright and breezy, just like him really.

'Wow, it looks great in here.'

'Thanks. Over here is the living room which isn't finished yet, I need to decide on a colour.'

I look in to see a newly plastered room, not painted yet but with beautifully restored beams, a brown leather sofa and a log burner in the centre of the room nestled into a large brick nook with a floating mantle in reclaimed timber.

'Everything had to be completely stripped out and redone from floor to ceiling. Through this room is my study.' Ben points to the door at the far end of the living room. We go back into the hallway and to the other side of the house.

'This is the kitchen. It's been the biggest job so far,' he says proudly, and I can see why.

I'm blown away. 'Wow – the hard work has certainly paid off.'

It's a very chic new kitchen. Bright white walls with contrasting dark-blue cabinets and a light oak worktop. In the centre is a large island with a Belfast sink on one side and black bar stools on the other. Three large copper lights hang gloriously over the centre, casting a dim glow across the counter. Ben has lit some candles and it all looks extremely romantic. 'You have a talent for interior design,' I say, impressed.

Ben chuckles. 'Thank you. My sister actually helped me with the design in here. She said the kitchen is the heart of the home. I hate to think what it would have looked like if it was left to me.'

'Something smells good, what are we having?' I ask as I hand Ben the bottle of wine. My nerves are twisting into a tight knot now, at this rate I won't be able to eat anything no matter how good it smells.

'Thank you,' he says, placing the wine in the fridge. 'Chicken alfredo. Do you like Italian food? I realised I didn't ask what you liked when I invited you but thought pasta was a safe option.'

'I love Italian food; I love Italy actually. I've been to Rome and Lake Garda but would love to visit Florence someday.' Shit, I went to both those places with Philip, he is not who I want to be thinking of right now.

'Would you like a drink?' Ben asks, pulling an already chilled bottle of wine out of the fridge.

'Yes please.' My mouth still feels so dry it's like I've gargled with sand, my lips keep sticking to my teeth – very unattractive.

He fumbles slightly trying to pop the cork, and it's endearing that he's a little nervous too. He's gorgeous but not cocky or obnoxious about it which is very appealing. I wonder if he's entertained many women here. Perhaps this is just a well-rehearsed part he plays every weekend to a steady stream of women, building up the notches on his bedpost. No, in a village like this where everyone knows everything, that would be damn near impossible to get away with.

'The house looks great, you've done so much already.'

'It's a been a hard slog but I'm really proud of it. Through there is the dining room,' Ben says, pointing to the back of the kitchen before handing me a glass of wine. 'The plan is to extend the dining room by adding an orangery which will give a lot more light. Upstairs are three bedrooms and the bathroom. The bathroom is finished, and my room is almost done, plastered and just waiting to be painted.'

I feel myself blush; will I see that room later? No, Violet, you will not! A stomach jerking image of him throwing me over his shoulder and taking me upstairs blasts through my mind and I need to sit down. I climb on one of the bar stools, but it's higher than I anticipated and I'm struggling to do it gracefully. I wobble and almost fall off as Ben catches me and steadies me back onto the seat. 'Sorry, it's not the best place to sit but I haven't bought a dining table yet,' he says, still holding on to me.

'No, it's fine.' He's tantalisingly close again, my body feels like it's on fire. His face is suspiciously close to mine, I think he's going to kiss me. Christ he's a fast mover, I haven't even finished my first drink yet.

'Dinner will be ready soon, hope you're hungry,' he says, suddenly backing away. Okay, so I may have misread the situation then.

'Great, I'm starving.'

'How are the dresses coming on?'

'Really well, thank you.' I begin to tell him all about Jenny's reaction to her dress earlier. Thinking about how elated Jenny was fills me with such a sense of satisfaction and pride that it reminds me I should have more confidence in myself. My nerves begin to drop a little and I start to settle into the atmosphere Ben has created.

'What is it you love about making clothes?' he asks me as he plates the food up. There is something very sexy about a man in the kitchen.

'I love being crafty, it's always been a passion of mine. Making something fabulous from just a roll of fabric. But it's what it does for the person too. I guess that's why I love designing and making bridal dresses so much. Seeing a customer's face when they see themselves in the dress that makes them feel special. It gives them an extra spring in their step and that extra push of confidence. I know they are just clothes but what you wear can change your entire mood.' That probably sounds ridiculous to him. 'What about you? What do you love about architecture?'

Ben looks thoughtful for a moment as he brings the plates over. 'I guess it's a similar sort of thing to you really. The concept of home is a powerful thought. It's someone's sanctuary. It's meant to be safe and comforting. I love helping someone create that, bringing their ideas and dreams to life in a way. I've been doing a few jobs with renovations recently and I really love it. Bringing something old that people have written off back to life. There is so much history in places that people are so quick to tear down when we should be bringing them back to their former glory, a celebration of history.' His face flashes with an ardent passion, and I don't feel as silly about my outburst because I think on some level he actually understands it. 'Sorry, I went on a bit there.'

'Don't be,' I reply with a reassuring smile, I can relate to that sort of passion.

'Is it just houses that you design?'

'No, we do all sorts: business premises, hotels, but houses and renovations are my favourite. They are why I got into architecture.'

The conversation continues to flow easily after that and as we both tuck into dinner the nervous energy completely subsides. Ben's easy to talk to. Over dinner he tells me about his family in Cumbria, his mother still lives there as does his sister and her family. We eat and drink, happily chatting and laughing about our interests and hobbies, where we've travelled and where we still want to go.

'That was lovely,' I say, feeling full at the end of the meal. He certainly knows his way around a kitchen. 'So, you're clearly talented in the DIY department and you can cook, is there anything you can't do?'

'I'm a rubbish gardener, I may have to get Fred round to sort the gardens out.'

'What about your dad, you haven't mentioned him?' I ask and instantly regret it as Ben's face drops. Shit, why did I ask that? He obviously would have mentioned him earlier if he wanted to. 'Sorry if that's personal, I shouldn't have asked.'

'No, it's fine to ask.' He takes a gulp of wine. 'We lost him about ten years ago.'

'I'm so sorry.' I feel terrible, we're having a lovely meal together and I go and bring up such a painful memory. What a way to ruin the night!

'Yeah me too, I just find it hard to talk about him even after ten years, it still feels raw.'

I don't know what to say, there aren't really any words, so I just put my hand on top of his and squeeze. He seems satisfied with the gesture because he squeezes my hand back. He changes the subject pretty quickly after that and clears the plates away.

25

'Fancy any pudding?'

'I'm so full I really shouldn't.' I'm not sure I could eat anything else.

'Oh, you should, it's Ethel's chocolate cake,' he says with a mischievous smile and I laugh.

'How can I resist?'

'It's a lovely evening. Come on, let's have it outside.' Ben gets the cake from the kitchen worktop, grabs two spoons and leads the way to the garden. I follow with our drinks. Ben wasn't wrong about his gardening skills; there is a patio with an outside sofa and table but the rest of the garden is bare and could do with some love. The majority of it is just grass with empty borders dug out, but the view... the view is something else entirely. The garden looks out onto a glorious landscape of fields and hills. Colours of orange and red dancing across the sky, merging seamlessly into each other from the slowly setting sun.

'Look at that view,' I gasp.

'It's amazing, isn't it? It was a massive part of why I bought the place,' Ben says, lighting a couple of candles on the table. He places the cake in the middle of us. 'Dig in.'

'So how long have you been single for?' I ask, taking a spoonful of cake. I find it unbelievable that a gorgeous talented sweet guy like him could be single. There must be a catch surely.

'About a year. I was with someone for three years. Everything was fine, and she was lovely, but as time went on she hinted at moving in together, which was the natural step. But it didn't feel right and I knew at that point it was over. I think we just became friends more than lovers.'

'Do you still keep in contact?'

'I sometimes see her around Lancaster, and we do the obligatory happy birthday messages when that time of year comes around.'

'It's good that you've stayed friendly.' I think of Philip and how we will never be friends. What a shame after all that time.

'What about you? I know things ended badly with your ex, were you together long?'

'Five years.' Interestingly I notice that the dreaded Philip-related stomach pang doesn't make itself known... nothing at all.

'A while then,' Ben says thoughtfully. 'I still can't believe you walked in on him shagging your boss.' Ben looks just as gobsmacked as the first time I told him.

'You and me both,' I say, taking a sip of wine.

'How does someone even do that? So, are you okay about it now?'

'Do you know what? I am. I'm glad I found out who he really was. It's made me worry about my own judgement, I mean he must have fooled me for a while, but I'm starting to realise that I wasn't who I wanted to be with him. I didn't feel good enough. He changed over time and I did too. I thought he was my happy place. I was wrong.'

'Your happy place?'

'Yeah, you know, that place where you feel at your happiest and most content. The place where you crave to be above anywhere else. It used to be with him, curled up, watching a movie and having a takeaway. I would look forward to that all week. Locking the door and it just being us.'

'And now?'

'I'm finding a new one. It scared me so much, the thought of having to start again. To find happiness somewhere else but all of a sudden now it seems exciting.'

'He must have been crazy to let you go,' Ben says looking at me, and I feel his eyes searching mine.

I gulp and I think I hold my breath for a second. I find myself looking at his neck, I imagine tracing my lips all over it slowly making their way down... no I can't go there. I must look away. Change the subject or something – but I can't because I feel like I'm falling under his spell again. Snap out of it, Violet. I blink a few times to break the spell but as I do, I swing the spoon forgetting there's cake sat on it. It flies across the air and hits Ben square in the face. Oh no, not again. I burst into hysterics. He looks so shocked with cake dripping off his face.

'Shit, I'm sorry,' I splutter through my laughter.

Ben's laughing too... thankfully. 'What is it with you and covering me in cake?' He sticks his finger in the chocolate fondant and rubs a line down my cheek.

'Ben,' I gasp.

'Payback.'

'Right you've asked for it now.' I scoop a handful of cake up but Ben's out of his seat and ducking behind the sofa before I can throw it. He peaks above the chair and I hurl it at him but miss. Luckily, I miss the chair in the process and the cakes splats down onto the patio.

'Ha ha, you missed!' he shouts jovially, running back around and scooping a handful himself. I grab some more and run to the back of the garden, Ben chasing after me. I turn and face him and with giddy smiles, we stand poised for action.

'One, two, three,' I yell and we throw. Mine hits Ben's shirt and his lands with a smack on my chest. We fall about laughing. There is only a little bit of the cake left on the plate but Ben hasn't noticed it yet. If I'm quick I could get it before him. I run back to the table and grab the last bit.

'This has escalated quickly,' he shouts, chasing after me. We start running around like excitable kids. I'm throwing bits of cake behind me, hoping I am actually hitting him.

'This isn't fair, I have no cake to throw at you.'

'You snooze you lose,' I call triumphantly, but I've run out of garden and I'm cornered. I turn to face him holding the cake in the air... what's left of it anyway.

'I surrender!' he shouts, holding up his hands. 'You win.'

'Good, because there isn't much cake left.' We stand at the base of the garden, both slightly out of breath. If anyone could see the state of us, what must we look like? I step forward and cheekily wipe what's left in my hands down the front of his shirt. Bloody hell he feels good, I feel slightly resentful that the shirt is in the way!

'Hey, I surrendered,' he says in a deep husky voice that vibrates deliciously around my body.

'Sorry, I couldn't resist.'

'I know the feeling.' He's looking at me hungrily and I have the biggest urge to jump into his arms and wrap my legs around his waist. Obviously I won't do that because I'm demure and classy, and not at all desperate to rip his clothes off. I move closer to him, lift my hand and wipe the cake off his cheek. I don't know what makes me do it but I lick my finger ever so slightly provocatively and Ben raises his eyebrow, his eyes wide with interest. I'm never normally this confident but something about the way he's looking at me makes me feel seductive.

'Tastes good though.'

Ben gently strokes back a loose tussle of hair that's fallen in front of my face and my breathing quickens. We're so close that I can feel his breath on my face. He places one hand on my waist and the other gently on the side of my neck tilting my face towards his. I close my eyes and wait for the delicious moment when our lips will meet – but instead I feel his forehead press against mine, my lips cold and empty – no kiss. I open my eyes and see his expression has changed, the hunger is gone and instead he looks almost pained. He steps back as if he's fighting some inner turmoil. Passion-killer or what? I'm so confused, what the hell has just happened? That was supposed to be it, the fairy-tale magic moment where we kiss, and I swoon in his arms. Did I do something wrong? He looked like he wanted me but then stopped – story of my bloody life.

'Perhaps we should go back inside and get cleaned up,' he says as he looks down at our cake-covered clothes. He holds my hand in his and walks us back up the garden and into the house. I'm baffled! He hands me a cloth and I clean myself up.

'Well, that's two shirts I owe you now, I guess,' I say, trying to cover the fact that I just feel so stupid, and now there's a horrible awkward tension between us.

'Then I guess I owe you a dress,' he replies looking forlorn as he watches me wipe the cake off it. I feel tears sting my eyes, how quickly the night has turned. I don't even know why. I was so busy wondering if I was going to take things further tonight, I didn't stop to think whether he might actually want to. What an idiot!

He takes the cloth from me and runs it under some water.

'You missed a bit,' he says softly as he wipes the cake from my cheek just like that first day we met in the tearoom. I meet his eyes with mine, I want to ask what's happened but instead I feel a charge in the atmosphere between us fizz again, like it always does when we look at each other. It's clearly one-sided though. Perhaps I've mistaken what I thought was a look of desire in his face for something else – indigestion maybe. Bloody hell. Only I could confuse lust for wind. I wait for him to pull away again only this time he doesn't. His eyes are burning into mine and he sighs as if he's resigning himself to something.

'I'm sorry, Violet, I've tried to but I can't.'

'Can't what?'

'Stop myself.' He leans forward and as his lips find mine, he's kissing me urgently as his hands clasp the sides of my neck. It's deep and passionate and I get my leg-swooning moment. I reciprocate that deep yearning as I feel myself melt into him. My hands are running up his chest to the back of his neck. His lips are soft but powerful and taste delicious from the chocolate. He pulls away gently and breathless but holds me close.

'I've been fighting with myself all night,' he tells me.

I try to concentrate on what he's saying but it's a struggle to keep track. His kiss seems to have awoken me from a slumber that I didn't know I was even in; heat is spreading through my thighs as my whole body tingles with downright lust. 'I have wanted to do that from the moment you walked through the front door.'

'Then why didn't you before?'

'I didn't want to scare you off, I didn't know if you thought it was too soon.'

He most certainly has not scared me off, in fact it's the opposite. I want him more. I ache to kiss him again. I know what I want to do, and I don't care what anyone else thinks. Lace underwear was most definitely the correct choice! My hands fly up to his face and I kiss him again. He responds eagerly, the passion escalating quickly. His arms wrap around my waist, my fingers winding through his thick hair. His body pushes up against mine, as his hands make their way up to my neck again. My skin comes alive with every touch.

I can feel our need for each other increasing by the second.

Ben slides his hands down my body to the back of my legs where in one swift move, he has lifted me up onto the kitchen side. I gasp as I wrap my legs tightly around his waist, my hands frantically moving to the buttons on his shirt. He kisses my neck, sending a charge of electricity down my spine and I hear myself moan with utter indulgent delight. I'm impressed with how quickly I've unbuttoned his shirt, I pull it over his shoulders, and it drops to the floor revealing his muscular chest – oh my! Ben's hands have found their way to my thighs as he runs them under my dress and up my back. Feeling his touch on my skin sends another glorious shiver through my body and I squeeze my legs tighter around him, pulling him towards me more.

'Wait.' He suddenly pulls away panting and holding me by the shoulders. 'Are you sure you want to do this? It's okay if you don't, we can take it slow. I don't want you to think that's why I invited you here.'

'I don't think that, and I want to. I really want to.' In fact, I can't think of anything I want more right now. He pauses for a moment as if he's checking that I'm sure, which only increases my desire, and then his arms are back around me, his mouth running over my neck. His hands grab my bottom and slide me forward towards him. My legs cling around his waist as he carries me up the stairs to his bedroom. I gently nibble his bottom lip and feel his body pulse against me as his thirst intensifies.

He lays me on the bed and holds himself up over me. He gently kisses my neck, making his way gloriously down towards my breasts, my body writhing in response to him. His lips are so light that it's as if he's teasing me, electric tingles course between my legs and I moan with pure pleasure. He kneels up and slowly lifts my dress up over my body. I arch my back helping him relieve me of it.

He looks at me lying in front of him with such an intense

craving, I feel I'm going to explode – I need him now! I reach down and undo his trousers and he groans with appreciation. I push him onto his back, kissing his chest, working my way back up to find his mouth, gently caressing his lips with mine.

The next few hours are a blissful delight... undeniable fireworks.

26

I wake up to sun streaming through the bedroom window. I open my eyes and see my dress and underwear flung on the floor. Memories of last night come flooding back and I can't help the big grin that is spreading across my face. Ben Matthews is certainly a passionate lover. My body aches slightly from the acrobatics of last night and I feel... happy. I roll over, but Ben isn't there.

I bolt up in panic. Christ, what was I thinking? Sleeping with someone on the first date? What must he think of me? He's probably downstairs waiting for me to wake up and leave. The bedroom door opens, and I quickly lift the covers up suddenly very aware that I'm naked. Ben walks in carrying a tray with some coffee, toast and a single pink rose in a little jug. He's smiling brightly and wearing nothing but his boxer shorts. A very welcome sight. Okay, panic over. I feel the heat rising in my face though as I look at his toned torso, it gives me a flashback to last night when it was leaning over me ever so impressively.

'Good morning,' he says, placing the tray down on the bedside table.

I probably look like I've been dragged through a hedge

backwards. I quickly pat my messy hair down. 'Morning,' I mumble. 'Breakfast and dinner, you are spoiling me.'

Ben kneels on the bed, puts his finger under my chin and tilts my face towards him. He kisses me gently and all insecurities of sex on the first date drift away. The covers fall slightly and I grasp hold, wrapping them tightly around my chest. I don't know why I feel so nervous about him seeing me naked, nothing was exactly left to the imagination last night when he was tracing his lips all over my body.

He sits down next to me. 'I have a late meeting today but wondered if you fancied coming with me to pick some paint tomorrow after work for the living room? I could do with a second opinion.'

Not just a one-night stand, he wants to see me again. Is it too obvious if I fist pump the air?

'Yeah sure, would love to.'

We sit on the bed for a while together chatting about colours while chomping on toast and drinking coffee. It all feels very relaxed and serene.

'I had a great night,' Ben says, looking at me in a way I'm not accustomed to; he looks so content.

'Me too.' I smile back.

'You don't regret it, do you?' he asks, his eyes wide with concern. I love how expressive his eyes are, they seem to do half the talking for him.

'No, not at all, do you?'

'Nope, in fact I'm struggling right now to keep my hands off you,' he says with a carnal gleam in his eye. I place my coffee on the bedside table and lay back down, letting go of the duvet. I'm not sure where this sudden freedom of inhibitions has come from, but I'm going with it.

'And you're stopping yourself why?' I ask in hope that he gives into temptation. Ben takes the invitation willingly; he pulls the covers back and I gasp as the cool air caresses me. It's a very different experience being this naked in the harsh light of day, but the longing look on Ben's face stirs my confidence as he traces a finger over my breasts and down my body.

'You are so very sexy, Violet, do you know that?'

The next hour is spent re-enacting the fun of the night before.

Two hours later I'm leaving Bracken Lodge with a spring in my step and a smile on my face. I'm going as quickly as I can back to Willow Cottage, hoping desperately not to bump into anyone. Doing the walk of shame with cake down your dress really gives the wrong impression.

'Violet, is that you?' Shit... Linda. As if being confronted the morning after isn't bad enough, it would have to be the local hairdresser and gossip queen who catches me in my dishevelled state.

'Hi, Linda, lovely morning, isn't it?' I say as if there is nothing at all strange about my appearance. Nothing to see here!

'Are you just coming from Ben's?' She's so brazen with interest.

'Erm...' There's no getting out of this one is there. 'Yes I am.' I'm determined not to give any more information than that, but I am secretly delighted that I'm leaving her open-mouthed, wanting more. That will certainly give her something to talk about in the salon. 'Won't keep you though, you must need to get to work. Bye,' I say, scuttling past.

That's that then, within a matter of minutes everyone will know I've spent the night with Ben now the village gossip has seen me.

. . .

I sneak through the front door hoping that Lilly and Fred are in the garden and won't witness my rather shameful entrance. I creep up the stairs and across the landing, my room is in sight. Christ, sneaking into my parents' house at my age!

'Good night?' Lilly bellows, making me jump a mile. I was so close to making it to my room. I turn and see Lilly leaning against the bathroom door, arms folded looking like the cat that's got the cream.

'Holy shit, Mother, you scared the life out of me.' I clutch my chest. I think my heart nearly exited through my mouth.

'And what time do you call this?' Lilly mocks, looking far too happy with herself. 'There was me thinking it was just dinner.'

'Mum, don't,' I groan as she follows me into my room.

'So how was the *non*-date?' she says with her impish grin emphasising the 'non' part.

'It was very good, thank you,' I say, playing it down.

'I bet it was... Details please.'

'Normal mothers would be embarrassed to have this conversation, Mum.' I sigh.

'Oh pish. You can't come in like that and not expect questions,' Lilly says, eyeing my cake-covered dress.

'We had a food fight,' I answer, unable to keep the smile from my face this time. 'Now please, no more questions.'

'Okay, okay... But are you seeing him again?'

'Mum! We're going paint shopping after work tomorrow.' That seems to quench her insatiable thirst for asking awkward questions because she doesn't press me for more information – thankfully. I can't exactly tell her that I had the most mind-blowing sex of my life last night followed by the very same this morning.

'Get ready, darling, Zumba in an hour,' she exclaims merrily as she leaves the room.

'Mum, do *not* tell any of the Golden Girls about this,' I say firmly. 'I mean it. Linda has already seen me sneaking across the road.'

'Tell them what? You haven't told me anything and I'm sorry but if Linda saw you then I won't need to say anything. Everyone knows she has a mouth the size of Etna,' Lilly announces very matter of fact. 'See you there, darling,' she calls as she waltzes downstairs.

I walk into my bedroom and shut the door as my phone beeps, it's Ben.

Great night... and morning!! X. I flop on the bed – it really was.

27

I sneak into Zumba with my head low. If I keep my head down and stay quiet no one will notice me and ask any questions about my date. Who am I kidding? All of the Golden Girls seem to have heard about my walk of shame already and are all sat waiting for me with bated breath. There is nothing quite like your mother and her friends basically asking about your sex life – entirely mortifying!

'Good night, I hear.' Olivia beams. I look to Lilly, furious.

'I didn't say a word,' she says, holding her hand up in the air defensively, noticing my look of pure anger.

'She's right, she didn't,' Jane says as she gives Lilly a frustrated look.

'So how did you hear?' I ask. Why is nothing private in this place? Oh God, what if they all think I'm some sort of hussy.

'I heard from Norah when I was walking the dog, who heard it from Ethel who heard it from Linda,' Jenny tells me. Linda... I should have known.

'Morning, ladies!' Roberto shouts walking into class. 'How are we all? I hear you're well, Violet.' He gives me a cheeky wink. 'You lucky girl, he's bloody gorgeous.'

'How the hell do you know? You don't even live here.'

'Popped into the post office on the way in. So, come on, tell all,' he says with a flick of his blond quiff.

'Could this be any more embarrassing?' I ask to no one in particular, closing my eyes. I knew I shouldn't have come to Zumba today.

'What did he cook?' Bonnie, one of the quieter women, asks.

'Pasta – can we get on now?'

'Did he kiss you, or did you kiss him first?' Rosalind asks, her eyes alight with curiosity. All the women are now circling me like a group of vultures waiting to pounce.

'I'm really not comfortable talking about this.'

'What was his–?'

'All right, that's it,' I interrupt forcefully, knowing exactly where Olivia's question is going. 'Can we just do the class, please?' My voice is so high-pitched that I'm not sure it is even audible to the human ear.

'Spoilsport,' Roberto says, looking disappointed. 'All right then, ladies, do some stretches while I set up the music.'

I manage to dodge as many questions as possible and make it through the class. I'm actually getting better at Zumba. I still seem to be putting my own flair on it, but I am remembering more of the routines. Once the class is over, we all reconvene at Jenny's house for cake club. I indulge myself in a large piece of carrot cake that Ethel's brought along. I'm starving. I've worked up quite an appetite from this morning's bedroom antics and then the Zumba class.

'So, come on, how was it?' Jane asks, sliding down next to me on the sofa. Really? Do these women ever give up?

'How was what?' Perhaps if I just play dumb, they will all leave me alone.

'You know what, come on, make a bunch of old ladies happy. We're living vicariously through you.'

'It was a lovely evening, thank you,' I say, relenting to their demands slightly.

'And...' Jane pushes. All the others seemed to have stopped talking and are now listening out for my answer. Even Rosalind and Olivia have stopped bickering about who makes a better Victoria sponge to hear the gossip.

'And he was a perfect gentleman.' That is all they are getting.

'Such a lovely boy,' Winnie says, tucking into a zesty lemon cake.

'We're glad to hear it. We're all very happy for you, I hope you will still have time for Zumba though. We all enjoy having you with us. Although we understand he is a rather dishy distraction,' Jane snorts.

'Of course I want to carry on.' I'm shocked they think that after welcoming me so warmly I would quit because of a new man. Although I guess that's what I did when I met Philip. I just upped and left. But I've learnt my lesson. Never again. Plus, things with Ben are only a bit of fun. Nothing serious. 'I would miss you all if I stopped with Zumba and cake club, besides, that would only leave Mum delving into my private life,' I tell them with a wry smile.

After that I sit quietly listening to them all chat and realise how comfortable I am in their presence. Going into that first class I did wonder what the hell I was doing. I only really did it to please Lilly but now they're not just my mother's friends, the Golden Girls have become mine too. I'm on the mend and beginning to find happiness again and they are a huge part of that. They have brought laughter back into my life and gave me a distraction with the dresses when I needed it most. I don't want to leave them.

My phone rings and it's the haberdashery in Lancaster

calling to tell me that my order has arrived. I excitably tell them I will be in tomorrow to collect it. I can finally get started on the wedding dress.

'Jenny, your dress is finished if you want to pop round tomorrow for one last try on to make sure you're happy.'

'How exciting. Yes please, I can't believe how quickly you've made it.'

'I've loved doing it. Jane, are you happy for me to get the material for your dress?'

'Yes, absolutely. Winters Gin has been nominated for a family business award in November, so I can wear it there. It's a black-tie event,' she says proudly.

'Brilliant. I'm picking up my order tomorrow in town, so I will see what material I can get for you.'

'Don't suppose you could squeeze me in too, could you?' Verity asks timidly.

'Of course, what for?' Another order, blimey this is great.

'A dress for Collette's wedding. Jenny has talked so much about the dress you made for her, I thought maybe you could help me. I don't really know what I want though.'

'Not a problem. Why don't you come tomorrow morning with Jenny and I can show you some patterns?'

'All these gorgeous dresses, it's a shame there isn't an event that we could all get dressed up together for,' Lilly says thoughtfully.

I decide to go home and shower then visit Hettie and Safiyah. I've already received messages from them both after hearing Linda's gossip. I've arranged to meet them in the tearoom and by the time I arrive, they are already sat waiting for me.

'Here she is, the dirty stop-out,' Safiyah jokes.

I beam at them both. I've spent the whole day dodging questions but I'm desperate to actually talk about it now.

'So how was it?' Hettie asks.

'Bloody brilliant... big huge fireworks,' I gush.

'You did do it then?' Hettie says delicately with a giggle.

'What Hettie means is, did you jump his bones?' Safiyah adds, more to the point. She really is just like her mother. I don't answer and instead let the sheer joy on my face give it away.

'You did!' Hettie squeaks. 'Was it good?'

'Oh my, so good, he is an Adonis.' I sound giddy. 'I'm seeing him again tomorrow night.'

Safiyah and Hettie look at each other smugly.

'Do you think it makes me look easy, me sleeping with him?'

'What? No. You're a grown woman, you can do whatever you like. If you were a man you wouldn't ask that question. Why should it be different for a woman?'

'True, it's just I haven't known him that long.'

'So what? You deserve some fun and you both clearly like each other. You should see your faces when you're around each other. It's sickening really,' Safiyah adds, pretending to gag.

'I need to remember to keep it fun and nothing more. No deep feelings.'

'What, like friends with benefits?'

'Yes exactly.'

'Because that always works out well for people! I'm going to get drinks and then I want more juicy details.' Safiyah jumps up and goes over to Tessa at the counter.

Hettie leans over while it's just the two of us. 'I, err, I spoke to Jack about the whole baby thing.'

'You did, and what did he say?' I'm so pleased she took my advice.

'Exactly what you said; understanding, supportive. He admitted he was scared too but we are in it together. We have agreed to take it slowly and not to put pressure on ourselves. Whatever happens happens, but that he will be there no matter what.'

'How do you feel now?'

'Much better now I know he feels the same too. Thank you for pushing me to talk to him.' I can see the relief on Hettie's face. I reach out and squeeze her hand. 'That's what friends are for.'

The door to the tearoom pings and a nervous-looking lad in his early twenties walks in. He stands to the side and runs his hands through his long messy hair in an attempt to smarten himself up. Once Safiyah is sat back down with us he marches over to the counter like a man on a mission, his face turning bright red. I recognise him from the village but don't know his name.

'Hi, Tessa.' His voice is shaking, and he's shuffling his feet.

Tessa's cheeks flush and I can see she is struggling to make eye contact with him. 'Hi, Sam,' she says shyly.

They're both quiet, taking glances at each other. Safiyah, Hettie and I are watching the awkward exchange like we're at the cinema, all we need now is popcorn. I feel like I might be intruding on quite a personal moment for them both but it's really hard to tear my eyes away.

'Can I get you anything?' Tessa finally asks.

'No, I mean yes, erm...' He wipes his brow that has started to sweat. 'I wondered if you were busy tonight?'

'Oh, erm... no, I'm not busy.' Tessa looks a little stunned because he has practically shouted the question at her with his very obvious nerves.

I'm thinking I should go over and rescue her, but something about her bashful smile and look of anticipation of his next sentence makes me think otherwise. I think there might have even been an eyelash flutter from young Tessa.

'Good. W-would you like to come for a drink at the pub… with me?'

'My God, they are so cute,' Safiyah whispers.

'I would love to,' Tessa replies, glowing.

'Great. I'll pick you up and we could walk together. Shall we say eight o'clock?'

'Yeah, great. See you later.'

Sam leaves the shop looking like he has won the lottery. Tessa looks up and notices that we've witnessed the whole conversation.

'Someone's got a date,' Hettie teases.

'I can't believe he's finally asked me out. I've liked him for ages,' Tessa says. 'Oh God, what am I going to wear? Do I get dressed up? I don't really date.' Bless her, she looks so worried.

'It's the pub so something cute but casual. How about a nice little summer dress?' Safiyah suggests.

'I don't own a dress,' Tessa says as she looks down at her jeans and vintage Red Hot Chili Peppers T-shirt.

'Really? I think I could help you with that. If you're interested?' I say, hoping I'm being helpful.

'Yes, I need help.'

'Give me ten minutes.' I run out of the little tea shop towards home. That's the great thing about a small village; home is never far away.

I go straight upstairs to the wardrobe and pull out a box that contains a few handmade dresses I made for stock. I pull out two that I think will be her size, she's quite petite. I choose a green floral shift with ruffles on thick straps and a mustard-coloured short-sleeved tea dress with buttons down the front, both suiting

Tessa's tanned skin and long hazel hair. I run back to the shop and hand both dresses over to Tessa.

'Go and try them on, I'll man the counter.'

Tessa goes to the bathroom and five minutes later walks out in the mustard tea dress.

'What do you think?' she asks, looking stiff and out of her comfort zone.

'I love it, it really suits you.' I think Tessa could wear a bin bag and look great, to be honest, if she could just look a little more comfortable and a little less like she's wearing a bomb.

'Sam's eyes are going to pop out of his head when he sees you in that,' Safiyah says with a chuckle.

'Do you think? I don't usually wear dresses,' she says, pulling uncomfortably at the bottom of the hem.

'If you're not comfortable or if it feels too short...' I say, not wanting Tessa to feel pressured into wearing something she doesn't like but she interrupts me before I can say any more.

'No, no I really want to wear it, I'm just not used to it.'

'You need a little confidence, that's all. Wear it proudly, relax your shoulders a little and lift your head. If you feel self-conscious, then you will look it. Your legs are amazing, and the colour is perfect for you, but you need to wear the dress, don't let the dress wear you.' Tessa does as she's told and relaxes her hunched up shoulders. 'See, that looks so much better. You honestly look great.'

'I always thought I couldn't really pull dresses off, I'm not very girly.'

'You most certainly can. It actually looks really good with your ankle boots. You can give it a more edgy vibe with your accessories.'

Tessa walks around swishing the dress, judging how it feels.

After a minute or two of anticipation, she turns to me resolute in her decision. 'How much do I owe you?'

'Nothing at all.'

'You can't do that.' Tessa frowns. 'Please let me give you something.'

'Honestly it was just sat in a cupboard. I would much rather it be worn and next time I'm in you can buy me a coffee.'

'Thank you,' Tessa says, looking grateful. She looks back down at the dress and gives a little squeal as she spins around in it and another burst of happiness erupts in my chest.

Later that evening Safiyah and I decide to have dinner together at the pub, purely for moral support in case Tessa needs us and not at all to be nosey!

'I feel really mean that we're doing this.' I scan the door, watching for Tessa and Sam to walk in.

'Doing what?'

'Being as bad as the rest of the mad lot that live in this place. All I've done is moan about nothing being private in the village and here we are waiting to spy on their date.'

'We're having a lovely meal together, that's all. It just so happens to be in the same place that Tessa and Sam are having a date but there's hardly anywhere else to go,' Safiyah answers, justifying our nosiness with a tone of indifference.

'Yeah you keep telling yourself that.'

Tessa and Sam walk through the door. Tessa looks amazing, she's teamed the mustard dress with a pair of brown ankle boots and lots of bangles up her arm which preserves her edgy cool style. Her long hair is flowing down her back with delicate little plaits dotted about. She looks happy and confident. She's heeded my words of encouragement with her shoulders back and head held high. Sam can't take his eyes off her, he looks like a deer caught in headlights. I'm about to hide behind the menu when Tessa sees us sat in the corner and gives us both a sly thumbs up as she walks by.

'Look at her go,' Safiyah says, impressed.

'I say it all the time but it's amazing what an outfit can do for your confidence.'

'Sure does.'

Right, I pull my eyes away from their date, determined to give them some privacy. 'Fiya, what's your happy place?' I ask. Seeing Tessa so happy and carefree reminds me I'm still on my quest to find out what makes a happy place.

'Slightly random change in conversation but, erm, on holiday on a lovely hot beach. I'm happiest by the sea, I think. I find it quite calming. I love hearing the water hitting the rocks and just relaxing. The distillery is so hectic that I love the break every now and then. Don't get me wrong, I love the farm but it's noisy and busy, so when Theo and I do get away and go to the sea, there's something soothing about it.'

'Sounds lovely.' For Hettie it's the comfort of home and for Safiyah, it's the relaxation away from normal life. Both sound so equally appealing. 'Oh, before I forget, do you still have that huge marquee for events at the farm?'

'Yes, why?'

'Just an idea I have.'

28

The next day, I wake bright and early. I stretch out my arms wide, and then it dawns on me. How had I not noticed yesterday, or the day before? For the last few mornings I have woken with no sign of the dreaded stomach pang. In fact, even now, thinking of Philip, nothing particularly stirs. I jump out of bed and do a little dance in delight. It feels bloody brilliant.

I down my breakfast, have a shower and get dressed. Another pleasant surprise is that my jeans feel a little looser. All this Zumba, however rubbish I am, seems to be making a difference. I hear a knock at the front door and run down to let Jenny and Verity in.

'Wow, look at you!' Jenny is standing before me with a new, very chic angled blonde bob. 'That looks amazing.'

'I love it, I went after Zumba yesterday and had it done. I feel twenty-five again.' Linda may be a blabbermouth, but she's a flipping good hair stylist. The finished dress is a success and Jenny loves it. I feel euphoric as I watch Jenny bounce about in her dress and hairdo, she's like a new woman. She has an energy I've never seen in her before and so much more life and confidence in herself than when we first talked about her dress.

She even pays me a little extra than what we agreed on, which I feel awful about accepting.

'Violet, please, I want you to have it. It may only be a dress, but you have made me feel like I did all those years ago. You've given me back a spark I thought I had lost. I was dreading the retirement party, but I can't wait now.' If that isn't success then I don't know what is.

I make a fresh pot of tea and the three of us set about looking through magazines and patterns for a dress for Verity.

'I like that one.' Verity points to a ruched chiffon dress in a printed sea-breeze blue and a pale lemon yellow. 'Although I don't really want my arms on show.'

'Why not?' I ask.

'I don't like the tops of them, they're all wobbly. The dress is pretty though.'

'I could make a little silk bolero to wear over the top. You'll be able to see the dress but still be covered up. Then you have the choice to take it off if you want.'

'That sounds great.'

'I have this pattern here which is a shift dress,' I say, passing the picture to Verity from my stash of patterns. 'I might struggle finding that exact fabric, but do you trust me to find something as close as possible?'

'Absolutely,' Verity replies.

'Brilliant. I'll see what I can find later today.' That was a very quick and painless decision.

After saying goodbye, I hop in the car and head towards Lancaster to pick up the material. As I'm driving through the village though, I spot Winnie sitting on the bench on the village green, tucking into a sandwich. It pulls on my heartstrings seeing her sat there. She looks so small and solitary. Winnie could be perfectly happy sitting there after enjoying a little walk in the sun, and yet I can't help but wonder if she's lonely. Ever since she told me about turning up early everywhere because home can be too quiet, it's really played on my mind. Maybe I could pop round later and have a little catch-up with her. If anything, it might ease my worry.

I park up and stroll into the little haberdashery.

I manage to find a beautiful emerald-green material for Jane's cocktail dress and order what I need for Verity's, which I opt to be delivered to Willow Cottage next week. I stash my two huge bags of goodies in the car and walk into town to treat myself to lunch. I stop at a little coffee shop in the town centre and sit in the window with a sandwich and drink, watching the world go by. I pull out my little notebook and start a to-do list.

If I'm staying in Elmsbourne-Hollow then I'm determined more than ever to make a go of my own business. I could up the promotion for my Etsy shop to bring in some money and start planning towards my own bridal shop. I could stock wedding dresses from other designers as well as offering my own bespoke designs. I only need to start off small and if there was ever a time to do it then now would be it. Nothing's holding me back anymore. Philip had hinted several times that it was just a pipe dream and I'm going to prove him wrong.

I finish my lunch and look out of the window to see a dashing man in a well-tailored navy-blue suit on the other side of the road. Is that Ben? I strain my eyes looking a little closer – it is him. He does work near here – perhaps he's on his lunch break. I grab my coffee and bag and go outside onto the street to surprise him. I haven't seen him in a suit before, he looks incredible, all professional and sexy – I might have to get him to wear that for me in the bedroom.

I'm about to call his name when I see him wave to someone else. A tall blonde supermodel in an expensive-looking black figure-hugging dress with a pair of killer heels is strutting towards him. She has a big beautiful grin with perfect teeth, her blonde hair bouncing elegantly behind and then falling perfectly into place. I think she's actually walking in slow motion – she is breathtaking. Ben kisses her on each cheek and they fall into deep conversation.

They look so good together – who the hell is she? They start walking towards me, talking animatedly to each other. Shit, he can't see me, I need to hide. In a blind panic, I duck down behind a sign that's on the side of the road. Ben and the mystery woman walk past me, chatting. She's laughing at something he's said and it sounds like a beautiful melodic song – crap, even her laugh is perfect. They turn into a restaurant right next to where I have ducked down. *Come on, Violet, don't think the worst, perhaps it's a business lunch.* He was very happy to see her though. Mind you, who wouldn't be?

'You okay, miss?' a deep voice booms from behind me and I almost jump out of my skin. I spin around to see five workmen standing in the road, watching me with a mixture of amusement and confusion. I jumped so hard I've spilt my coffee down my white top, and you can now see my bra showing through. Bad day to wear a pink bra and white top combo – breaking a cardinal fashion rule right there, so it's probably karma. I look at the sign that I've squatted behind which is actually a roadworks warning. I was so distracted that I've only gone and bent down smack bang in the middle of where five burly workmen are trying to resurface a road – oops!

'Err, yes, sorry. Good work, carry on,' I say, stepping back onto the pavement and hurrying away from the restaurant window with my arms tightly folded around my chest, trying to regain some sort of modesty. I jump in my car and let out a deep sigh as I realise that Ben could possibly be on a date with someone else. Oh, I knew he was too good to be true. But he asked to see me later, is he really the type to date two women in one day? The answer to that is I don't know because I don't really know him that well, do I? Maybe it's a business lunch with a gorgeous woman who has angel-like features... Shit...

No come on, snap out of it, I'm reading too much into things again. It shouldn't matter anyway. Ben is a bit of fun, nothing serious, we've only had one date, we're not *together*. He can do what he wants. Friends with benefits, that's all. I don't even know why I hid from them both. It was probably because stood next to her in the street I would have felt like a dowdy shit tip. Ben would have compared the two of us and instantly regretted hopping into bed with me.

I drive back home to Elmsbourne-Hollow trying to forget all about my little escapade in town but as I pull up at home my phone buzzes with a message from Ben – *Still on for later? Don't forget your paintbrush X*

God, what if he's dating numerous women and I'm a name at the bottom of a long list of women? Perhaps I could do the same, date numerous people too. Be easy-going and aloof, not getting attached. Lots of fun and sex, a man at each port as it were – perhaps not.

I reply – *Yep, see you later x* – as I desperately hope he isn't only after free labour in the form of decorating. I decide not to think about it anymore. I promised myself fun and fun I shall have. I'm pretty sure that the happy place I'm so desperately seeking lies in getting my business going. That's my main priority and there is no room for worrying about anything else, in particular gorgeous architects and their leggy perfect blonde lunch dates.

29

It's only two o'clock when I get home, I've changed out of my coffee-stained top and I'm unpacking the mounds of material. The satin feels so luxurious as it slips through my fingers. I feel a burst of excitement to start Collette's dress but that's going to have to wait an hour or so. Ever since I saw Winnie this morning sat on the bench, I've been keen to go and see her. I could pop in for an hour and still have time to come back and make a start on the dress. I grab my bag and walk towards Winnie's.

She lives just off the village high street, down a pretty little side road of terraced stone houses. The house is beautifully adorned with window boxes filled with vibrant petunias and zinnias. I open the little wooden gate and knock on the door.

A few seconds later Winnie appears looking delighted to see me. 'Hello, dear, what a lovely surprise.'

'I hope you don't mind me turning up unannounced but I just wondered if you fancied having a cup of tea together.'

'What a lovely idea, come in.' I instantly feel at home, the house exudes the same openness and warmth that sums Winnie up. She shows me into the lounge, a large room with two floral armchairs and matching sofa. It's airy and smells like freshly washed laundry, the room has a perfect combination of chintz and rustic charm.

'I'll make a pot of tea, you make yourself at home.' She scuttles off to the kitchen.

I sit down and look around the room that's filled with photos of Winnie's children and grandchildren, happy little faces looking back. Winnie returns with a tray of tea and biscuits and places them on a coffee table in the middle of the room.

'I love your home, Winnie,' I say, pouring myself a cup of tea.

'Thank you,' she replies proudly.

'Are these your grandchildren?' I get up to look closer at a photo of three giggling children sat in a row on a sledge in the snow.

'Yes, that's Daisy, she's nine, James who's six and Zach who's four.' I can see the love pouring out of Winnie as she looks at the photo. I can imagine she's such a loving grandmother.

'They're beautiful.'

'They're my pride and joy. Daisy phones me every other day and tells me all about school. I'm seeing them this weekend.' Winnie beams.

'That's lovely.' See, I knew I was just being silly, assuming that Winnie was lonely.

'I'm hoping my Nathan and his girlfriend settle down soon and have children, but I think that's a little way off yet. They love jet-setting about. They've just come back from a long weekend in New York.' Winnie passes her phone to me and I see a picture of Nathan and his girlfriend stood on top of a tall building with the New York skyline in the background.

'He looks so much like you,' I say, seeing the familiarity in Nathan's face. The two of them have the same round face with pink cheeks, big brown eyes and engaging smiles.

'Everyone says that,' she says, gazing at the photo adoringly. 'Keira is just like her father.'

Winnie passes the phone back and this time it shows a photo of a woman in her thirties with hazel eyes, and dimples in both cheeks. Winnie walks over to the sideboard and comes back over with a photo in an ornate gold frame of her late husband.

'Wow, she does,' I say. The same eyes and dimples that I have just seen in Keira are looking back at me, so charming and cheeky. 'They both look quite mischievous with those gorgeous dimples.'

'Oh yes, Keira is forever playing tricks on the children just like Arthur did,' she tells me, reminiscently staring at the photo I've handed back to her. 'He was very playful.'

'Where did you meet?' I hope she doesn't mind me asking but I would love to know how her love story began.

'The London Coliseum,' Winnie says, getting up and walking back over to the sideboard. She opens a drawer and pulls out a small well-worn dark-red leather box. She sits back down, takes the lid off and I see it's full of old photos. 'I was a ballet dancer for a short time when I was younger, believe it or not.' I can most definitely believe it, Winnie has a lovely lithe figure and she moves in such a graceful, delicate way. She hands me a photo. 'I was eighteen.'

The black-and-white photo is of a young woman in a tutu, stood with her legs crossed, high up on her toes, her arms held gracefully up in the air over her head. She looks so beautiful and elegant, it takes my breath away. It's the Winnie I know now but just younger. Her eyes though, they haven't aged at all. They are still the sparkly bright windows of a gentle soul that I can see today.

'You look beautiful.'

'Thank you. I was in a production of *Swan Lake*. Arthur was a couple of years older and was working as an accountant. He had never wanted to be, but his father had been one, and pushed him to do the same. In those days you did as your parents told you,' she says wistfully as if she's falling back through time. 'He'd taken his mum to the ballet for her birthday. He said that as soon as he saw me, he knew he wanted to marry me.'

'How romantic,' I say, listening intently.

'I noticed him in the audience at the end, he gave me a standing ovation. He was so handsome, I remember my stomach fluttering. He came back the next day to the stage door and asked to see me. I, of course, said no but after a week of him turning up, I finally relented and spoke to him. He asked to take me for a drink. He was so striking, I couldn't turn those dimples down.'

She strokes his face on the photo and a lump forms in my throat as I listen to Winnie talk so pensively about her husband. 'My friend came with me the next day for a double date. Arthur's parents didn't agree with our partnership; they didn't think a dancer was good enough for their son, which made it all the more romantic. Forbidden love and all that.' She smiles gently. 'He proposed after two months and we got married two months after that.'

'So quickly?' To know so fast that you want to spend your whole life with someone sounds so romantic and dreamy, something you see in a film or read in a book.

'By today's standards I suppose so, but it was so different back then. I gave up ballet and we travelled. We visited so many places and then we eventually settled and had Keira and Nathan. We were married forty-five years when Arthur died, he had a heart attack, and that was... gosh, five years ago now.' Winnie passes me a photo of them both on their wedding day. Winnie is wearing an A-line white V-neck wedding dress that stops just below her knees with three-quarter-length sleeves, her hair up in a beehive hairdo with a white ribbon tied around it and a little posy of white roses. Arthur's wearing a very retro brown suit, they both look undeniably happy.

'I love the dress.' My heart gives a little thump of sadness as I see Winnie's eyes sparkling with tears and I have to blink back my own that are threatening to fall. Winnie does a little cough to clear her throat and takes a sip of tea. I don't know what to say. What can you say when someone talks so tenderly about the love of their life who they've lost?

'Did his parents approve in the end?'

'It took a while, but I think they did, especially when I had the children.' Winnie hands me the box of photos and it's a time capsule of Winnie's life over a forty-year period. Pictures of them smiling at different places around the world, they look so happy and in love. There are pictures of them bouncing a baby on their knee, chasing a toddler around a park – then two children. Pictures with teenagers and graduations. A beautiful life. Winnie's happy place was here in that box.

'You both look very much in love.' The emotion seeps out of my voice. 'A truly beautiful love story.'

'It was, I was very lucky. We had so many wonderful years together and I have all the memories to look back on.'

'You must miss him.' That sounds like such a stupid thing to say, of course she misses him.

'I do, I miss the mayhem of it all really. Life with him and the children was manic and wonderfully noisy, the house was full. You spend all these years looking after a family, having this purpose and then all of a sudden life is... quiet.' Winnie stops talking and the enormity of the silence hits me, and I understand why she is always so eager to get out and about. 'Don't get me wrong, I see my family a lot and as often as we all can. It's just not the same when it isn't every day. That's why I like to go out and see people, I love the noise.'

'I'm sure there will be plenty of that this weekend when you see your family.'

'Absolutely,' Winnie says, taking the box back and putting it away. 'I can't wait. What about you? You and Ben looked quite smitten together at the fayre.'

I feel suddenly very reticent talking about him to Winnie. It seems so small compared to talking about her great love story. 'Oh, it's nothing really and I guess quite soon after Philip.'

'Take it from an old bird who knows, love can hit you when you least expect it.'

'Where have you been, darling?' Lilly asks as I walk into the kitchen.

'I went to see Winnie.'

'Is she okay?'

'She's fine, just wanted to give her some company. Did you know she used to be a ballet dancer?'

'Yes, when she first joined Zumba she said she was looking for something to keep her active and explained that she was a ballet dancer before she was married.'

'I might make it a regular thing, popping round for a brew. She's so lovely to talk to and I don't like the thought of her being on her own too much.' Winnie seemed pleased I visited so I don't think I was in the way.

'What a lovely idea, she'll enjoy that.'

'How are the paintings coming on for the exhibition?' I ask. Lilly's been working her socks off. When she gets into a creative bubble, there's no stopping her.

'Wonderfully. The collection is turning out better than I thought. Fred and I are popping out in a bit for a walk to take some more photos for me to paint. I love the late summer sunsets,' she says, bouncing around like a loveable puppy. I swear that woman has more energy than anyone I know.

'Have fun. I have the material for Collette's dress so I'm going to go and make a start before I see Ben later,' I shout, running up to my room eagerly. In the excitement of the project, the rest of the day passes by in a blur of dress material. Before I know it, it's time to head to Ben's. I have made a good start though. I've cut a couple of pieces out in lining fabric, purposely going slowly to make sure I'm getting it right. Measure twice, cut once, that's what Lilly always taught me. I get changed into a fitted black and white striped T-shirt and pull on my black cropped dungarees with some comfy ballet shoes... black! I certainly look the part of a decorator.

'I come dressed for work,' I say, striking a pose with the paintbrush I swiped from Lilly's studio as Ben opens the front door.

'Looking good, Miss Brown,' Ben says, laughing. As soon as the front door shuts, he immediately pulls me in for a blow-your-socks-off kiss. Who knew dungarees would have such an effect on a man!

'I have been thinking of doing that all day,' he says as we finally pull our mouths apart. He has a knack for making me breathless every time we kiss, and it takes me a second to get my mind back on track. We walk into the kitchen together and heat spreads through my thighs as I remember what we were doing the last time we were in this room. Ben's thoughts seem to be similar to mine because he walks up right behind me and gently kisses my neck.

'I think we should head to the shops now before we get too carried away,' I say, trying to keep both our heads in the game, we are supposed to be decorating after all.

'Really? We could just forget about the painting. Who needs a finished living room anyway?' Ben says, nuzzling into my neck.

'You do. Now come on,' I say, playfully pulling him towards the door. He reluctantly does as he's told, and we jump in his car and head for the shops.

'So how was work today?' I ask as I watch him drive.

'Good, thank you. How was your day?'

'Pretty good. Finished Jenny's dress and had a catch-up with Winnie from Zumba. I popped into Lancaster to pick up my order for Collette's dress.' Oh, and I saw you in the street with a goddess!

'You were? You should have said, I was in town too.'

'Oh really?' My shock sounds rather convincing.

'Yeah, business lunch with a possible new client.'

So it was business and not a date – not that I care anyway because I'm cool and aloof now. 'Did it go well?'

'I think so, should hear tomorrow if we've won the contract.' He doesn't seem to be hiding anything, not that he needs to anyway. He can have lunch with as many drop-dead gorgeous women as he wants. He is actually single.

We arrive at the shop and I help Ben pick a yellow geometric wallpaper for an accent wall and a soft blue paint called First Dawn for the others. We go back to Ben's, order pizza and get to work painting. After two and a half hours of hard graft, we stand back and check out our handiwork.

'Looks pretty good, if I do say so myself,' I say, wiping my forehead.

'We make an excellent team,' Ben replies.

A pleasant buzz shoots through me, followed quickly by alarm – no, we aren't a team we're just friends. Friends who have fun with no strings – friends who pick wallpaper together. Oh crap, why did I agree to this? We should be having casual drinks, dinner and mind-blowing sex not decorating, that's relationship stuff. 'I'll wallpaper tomorrow night when the paint is dry and then it's done. I just need to hang the television and the room is good to go.' He steps closer to me. 'You have paint all over your head.'

'So do you,' I say as I quickly try to wipe off the paint.

'Do I? Right, I'd better go for a shower then.' He takes his top off in front of me and my legs go weak at the sight of his buff torso that I would quite frankly like to be rubbing up against right now. 'Fancy joining me?'

Now that's more like it. I don't need asking twice.

30

I step back from the dressmakers mannequin and stretch. I've spent the whole day busily working away on Collette's dress, in fact I've spent a busy few days working on it. I've finished cutting out all the pieces in a lining fabric and have pinned them into shape on the mannequin to create the pattern for the finished dress, the next step will be to start cutting the silk.

After being indoors all day though I need some fresh air. I've decided to go for a run. In my head I have visions of a super-cool Nike advert where I pound the road looking athletic and fit and come home feeling exhilarated. I thoroughly enjoy Zumba twice a week, surely running will be just as fun. I throw on my gym kit and trainers, fill up a water bottle and plug some earphones into my phone. I look the part, so I take a deep breath and run down the road heading out of Elmsbourne-Hollow towards the woods.

As I run down the steep footpath, towards the river, I can feel my heart pumping hard already. I have a running playlist on my phone and I'm trying to jog to the beat. Shit this is harder than I thought, I am so not cut out to be a runner.

. . .

How long have I been running for? Bloody hell, how has it only been five minutes? I push on for fifteen more until I get to the bridge that crosses the river. I probably should have stretched before I set off! I can feel myself panting, I have an awful burning dryness in my throat and a stitch creeping across my sides. I cross the bridge but can't take any more running. I stop at a bench to catch my breath. Oh God, the pain. Sweat is dripping off my face and all I want to do is climb into a cold shower. Maybe I could throw myself in the river to cool down. Definitely not as fit as I thought. I yank out my earphones.

'Never did I think I would see the day when Violet Brown would be running.'

'Shit, Josh, you scared the crap out of me.'

'I've been calling your name for the past five minutes,' Josh says, laughing. He too is out for a run but looks a lot more professional in his shorts and running top with a band fitted around his bicep that's holding his phone. He's sweating but doesn't appear to be in the pain that I'm in – I bet he stretched beforehand!

'I think I've only ever seen you run to the bar.'

'Shut up.' I try not to smile. 'I'll have you know I'm a serious exercise enthusiast these days.' Exaggeration, I know.

'Yeah, Mum said you were an avid member of the over-fifties Zumba class.'

'It's harder than you think,' I say, still struggling to get my breath back. 'They're a feisty bunch.'

'I bet they are.'

'Anyway, I'm working on the new me.' I lift my arms above my head, trying to stretch the pain away. 'This is all part of the life makeover, a new Violet.' Crap, I need to sit down. I practically fall onto the bench. 'Why does running have to be so bloody hard?'

'I think that's the point of it, to push yourself.' He sits down next to me. 'So why a new Violet? I quite like the old one,' he questions, flashing his sapphire-blue eyes at me.

'Because old Violet was a pushover who got her heart broken. She let people walk all over her, use her and make a fool of her. She was far too trusting.'

'Really? That's not the Violet I remember. The one I knew was far from being a pushover. She once punched a boy in her class because he laughed at Hettie for wearing glasses. She stood up to a teacher who told her that she couldn't play football because it was a boys' sport. So she set up a girls' school football team, even though she hated the sport, just to prove a point.' He laughs. 'She moved to London and fought her way to get an interview at the bridal house she wanted to work at. She doesn't sound like a pushover to me. She sounds pretty special actually.'

That's sweet of him to say and I may have done all those things but somehow along the way I stopped being that girl. 'You would say that, you're one of my oldest friends and my best friend's brother.' My breathing is starting to steady and my heart rate is returning to a less-frightening speed.

'I'm not saying it as your friend or your best friend's brother. I'm saying it as someone who was loved by you once... and loved you back.' He leans forward placing his elbows on his knees, looking at the floor.

'Oh.' We've never really spoken about our past relationship. Once we realised that long distance would never work and we finally made the decision to break-up, we avoided each other when Josh returned for holidays. I found it too hard to be around him, I was crushed that we weren't together anymore. After time though our friendship grew. It became easy to still be a part of each other's lives, still caring for each other but never really mentioning what we once had.

'You were never a pushover when we were together, you always put me in my place when I needed someone to.'

'I changed, I ended up being one with Philip.'

'He hid his affair, Violet. It wasn't your fault you didn't see it.'

Did I see it though? Did I see the signs and choose to ignore them? Because I'm not sure anymore. I don't know what's worse. Seeing it but ignoring it or being completely oblivious.

'It's not just the affair though, I'd become someone I don't recognise. I took so much crap off him. He controlled my life. I didn't come home because he didn't want me to, he would make up plans we didn't have beforehand just to keep me around and I fell for it. Everything had to revolve around him. I didn't feel good enough because of his horrible little remarks about the way I looked and the things I liked. Even the apartment, there was almost nothing of mine in there. I backed away from designing more because to him it was just a silly dream. I lost all my confidence, he took who I was, piece by piece, until there was nothing left, and I didn't see it.'

Hearing all those words out loud shocks me to my very soul. Until this moment I didn't realise the extent of his damage.

'I don't think you're giving yourself enough credit. From what Safiyah said, the moment you found out about his affair, you were out of there. You didn't stick around, that doesn't sound like a pushover to me.'

I haven't really thought about it like that before. The truth is that maybe there was nothing else left to give. He had taken everything, I had no choice but to leave. Josh twists his body to face me, he looks so serious.

'I know you pretty well, Vi. When we were together you were confident and vivacious, so sure of yourself. So you may have got a little off track but you're away from him now. Who you are is still in there and please don't change that. You are one of the most caring and thoughtful people I have ever met, you put your whole heart into everything and you want to make everyone around you happy. But that isn't the reason he did those things to you. He did them because he's a bad person. Those things that you are, are actually the things that make it so easy for people to love you, they're why I loved you.'

I'm taken aback, I so want everything he has said to be true. I want the Violet that I was all those years ago when we were together to still be here. I don't want Philip to have taken that person away.

'That seems like so long ago now.'

'It was but it still doesn't change the facts. He hurt you, and I get that you don't want it to happen again. You're bound to be cautious but don't lose all the parts of you that make you you. That openness and warmth is so special, don't close it off. He was a fool to try to take that from you.' Josh squeezes my hand and for a split second I'm eighteen again.

'Do you ever wonder what could have happened if you had gone to university in Lancaster rather than Southampton?'

'I did a lot at first. I even contemplated transferring the first summer I came back for the holidays; we'd just broken up and I missed you so much,' he says, looking out at the river.

'You did?' I'm shocked, I never knew he felt that way, I thought he got over me the second he left. I knew it was a tough decision for him to move away at the time, but it was his chance at seeing what life would be like away from the farm. I figured once he left, he forgot all about us.

'Yeah of course, don't look so shocked, you weren't easy to get over, you know. I had to see you so much with Fiya that summer it was torture. Sunbathing in the garden at the farm and nights out in the pub.'

'It was torture for me too, you kept showing up around the village looking all brooding and hot.'

'I wasn't brooding.' Josh laughs.

'You were and you were good at it.' I smile, remembering it like it was yesterday. 'It worked out in the end though, didn't it?'

'Absolutely, we realised it was the right choice. I went on to meet Ayda and have Hector.'

'I got to move away and experience life away from the village, work for Anna Pemberton,' I say nostalgically. 'The only good thing to come out of moving there was the experience I got from her. Actually, that's not true, for a while there Philip and I were happy.'

'And now there's Ben. I hear things are going well there,' Josh says, gently nudging my shoulder.

'It's only two dates and we're just friends. We have more of a physical relationship.' Thinking of Ben makes me feel all warm and fuzzy inside though – Goddammit.

'As I said before, you're a heart-all-in kind of girl. I like him, I think you're both well-suited. Don't fight it.'

I rest my head on his shoulder. I want to stay here for a few more minutes pretending I'm still eighteen when life was a little easier.

'Can I ask you something? What's your happy place? Where are you most happy?'

'Easy. Anytime I'm at the farm with Ayda and Hector. But my most favourite is when we've been playing out in the fresh air and then we go inside and there's a stew cooking away. Mum and Dad come over, Fiya and Theo too, and we all sit together around the table eating and talking. No TV on, no phones, just all of us together.'

'That sounds nice.' Family is Josh's happy place and that sounds pretty special. I think that is probably most people's definition of happy.

'What about yours?'

'I'm still working on it,' I say thoughtfully.

'Come on, race you to Ethel's – loser buys the coffee.'

. . .

'You win!' I pant as we stop outside the tearoom. Josh and I raced back to town, well, raced is a loose term. Josh sprinted off very athletically while I dragged my sorry arse after him.

'Coffee's on you then,' Josh says, gulping the last of his water, looking rather triumphant.

I feel utterly exhausted as we walk into the tearoom and there's a weird gushing noise rushing through my ears which I think is from my heart thumping so hard. The rich sweet smell of cakes hits me, and I salivate, which is quite an achievement considering how dry my mouth is from running. I'm so hungry after all that.

'Violet, darling, are you okay? You look like you're about to be sick,' Lilly calls from the back of the tearoom. I feel like I might be sick, to be honest. Running is not for me; I'm sticking with Zumba.

'Hey, Mum. I'm... fine... Been for a... run.' I wheeze between words. 'Josh decided... to try to kill me.'

'It was only a gentle jog,' Josh says innocently, passing me a glass of water. He can bugger off, that was not gentle. Lilly, Winnie, Jane and Mary are sat in the tearoom having a late lunch.

'Hi, Mum, I didn't know you would be here,' Josh says, giving Jane a kiss on the cheek.

'Needed a break from your father so having a good natter with the girls,' she replies, shifting her chair over so her son can squeeze in next to her.

I fall into a chair next to Lilly and after what feels like a trillion hours, finally get my breath back and heart rate under control. I order a peanut butter flapjack – peanuts give you energy, right? I think I've heard that somewhere.

'Perhaps we could all find somewhere to go together,' Lilly says, looking around at the rest of the women.

'Go where?' I ask, finally having the energy to take note of the conversation.

'We were just talking about all getting dressed up and going somewhere together. You making dresses has got us in the mood for a good-old-knees-up where we can show them off.'

'Funny you should say that, I have actually been thinking about something. Why don't we put an event on?'

'What do you mean?' Winnie asks.

'We could organise a dance for the village, sell tickets and donate the money to a charity. Josh, the distillery has that huge marquee still, perhaps we could borrow it for a small charge. We could set up a bar and put out some tables, hire a DJ and a few of the local bands. We don't need to charge a lot – enough to cover costs and then donate the rest.'

'What a marvellous idea.' Jane claps.

'Verity, I thought maybe you could have a word with the rest of the council and check what permission we might need to hold it on the village green, and, Winnie, I was wondering if you would like to help me organise it. I'm quite busy with the dresses so thought you could be the head of the dance committee. Only if you want to though of course,' I say.

Winnie's eyes light up. 'Oh yes, I would love to,' she answers rather proudly.

'We could have weekly meetings to get everything organised,' I suggest. Another excuse to keep meeting up with Winnie.

'That's settled then,' Lilly exclaims energetically. 'We could have it say mid-October before it starts getting too cold, and that gives us enough time to organise it. We could do an autumnal theme.'

There's a buzz of excitement as the ladies start discussing plans.

.   .   .

'That was nice of you to include Winnie,' Lilly says as we're walking home. She's looking at me very quizzically.

'I feel a bit sad for her, being on her own. She arrives early for Zumba because she wants to get out and about. I often see her in town walking on her own. When I went round for a brew the other day, she mentioned feeling like she didn't have a purpose now the children are grown, and Arthur's gone. I thought this might give her something to do and get excited about.'

'It's a great idea, perhaps we could set up a village events group that she could chair,' Lilly says. 'By the way I'm going to need you to make me a dress now too.'

31

For the next few weeks I dedicate my time to Collette's wedding dress which is coming along nicely. The silk has been cut and carefully machined together. The lace and embellishments haven't been added yet, but the main base of the dress is finished. Collette has visited to see the progress and to try it on at various stages, making sure the size is right.

I've been promoting my Etsy shop a lot more and through the wonders of social media, I've managed to get a few more orders, mainly last-minute summer dresses. I've made a few thicker winter pinafore dresses that look great with tights and thin jumpers underneath which I've taken photos of and added to the online shop. In between making the wedding dress, I completed Jane's cocktail dress which was an instant hit with all the Golden Girls. Jane's promised that if Winters Gin wins the award and they make it into the papers she will make sure the dress gets a mention.

With news of the dance spreading, a couple more of the Golden Girls have requested bespoke dresses especially after the success of Jenny and Jane's. They are even thinking about Christmas parties too, so are choosing outfits that they can wear for both events. Verity's ruched dress is finished and hung on a hanger in my bedroom waiting to be delivered, so all in all it's been a busy few weeks. I cross the dress out of my order book with immense satisfaction. The thought has occurred to me that the Golden Girls are asking for dresses purely out of the kindness of their own hearts, wanting to give me work, but they insisted that isn't the case when I asked them at Zumba. Whatever the reason is, I'm very grateful.

I've begun to regularly visit Winnie at home where we discuss plans for the dance and normal day-to-day life chit-chat and I love it. She's such a beautiful character and a joy to be around. My ulterior motive of asking Winnie for help seems to have worked and she has a new lease of life. She has so many ideas for themes and has been busy looking at ideas for home-made decorations. I've also carried on with Zumba and I have to say I'm nailing all the moves which makes me feel less guilty about indulging at cake club. I adore the company of the Golden Girls, they're cheeky and funny, and I always come away with my face hurting from lots of laughter.

My evenings have been spent going for leisurely walks around the woods with Ben and helping him decorate his bedroom although that is proving hard as we do get sidetracked... a lot. We seem to have an insatiable thirst for each other whenever there's a bed nearby, or a sofa or kitchen worktop, for that matter. I'm determined to keep it very casual between us and this whole friends with benefits thing seems to be working out quite well for the both of us.

Being back with Hettie and Safiyah, getting to spend more time with them, is the cherry on the cake. Five years of being so far from them, it feels great to be able to pop down the road for a quick cup of tea or catch-up at the pub over a gin. Life has fallen into a lovely flow. I can't believe I'm saying this but I'm thoroughly enjoying village life. Why had I been so miserable about coming home?

'Hello, love.' Winnie opens the door to me practically bouncing. It's Saturday in late August and I've arrived for our weekly chat. 'Come and see what we have made,' she says, hurrying me into the living room. Verity and Jenny are sat down on the sofa although it's pretty hard to see them as they are covered in huge red, orange and yellow paper pom-poms.

'Wow, look at them,' I say, fighting my way through the living room. 'They're great.'

'And really cheap to make, we went and bought a load of tissue paper and spent the morning making them. We can hang them from the top of the marquee on long string,' Jenny says, clearing the pom-poms off the sofa so I can sit down.

'I was telling my granddaughter about the dance and she came up with the idea. They're going to come by the way.' Winnie's flushed with excitement.

'Fantastic, I can't wait to meet them.' I've heard so much about Winnie's family, I feel like I know them already. 'It's a while till the dance though, where are we going to store them all?' I say, looking at the mounds of paper pom-poms that Verity and Jenny are currently drowning in.

'Oh, they can go in my spare room,' Winnie tells me with an absent-minded wave of her hands. Clearly, she has already thought it all through. 'I've booked the DJ you gave me the details of and two local bands as well,' she says as she checks off her list. There's no hanging around with this lot!

'I spoke to Safiyah and she's going to set up the bar and use the staff they hire for events as well as putting on a hog roast,' I tell them all so another job can be ticked off. 'Everything seems like it's in hand. I'll print off some flyers and sort out tickets and we can start selling them around the village.' I jot it down in my notebook so I don't forget. I'm swamped with jobs at the moment that if I don't write it down, it doesn't get done. 'It would look really pretty if we hung lots of fairy lights around the marquee. I'll see what we have in the attic at home.'

'I have some too,' Verity adds.

'Me too,' says Winnie. Fantastic, the less money we have to spend on decorations, the more there will be for charity.

'Great! Between us all we should have enough.' I suddenly remember the package I have with me. 'Oh, here you go, Verity, I almost forgot. Special delivery,' I say, passing her the large paper carrier bag. Verity delves in like an excited child opening a birthday present.

'Oh, Violet, it's perfect,' Verity says, holding the blue and yellow dress up in front of her. She reaches in further and pulls out the little silk blue bolero. 'Just perfect.'

'If there are any problems with it, let me know.'

'Based on my last fitting, I'm sure there won't be any problems. I can't wait to strut my stuff in it,' she says, doing a little dance, trying not to crush all the paper pom-poms.

'Are you all coming to the rugby match later?' I ask hopefully. Elmsbourne-Hollow are playing in a charity match and they are so much fun when everyone comes along.

'Yes, I think so,' Winnie says.

'Ooh yes,' Jenny agrees. 'Definitely worth a visit seeing all those lovely legs in shorts.'

I can't argue with that. There's a certain pair of legs I'll have my eye on.

Safiyah and I have joined Fred at the rugby field to watch Elmsbourne-Hollow play the annual charity match against Hollymere, the neighbouring village. The three of us are sat on the sidelines cheering Ben, Theo and the rest of the team on. Elmsbourne-Hollow are in the lead and the game has been rather exciting even for me who literally has no interest in rugby whatsoever. Mainly I'm just appreciating the view of seeing Ben running around in shorts, he does have lovely legs. Hettie's busy manning the refreshment stand with Lilly serving the villagers while cheering Jack on from the table.

I can hear random yells of 'Come on, love, show them what you're made of!' and 'Ref, are you blind?' coming from the table as Hettie shows her support rather enthusiastically and much to the displeasure of Mr Thompson who's volunteered to referee the match.

'Hettie gets into it, doesn't she?' Fred says with a chuckle. I watch as Hettie accidentally throws a drink in the air as she sees Jack get tackled to the floor. She's normally so mild-mannered.

'Certainly does, we're going to have to be careful she doesn't run onto the pitch in a minute,' I answer, genuinely worried for the Hollymere team.

'Luckily there's only a few minutes left,' Safiyah says, getting up. 'I'll go over and help pack everything away. I'll tackle her to the ground if she makes a move to invade the pitch.'

My phone buzzes with a message. 'I'll be there in a second to help,' I tell her as I grab my phone. What I didn't expect was for my blood to run cold as I read the sender's name. I've haven't heard from him once since I left London. It has been over two months, why on earth is he contacting me now? My heart thuds as I open the message, *I know I'm probably the last person you want to hear from but just wanted to see how you are. X*

How am I? Anger erupts in my stomach, who the hell does he think he is after all this time. Five years together and then nothing for months. I'm just getting my life back together and he now decides to make contact. He's still a complete shit pig.

'Are you okay, Vi?' Fred asks. 'You look like you've seen a

ghost.'

I feel like I have. I ram my phone back into my bag and force myself to remain composed. 'That was Philip.'

'What did he want?' Fred spits as his brow furrows angrily.

'He asked how I am.' Yet again, Philip leaves me utterly dumbfounded. I need to laugh or cry and I promised myself that there would be no more tears spilled over Philip flipping Miller – so I laugh. It's not funny at all but I can't stop myself.

'Are you okay?' Fred asks, clearly shocked at my strange reaction.

'I'm fine, Dad, I promise. I'm stunned that Philip thinks he would get a reply after all this time. Although actually he is so up his own arse, he probably still thinks I'm sat here pining for him.'

'You're not going to reply, are you?'

'What? No, I'm not.' I may have acted like I lost all respect for myself when I was with him but not again. Quite frankly Philip can sod right off. There's a cheer from the crowd and I look up to see that Ben has scored a try, crap I missed it. Ben looks over, waving and looking exceptionally pleased with himself. I smile back pretending I saw it all.

'Dad, please don't worry about me.'

'I will always worry about you.' Fred pauses, considering his next words carefully. 'I don't want that pompous prick ruining anything else for you, you seem so much happier recently and I don't just mean since the break-up. The last few months before that you didn't sound right on the phone. You didn't seem yourself and now you do again. I have my girl back.'

I feel a lump in my throat, I don't want to cry. 'You're right, Dad. I never admitted it to myself at the time, but I wasn't happy. I think I could sense that there was something wrong but that's over now. Philip Miller is history and I am very much looking forward to my future.'

32

The Chugging Bull is heaving; celebrations for the Elmsbourne-Hollow win started pretty swiftly after the match ended and after walking Fred and Lilly home, I have come to join in the festivities. I squeeze my way through the crowd and find Ben at the bar. He kisses me hello and points to a table in the corner where Hettie, Jack, Safiyah and Theo are sitting.

'Be there in a minute,' I say. 'Norah, can I give you these?' I hand her a pile of tickets for the dance that I printed after the rugby match.

'Of course, love,' Norah says, taking them. I join Ben and the rest of the group at the table and Ben slips his arm around my waist. I wish it didn't feel so good, but it does.

'Well done on the win. I must say it was a very enjoyable game,' I say, leaning into him.

'Thank you for coming to watch.'

'It was most certainly my pleasure.' I give his thigh a little squeeze and flash my best look of seduction. It probably looks more like I have trapped wind than seduction, but Ben seems to disagree. He raises his eyebrows in response, with a gleam in his eye. I check no one is listening then lean even closer and whisper, 'I might just show you how pleasurable later.'

'Miss Brown, you are a tease. How am I supposed to concentrate on anything else for the rest of the night?' His eyes are sparkling with hunger and I suddenly want him to throw me over his shoulder and march me back to Bracken Lodge.

The night continues with playful looks between the two of us and I'm eagerly awaiting the end of the night when we can sneak off. After one of the local bands called The Purple Monkeys plays a set, the boys slope away to the pool table and leave me and the girls to talk.

'Thanks again for loaning the marquee and bar to the dance, Fiya.'

'My pleasure, it's good for promoting the gin and I'm actually really looking forward to it.'

'Me too,' Hettie agrees. 'I can't remember the last time I had the excuse to get really dressed up.'

'Shit, Violet, I completely forgot, I have some news you may find interesting. I can't believe I haven't mentioned it yet,' Safiyah blurts out, hitting her hand against her head in frustration.

'Do tell!'

'I was talking to Patrick today who has the antique furniture shop in the middle of the high street and he mentioned he's decided to move to Canada to be nearer his daughter. He will be looking for someone to rent the shop.'

'Really? Oh my God, that would be perfect.'

'He said he would even be interested in selling it at some point too. To the right person of course.'

'It's quite a big space, isn't it?' Shit a brick, an available shop and here in the village. 'It will need some work doing to it though, to turn it from an antiques store into a bridal shop.'

'You could talk to him about it,' Hettie says excitedly. 'Just think, we could be shop neighbours.'

'It would be perfect,' I answer, my mind whirling with all the possibilities. I shouldn't get my hopes up though, it sounds too good to be true. 'There would be room for me to stock lots of wedding dresses and space in the back and upstairs for alterations and making my own gowns. And renting would be much better at first to see if I can actually make any money.' Okay so perhaps I am getting my hopes up!

'I said that I thought you would be interested and that you might see him tomorrow, was that okay?'

'Of course it's okay, I can't believe my luck.' I really can't. Everything seems to be falling into place. My wonderful family and friends have helped build me back up from the shattered person I was when I came home. My broken heart is mending and now the possibility of a shop – that could be my happy place. The boys come back over jostling each other about who's won.

'You look like you have a sudden fire in your eyes,' Ben says, noticing the flush of adrenalin that must be written across my whole face.

'There might be a shop available for me to rent here in the high street.'

'That's great, where?'

'Opposite Hettie's bakery. It's Patrick's Antiques, I'm going to see him about it tomorrow. It'll need some work to maybe reorganise the space, but it could be perfect.' So bloody perfect in fact.

'Lucky for you, you know a guy who is pretty good with a hammer and saw.' He smiles, pulling me into his arms. He wants to help me. That's so kind. I reach up and kiss him.

'It's sooner than I had planned though and it will take up all my savings but another shop might not become available here for years.'

'Sometimes you have to grab opportunities when they come. This is what you've been saving for.'

'I can't believe it might actually happen,' I say as I feel myself floating up to cloud nine. Life is feeling pretty damn good right now.

'Violet!' I turn to see whose urgent voice is calling my name.

Dean's making his way towards me. His face is pale and distressed.

'Dean, mate, are you okay?' Ben asks.

'No,' Dean says, not taking his eyes from me. My heart stops. The wind suddenly feels like it's been knocked out of me as I fall from my happy little cloud of excitement. I know this can't be good.

'Violet, it's Fred.'

'Dad.'

33

The following two weeks pass by in a blur. Looking back on it now, it's a confused foggy memory. Different scenes flashing and merging into one. Running home from the pub the moment Dean said Fred's name. In that very moment my world flipped upside down. I ran as fast as I could, hearing Ben and everyone else trailing after me. The ambulance in front of the house, Fred being taken out on a stretcher, Lilly walking next to him holding his hand. In the hospital seeing my father attached to machinery, doctors and nurses busily working around him. Holding Lilly's hand as we waited for news, no one really speaking to each other. Just waiting... and waiting. I know Ben, Hettie and Safiyah were there in the background but I can't grasp any clear vision of them, only flashes of colour here and there.

The following days, neighbours appeared, dropping off food parcels, the fridge filling with lasagnes and pies. Lilly and I took it in turns to sit next to Fred's bed pleading with him to wake up. I kept everyone up to date with news, as well as making sure that Lilly was getting enough rest and eating. In those uncertain days I honestly felt bereft. Darkness seemed to take a hold of me, and

I was lost in waves of pain that were hitting me one after the other viciously to the point where I felt like I couldn't breathe any longer. I was drowning.

After four days of waiting, I sent Lilly home for some sleep. I sat in the chair watching his chest rise up and down, holding his hand in mine. I wanted him to know I was there with him. I somehow drifted off to sleep next to the bed and woke with a start as I felt someone squeeze my fingers.

'Dad.' I wept as I looked into his green drowsy eyes. 'You're awake.'

Four days after that dreadful night when Fred had dropped to the floor after suffering a heart attack, he had finally woken up. I shouted for the doctors and called Lilly. When she arrived at the hospital, Fred's eyes were open. I couldn't be more grateful for anything.

The next few days we didn't leave his side. His strength began to return, his health slowly improved and after another week, he was allowed home under strict instructions of taking it easy, lots of medication and a special diet.

So here we are, Fred's home but on bed rest which he is getting increasingly irritated about. I'm sat upstairs in the bedroom with him, watching a daytime quiz show, seeing who can answer the most questions. With every sound and movement he makes, I flinch, questioning if he's all right and fluffing his pillows. His complexion is still a little pallid and he has dark circles under his eyes... but he's with us.

'Violet, can you please stop looking at me like that?' He sighs.

'Like what?'

'Like I'm a porcelain cup that you're worried is about to

smash. I feel good. I would be in that garden now if your bloody mother would let me.'

'No you bloody wouldn't because I'd stop you. Dad, you had a heart attack, you must rest.'

'I am resting but I'm bored, and the doctor did say I can move around.' Fred sounds like a whiney child desperate to go and play with his toys. It's so good to hear.

'Tough shit, you scared the hell out of us, I thought I'd lost you.' Tears pour down my cheeks. I've done so well keeping it together in the hospital, wanting to stay strong for Lilly but now it seems the flood gates have opened.

'Don't cry, Violet. I'm still here, I'm okay.'

'Dad, I love you. I don't know if I've said it enough but when you were lying there, I wasn't sure I would ever be able to tell you again. I promised that if I did get to, I would make sure that you know how much you mean to me.'

'I do know, Violet, and I love you too.' He holds my hands. I climb onto the bed next to Fred and snuggle into his chest while we finish watching the show. I feel like a child again, wrapped up in his strong arms. Life is so fragile, how quickly it can suddenly change.

'I'll go and make you some lunch,' I tell him as the programme finishes.

I go to the kitchen and find Lilly sitting at the table; she looks tired. For the first time ever my vivacious and bright mother looks quiet and old. Her bright spark has gone as she sits mindlessly stirring a cup of tea. She's wearing grey trousers and a plain black jumper. I don't think I have ever seen Lilly in such dull colours before, I'm actually wondering where the hell she got the outfit from. Her normally bright lipstick is nowhere to be seen either. In fact, the Lilly I know so well seems to have evaporated into the ether.

'Mum, are you okay?' I ask as I sit in the chair next to her and put my arm around her shoulders.

'Yes, darling, I'm fine, I just... I thought we had lost him. I thought my time with him was up,' Lilly says quietly. Her eyes are fixed on the cup of tea. Her words are so calm and yet the meaning behind them packs quite a punch. My heart breaks for her.

'Me too, but we didn't. He's upstairs now moaning about not being in the garden,' I say, holding Lilly tightly. She bursts into tears. She's been an absolute trooper through this whole ordeal, holding in her emotions, but she needs to get it out of her system so as her tears fall, I say nothing. I just keep her in my arms.

'Oh, look at me,' Lilly says, wiping her eyes and forcing a smile. I know it's forced because her eyes don't light up like they normally do. 'Silly old bird, don't you tell your father that I was crying, he will never let me live it down. Thank you for all your help these last few weeks.'

'Me? I haven't done anything.'

'Oh you have, just being here. I couldn't have got through it without you. You looked after the house and me. Even this last week, Fred's diet and medication, you've sorted all that out. I thank my lucky stars you came home.' Lilly kisses me on the cheek.

'Why don't you go up and sit with Dad,' I suggest, 'and I will bring you both some soup.'

Lilly goes upstairs and I put the hob on and heat through some of the tomato and basil soup Jane dropped off earlier. The village has really come together to support us. It may be frustrating everyone here knowing your business but boy do they have your back when trouble strikes. I pour the soup into two bowls, make a fresh pot of tea and carry the tray upstairs.

I pause as I get to the bedroom door though. Lilly is lying on the bed exactly where I was lying before, she's wrapped in Fred's arms sobbing into his chest. As I watch the heart-wrenching embrace between my parents my own tears silently fall. I've never seen Lilly so frightened than when we were in the hospital, it's taken so much out of them both. Seeing them now lying together, so in love and vulnerable to each other, it's beautiful and sad all at once.

Fred and Lilly are each other's happy place. It doesn't matter where they are or what they're doing as long as they're together. I creep into the room and put the tray down on the dresser. Fred gives me a thumbs up and I creep out not wanting Lilly to know I've witnessed such a tender moment.

I go back downstairs and walk into the living room. I find myself in front of the old wooden dresser where all the photos of Lilly and Fred's life are on show. Younger versions of them staring back in a wedding dress and suit, on beaches, sat in the garden or at parties. Holding a newborn baby, pictures of me at various ages. Each picture has something in common; beaming smiles so full of love, like Winnie's treasure trove of photos.

I hear a gentle knock and Ben walks in the front door. I see him and without saying anything, I walk straight into his open arms. He smells as good as always. I bury myself in his neck, feeling the safety and comfort of his hold. I haven't known him long, not really, and yet here he is. He's been here through the worst few weeks of my life and I want him to stay.

'Want to go for a walk?' he asks gently.

We leave the house and walk towards the woods. We stroll down the riverbank next to the towering trees and I breathe in the fresh air. It's like I've been holding my breath for the past few weeks and only now just coming up for air.

'How's Fred today?'

'He's doing well, moaning about wanting to get back into the garden so he must be feeling better.' I chuckle.

'That sounds like Fred. What about Lilly?'

'She had a bit of a moment before. She's done so well keeping it together that I'm glad she let go a bit. I think she needed to get it out of her system.'

'And what about you?' he says as we stop and sit down in the grass next to the river, watching a family of ducks swimming around.

'Tired, relieved, grateful that I still have him.'

Ben puts his arm around me and kisses my head.

'Thank you for being here, I don't think I said it at the time, but it really means a lot.'

'You don't have to thank me, I want to help.' He looks deep into my eyes and I kiss him gently. His soft lips bring a warmth that spreads through my whole body, lifting my heart from the slump it's been in. I've missed kissing him. In the short time we've known each other I've tried to keep him at arm's-length and not get too attached – friends with benefits – but Safiyah was right... again. That never works out well, someone always develops feelings. I fear this time that person is me.

'Can I ask, what happened to your dad?' I feel Ben's body stiffen. 'If you don't want to talk about it you don't have to. After everything that happened... well, I'm here if you want to talk, like you've been for me.'

Ben takes a deep breath. 'He had cancer, it was pretty quick from when we found out to him passing,' he says sadly. 'I was at work when Layla, my sister, called to say he had taken a turn for the worse. I didn't get home in time to say goodbye.'

'Ben, I'm so sorry.'

'It's okay, I mean it's not okay but I don't have any regrets. I knew how much he loved me, and he knew how much I loved him. I really miss him. It's the little things you miss, hearing his voice, the look of his hands. I know that sounds strange but as a kid I always looked at his hands, they seemed so strong. They could do anything, he was a real hands-on person, DIY and stuff... he was my hero. I wish he had seen my nephew and niece, he would have made a brilliant grandfather. It's cruel that he was taken when there was still so much for him to see and do.'

There's nothing I can say, and I know he doesn't want me to try. My eyes fill up, I pull his arm around my shoulder and snuggle into him. He leans his head on mine and we quietly watch the water flow by reminding me that even when your own world comes to a sudden halt, life carries on around you regardless. Even in the silence with Ben, I feel comfortable and safe. I'm falling for him. I can't stop it and I'm not sure I even want to. If the last few weeks have taught me anything, it's that you should take every chance you get because it could be gone in a second.

We go back to the cottage and spend a couple of hours with Lilly and Fred. After dinner, Lilly suggests Ben and I go back to his and have some time together. I don't want to leave them but Lilly gives me a very stern talking to so I agree to go. I hate leaving them both but I am relishing in the normality of such a restful easy evening after a manic few weeks. The nights are getting a little cooler; we're well into September so Ben fires up the log burner. There is something very romantic about sitting in front of a crackling fire.

'Think I'll message Mum to make sure everything is all right,' I say, reaching for my phone. It's been on silent and when I look, I notice a missed call. Shit. Fred, what if something's happened, how did I forget to turn the sound on? But then I see Philip's name. Now I come to think of it, in the blur of the last few weeks I vaguely remember reading a text from him. I open my messages and see Philip's name towards the top of the list, asking if it was okay to call. I check and there are missed calls from him over two consecutive days.

'Are you okay?' Ben asks, sitting back down next to me. Do I tell him? Of course I should, there is no reason not to.

'I have some missed calls from Philip.'

'Your ex?' Ben asks acting cool, but I can tell he looks a little ruffled about it by the way he is suddenly playing with the edge of the pillow next to him.

'Yeah, he's texted a couple of times, but I haven't responded.' I feel a sense of urgency to make sure Ben knows I have no intention of getting in touch with Philip. I don't even know why I need Ben to know that. We're both single, we don't owe each other explanations. Or maybe we're not single. Maybe we've moved seamlessly into a relationship. We spend so much time together I doubt he would have time to date other women. Maybe at a certain age you just don't have the awkward boyfriend/girlfriend conversation, it sort of goes without saying.

'What do you think he wants?'

'No idea,' I answer honestly. 'And I couldn't care less.' I fire off a quick text to Lilly, checking everything is okay and huddle back into Ben's arms.

The next morning, I wake up early and blissfully lie stroking Ben's back as he sleeps. He looks peaceful. I lean down and gently kiss his back which makes him stir.

'Good morning,' he says sleepily as he slides over onto his back. 'That's a wake-up call I could get used to.'

'This is a view I could get used to. What are your plans today?' I ask, kissing his chest, and the hairs tickle my nose. The answer I'm hoping to hear is staying in bed with me all morning.

'I have work,' he answers, which is disappointing. He sits up and looks over at the time. 'But I have an hour before I have to get up and I know just the thing to fill the time,' he says, playfully rolling me onto my back and lifting the covers over his head. I'm a little less disappointed now. He makes his way deliciously down my body until he settles between my legs.

OH. MY. GOD. I gasp and bite down on my lip in delight as I squeeze the duvet in my hand. Ben Matthews is so very talented in ALL his endeavours.

34

After a deliriously enjoyable hour in bed with Ben, I go home with just enough time to shower and get ready before Collette arrives, with her mum, Esme, in tow, ready to try on her wedding dress. Once Fred was home and starting to feel better, I had cracked on with the gown and it's pretty much finished. Collette follows me upstairs and I have to say I'm nervous as hell for her to see the finished dress. I help her into it and cover her eyes as I guide her over to the mirror.

'Okay, are you ready?' I ask. I hope she loves it as much as she has on her other fittings because the pearls and lace have been sewn into place now so there's no going back. I cross my fingers behind me.

'One, two, three open.' Collette opens her eyes and she stares at her reflection silently. Oh heck, please say something.

'Violet, I–' Collette's words stumble. 'I love it, it's everything I imagined and more.'

'You do?' Phew, thank God for that. I stand back and admire my work. The satin looks rich against her creamy skin, the lace-capped sleeves with little flecks of silver are delicate and glimmer in the light. It has an air of vintage romance with a train that is just long enough to showcase the delicate twinkle of crystals and pearls that I painstakingly hand-stitched on.

I thought I would feel something with it being the dress I had originally wanted for myself but no, it's as if it has always been meant for Collette.

'You look amazing.' The lace-capped sleeves fall beautifully on her shoulders and the fishtail silhouette shows off her curves magnificently. She looks every bit the perfect bride.

'How does it feel?'

'It feels like – the one,' Collette answers with a radiant glow as she looks down at the dress and runs her hands over the lace detailing.

'Do you feel like a bride?'

'I do, I really do.' I'm thrilled, that's what I set out to do and I've done it – job done.

'Let's go and show your mum.' I help Collette down the stairs to show Esme. Lilly has joined her in the living room and they both weep with delight as Collette floats angelically into the room.

'I might just raise the hem at the front ever so slightly,' I say, opening a box of pins. 'Do you have your grandmother's brooch with you, I could fix it on now to give you the finished look.' Esme passes the beautiful antique brooch to me. It's silver and in the shape of two feathers with a pearl and two small diamonds grouped together in the middle.

'Wow, that's beautiful.' And so perfect for the dress. I disappear upstairs to get the mirror and the one-inch-thick deep-burgundy ribbon that will sit around Collette's waist. I pin the brooch to the middle of the ribbon and then place it around Collette's middle. I tie a small bow and let the long stems of ribbon fall down behind the dress. 'I'll stitch it into place, so you won't need to worry about it falling off.' The brooch finishes the dress off flawlessly. Esme wipes a tear away and she looks at her daughter in utter admiration.

'Your grandmother would be so happy you have her brooch for your big day. Violet, you are an angel making this, thank you,' Esme says.

Collette smiles as she looks back at her reflection again.

'I'll sort the adjustments and then two weeks before the wedding, you can come back to try it on again. Would you allow me to take some photos on your last fitting for my portfolio?' I ask as I kneel down and pin the hem.

'Of course you can. I'll be recommending you to everyone.'

After I finish pinning the hem, Collette gets dressed and leaves with Esme after paying half of the money for the dress. I had told them no and that they should wait until it's finished but they insisted, not wanting me to be out of pocket for the material and time I've spent on it already. The money will be very handy towards the shop though so I'm extremely grateful. Oh no, the shop – shit – with Fred falling ill, I never made it over to see Patrick. What if he's already let it to someone else?

'Mum, are you going to Zumba today?'

'Yes, I think so. Dave's popping round to keep your dad company for a few hours. I've told him that under no circumstances is he to let Fred pick up a trowel. They are to sit in the garden only or I will bash his head in with said trowel.'

I laugh. 'That's told him then. I need to pop into the village, so I will meet you there.'

I get changed, ready for Zumba, and head for the village centre. My heart drops though as I get to Patrick's antiques shop. It's dark and empty. He's already packed up. I knock on the door hoping he might be in the back but there's no answer. I press myself up against the window looking around at the empty floor. What if he's already left for Canada? I'm too late. Oh, it would have been perfect. I know I can always rent a shop elsewhere but the dream of doing it in Elmsbourne-Hollow opposite Hettie was... well, too good to be true.

'Is everything all right, Violet?' Ivy the florist asks as she comes out of her shop which is next door, to see me with my face squashed up against the window like a mad woman.

'Ivy, I don't suppose you know if Patrick has let the shop, do you?'

'Yes, I saw him packing up last week. He said someone has taken it over although he didn't divulge what it was going to be.'

Shit, I really am too late. That's just bloody marvellous.

'That's that then, dream over. Thanks, Ivy, I better go. I'll see you soon. Good luck with whoever your new neighbour is.'

'Are you sure you're okay?' Ivy asks, confused, but I don't answer because I'm too upset to talk and just nod as I walk away. Gutted would be an understatement.

35

With my head hung low, I drag my feet back towards the village hall. As I walk past the tearoom, I look through the window. Did I just see what I think I saw? No, surely not. I double back, look again and give a sharp intake of breath. I had seen him! Ben is sitting with the supermodel I saw him with all those weeks ago back in Lancaster. She's the possible new client he told me about but what is she doing here? They look like they're having a heated conversation with their heads close together.

I jump away from the door, so my back is against the wall and then peek through the window like a rubbish undercover agent from an old spy movie, all I need now is a trench coat and fedora. Ben said he had work, but he didn't mention having a meeting here. I watch as the woman puts her hands on his arm as she talks to him and my mouth drops open aghast, he lets her arms linger there. Today is getting worse by the second. Is the universe mad at me for something?

I should go in and introduce myself, let this goddess-like creature know that Ben is mine and very much taken. Although is he taken? We still haven't had the conversation, so God knows what we are. I really need to talk to him about this so there's no confusion going forward.

I hold the door handle of the tearoom. I look down at my tatty trainers, leggings and zip-up hoody. There's no way I can go in there feeling like a messy hag and throw the gauntlet down to a woman who quite frankly even I would have a hard time saying no to.

I step away from the door and walk dejectedly to the Zumba class. It's probably for the best I didn't go in and confront them. How embarrassing would it be if he really is just having a business meeting and I walk in like some scary bunny boiler. I should give the guy a chance, he isn't Philip. There could be a million reasons why they're having their meeting here, near his home, although I'm struggling to think of any right now. His car's broken down perhaps.

Bloody hell, how has this happened? How has it gone from fun and no strings to worrying over his business lunch with another woman so quickly. I can hardly blame her for fancying Ben if she does, he's gorgeous and lovely. I puff out a sigh, this is exactly the reason why I didn't want to get serious with anybody. Perhaps my head still isn't in the right place after Philip. Is it too early for gin?

I walk into the hall, feeling completely downtrodden. No shop and now Miss Fancy Pants has her hands all over Ben. I'm going to have to really pummel my emotions into this workout today.

'Violet, there you are!' Hettie shouts as I walk in.

'What are you doing here?' I'm confused, why are Hettie and Safiyah sitting with the Golden Girls? 'Are you joining us for Zumba?'

'God no,' Safiyah says with the same amount of disdain you would give someone if they asked you if you wanted a punch in the face. Her face suddenly jumps into a beaming smile though. 'We wanted to surprise you.'

I look at Lilly who looks as baffled as I feel. 'Surprise me with what?'

'Should we wait for Ben?' Safiyah asks, looking to Hettie for an answer.

'He messaged to say he might be caught up with a meeting and to carry on,' Hettie replies, grinning from ear to ear.

'Okay so we have something for you,' Safiyah says, stepping forward and placing something small in my hand. I see that I'm holding a set of keys, but I don't know what for. 'They're yours, for Patrick's Antiques. Well, I guess it won't be called that now, but they're for whatever you decide to call it.'

'I-I don't understand, I missed my chance, I didn't speak to Patrick and Ivy said he's let it to someone else.'

'You didn't talk to him but we did,' Hettie says. 'With Ben. It was his idea actually. A few days after Fred got taken ill, we realised you wouldn't have spoken to Patrick. Ben didn't want you to lose the shop and we all felt so helpless. You'd been so excited, so we went to see Patrick and he said he was thrilled for you to rent it from him. He even said he's happy for you to crack on with any alterations that you might need to make.' I'm speechless, I can't believe what they're saying. 'I think he's pleased it will be rented by someone local.'

'Patrick was really understanding about Fred and the whole situation, what with them being friends,' Safiyah adds. 'And when I told Mum that Ben was going to pay the first month's rent for you to hold the place, she spoke to the rest of the ladies who all wanted to chip in and help. Ben topped the rest up, but Patrick wasn't having any of it, he said he had known Fred for far too many years and was happy for you to have the first two months free. So with the one we all paid, you have three months to get yourself up and running.'

Hettie finishes off the pitch. 'He said he would chat to you in a year's time and discuss the possibility of you buying the property, if you feel it's what you want.'

That's a lot of information to take in. Ben was willing to pay all that money for me. The Golden Girls, Hettie and Safiyah, they've all been so generous.

I haven't lost the shop. My heart is fit to bursting, I'm unbelievably touched by the gesture.

'I-I don't know what to say, I'm speechless.'

I'm crying tears of happiness as I clutch the keys to my chest. My voice catches in my throat. 'I don't know how to ever thank you all, you must let me pay you back.'

'You can make us dresses,' Safiyah says with a smile as she hugs me. I go around the room giving each and every one of them a hug because I don't know what else to do. They've pretty much just made my dream come true – how do you thank someone for that?

'I can't believe you've done that for me,' I say through blurry eyes.

'You have helped quite a few of us out,' Jenny says, stepping forward. 'You helped me so much with my confidence. I know it was only a dress and it sounds silly, but I feel like a new woman. I wanted to repay the favour.'

'Me too,' Winnie agrees. 'You might not realise it, but you've helped me too. Our little coffee catch-ups and getting me to help with the dance, it's given me a whole new purpose, I don't feel as lonely as I used to. I've even been asked to join the village committee,' she says, smiling at Verity.

'You're so talented, we all thought you deserved a break,' Olivia says, swinging her arm over my shoulder.

'Shall we go and have a look?' Hettie asks, jumping up and down. It's hard to tell who's more excited, me or her.

'Do you all mind if I miss Zumba?'

'You have to work extra hard next class,' Roberto says with a grin as he walks over to the speakers to plug in his phone.

I run out of the hall with Hettie and Safiyah and I'm still in total shock. We find Ben running towards us, looking flustered in an immaculate grey suit but as handsome as ever.

'I'm so sorry I missed it,' he says, looking gutted, his eyes giving away his feelings again, but I don't care. He's here now and that's all that matters. I fly towards him and without missing a beat and forgetting I have an audience my hands grasp the back of his neck and I kiss him. And I mean really kiss him.

'I can't believe you did that for me,' I say breathlessly. 'I can't ever thank you enough.'

'I think you just did,' he says, fluttering his eyes, bringing himself back down to ground after the earth-spinning kiss I planted on him. 'Are you happy?'

'So happy. I will be paying you back though.'

'I don't want it back.' He squeezes me tight and I'm filled with emotion again. 'Call it a thank you for all the decorating you've been doing.'

'Okay, okay, put each other down,' Safiyah calls. 'Are you coming to the shop, Ben?'

'I can't. I'm so sorry, I need to get to the office. I really am sorry I missed the big reveal.'

'It's okay,' I say gently. 'Hettie said a meeting came up?' I miss out the fact that I saw him earlier with the blonde goddess.

'Yeah, I asked the client to meet me here, so I could be there to see you get the keys but it ran over.' He looks sad and I sense he wants to say something but stops himself.

'Don't worry, we can celebrate later.' I don't want him to feel bad, he's done such a wonderful thing in securing Patrick's shop.

'Definitely, come around tonight and give me the list of things that need doing to YOUR shop.'

My shop. That sounds bloody amazing. I have a shop – eek!

. . .

My adrenalin is in overdrive as the three of us stand looking at the little shop that is nestled in between Ivy's Florist and the local craft and ale shop. It's a pretty row of buildings, all Cotswold stone with large display windows and little window boxes underneath them.

I push the key into the door and open up. This is mine. I want to get on my hands and knees and kiss the floor.

An hour ago, I was stood pressed up against the window, pining after what could have been and now here I am, with the keys, planning my own little empire. Hettie, Safiyah and I stand in the centre, looking around the large open space.

The walls need a freshen up and I instantly decide to paint them light grey, so the white and ivory gowns stand out against the wall. The ceiling and skirting could do with a lick of paint too and bright white would be a perfect counterbalance of colour. The room has a beautiful wooden floor that just needs a good polish. I wander around the shop, imagining beautiful gowns hanging on vintage rails.

'I could put spotlighting along the celling on this side so the light shines down on the dresses and look at this counter, it's perfect.' I stand behind the pristine white counter that Patrick's left behind, imagining myself welcoming a customer.

'There's a cute little kitchen back here,' Hettie calls. 'You could stock a little fridge with Prosecco for customers.'

'And these two rooms could be made into changing rooms,' I say, checking out the two smaller areas opposite the kitchen. The layout couldn't be better.

We go upstairs to see what's there and find two more rooms. The larger one at the front could be the sewing and office area, that way I can see the high street while I'm working. The room at the back could hold stock and the cupboard space in the middle is just big enough to store material, but it will need shelving installed. Perhaps Ben could help with that. Overall the shop is bigger than I thought.

'What are you going to call it?' Safiyah asks.

'I'm not too sure yet but I have a few ideas.'

36

A week has passed and I've done so much already. The electrician has been in to sort out the spotlights and Ben has helped after work to paint the changing rooms a very pale china blue and hang the large mirrors that I found online. I've ordered a selection of wedding dresses as well as bridesmaid and mother-of-the-bride outfits from contacts I met through Anna Pemberton.

The beautiful wooden floor has come up a treat after a deep polish, and Dean popped in the other day and painted the ceiling and skirtings for me, charging a minimal amount. Hettie and myself had a painting party and got the main room all finished in a very classy mist grey and I'm really pleased with the fresh and clean outcome. I also found some beautiful vintage-looking silver rails online that I bought at an absolute steal. They will look great housing the dresses which are due to be delivered in the next few days. Ivy, whose shop is next door, kindly popped in to give me a peace lily as a friendly 'hello neighbour' gesture, which I've popped on the counter. How lucky to have such a thoughtful neighbour. How lucky to have the shop full stop, to be honest.

The day after I got the keys, I turned up at Patrick's house with a huge bottle of wine to say thank you for his kind offer and signed the paperwork. He's delighted I've taken over the shop. He's off to Canada in a few short weeks but has promised to keep in contact to discuss the sale at a later date. I baked a load of yummy vanilla cupcakes and took them with me to Zumba for the Golden Girls as a thank you. It seems like such a small gesture for their generosity, but I needed to do something. I've of course invited them all to my planned grand opening in a few weeks and promised them lots of free wine and Prosecco. The shop's coming together nicely, and I'm busy moving some of the material that's been covering my bedroom floor into the stockroom upstairs when my phone buzzes.

'Hey, you,' I say, answering the phone in the sexiest voice I can muster.

'Hey, I was just sat here thinking about you so thought I would call to see how you were getting on,' Ben says. His deep, husky voice transcends over the phone and manages to send a tingle down my legs which I'm pretty sure he's done on purpose.

'Thinking something nice, I hope.'

'Of course. What are you up to today?'

'I'm actually popping into Lancaster later, I have some more material to pick up.'

'Why don't you come to the office, maybe we could get a late lunch together?'

'That sounds perfect, would be nice to see where you work. Two o'clock?'

'It's a date, see you soon.' I still haven't brought up the whole relationship status. Obviously after his gesture with the shop I would say we are firmly past friends with benefits although I can't honestly say it has ever really been that casual between us. Still, my main focus does need to be the shop if I'm going to make a success out of it.

. . .

I pop home and check on Lilly and Fred, Lilly's in her studio working on her last piece for the art exhibition which is in a few days. She still isn't back to her sparkly self, there's no make-up in sight, but she is donning a bright pink T-shirt with some black linen trousers while she paints so that's progress.

Fred has been allowed to potter in the garden to do some very light pruning. I make sure he isn't doing anything too strenuous which frustrates the hell out of him and then I head into Lancaster. The haberdashery is quiet, and I manage to get everything I need. I also leave a few business cards, ready for when I open to hopefully drum up some interest.

With my material loaded into two large bags I head back to my car and drive out of the town centre towards Nexus Architecture where Ben works. It's closer than I realised and I pull up into the car park earlier than expected. The building is impressive, although I suppose it should be really considering an architect's office is inside. It's a modern square block covered in reflective glass, sat in the middle of a forest of trees. In front of the building is a huge pond with a thin wall in the centre of it, water is trickling down, creating an elaborate feature. With the trees reflecting in the glass, the building itself disappears into the scenery like an illusion.

I step into the large open reception; it has pristine white furniture and walls and a striking turquoise carpet. I couldn't be more out of my comfort zone. The reception is so modern and sophisticated, you can see all the way up to the top of the building, the six floors on display are all open-plan. It certainly gives the impression of grandeur.

Everyone around me is wearing sleek suits with perfect hair and make-up, a direct comparison to my casual look. I opted for a red and blue check shirt tucked into a pair of dark-blue skinny jeans. My hair is down with my attempt at loose beach curls as I had no time to straighten it this morning and instead just chucked in some hair oil to tame it.

'Can I help you?' a snippy receptionist asks as she looks me up and down rather rudely. Her beady eyes are judging my informal choice of clothes.

'Oh yes, erm, I'm meeting Ben Matthews.'

'Third floor, sign in here and the lift is to your left,' she says with the air of a school headmistress, so I do as I'm told.

I press the button for the third floor and twenty seconds later, the door pings open onto a bustling office floor. The space again is very modern, the white decor has continued upstairs, the ceiling is high and open, so all the dark-blue pipes are on show, giving it a funky industrial vibe. There are lots of desks in the middle of the floor with glass-fronted offices along both sides. It's all very trendy. Next to the lift is another reception desk only this time Georgia, as her gold name badge states, seems much more approachable than the ice queen downstairs.

'Hello, can I help you?'

'Yes, I'm here to see Ben Matthews. I'm a little early but he should be expecting me.'

'His office is the third one on the right,' she says brightly, pointing in that direction. 'I think he has someone with him at the moment but if you want to sit in the waiting area over there, I will let him know he has a visitor. Can I take your name?'

'Yes, it's Violet.' I walk over to the seating by Ben's office. Lots of people are busily working around me, phones ringing and printers running off piles of paper, everyone looking very important. I have a sudden urge to grab the pile of paper that has just finished printing on the table next to me and shout 'HOT OFF THE PRESS!' but that would be weird seeing as this isn't a newspaper office – and I don't work here.

I look over at Ben's glass-fronted office, he's sat at a desk with a computer in front of him. He looks very dapper in a white shirt and bronze tie, however, the smile on my face quickly disappears when I see the blonde bombshell is back – again. She glides up next to him and bends over, rather seductively in my opinion, pointing to something on the computer screen. She looks flawless once again in a white shirt and pink high-waisted jacquard skirt. How does she manage to look so catwalk-worthy all the time? I swear she could wear a potato sack and still look stylish and jaw-droppingly gorgeous. Her hair's in a low bun with a few wispy trestles hanging down on her face which on me would look messy but on her is elegantly chic. I can hear her angelic laugh ringing out of the glass walls.

She places her hand on the back of Ben's chair, still bent over, and angles her body towards him. If he was looking, he would have a perfect view down her shirt. She glances at Ben to see if he's looking but luckily, he's busy studying the computer screen. She's doing it on purpose. Oh, she's good, I'll give her that. I hear Ben's phone ring, he answers it and a few seconds later shoots his head up, quickly scanning the waiting area. Georgia from reception must have called to tell him he has a visitor. His eyes fall on mine and he does a nervous-looking little wave. Why does he look so uncomfortable, surely it's me who should be? He motions me to come in and as I open the door, the woman looks in my direction.

'Hi. Sorry, I know I'm early,' I say apologetically as Ben gets up and walks around his desk.

'No, it's fine. I think time got a bit away from us,' he says, looking at his watch. He kisses me on the cheek.

'Sorry, this is Zoe, one of our clients. Zoe, this is Violet.' So the leggy blonde finally has a name!

'We're designing some new premises for the company Zoe works for.'

'Nice to meet you,' I say pleasantly, even though it isn't at all.

'You too,' Zoe replies rather overenthusiastically. I'm sure I see a flash of bitterness on her face, but she quickly covers it with a sweet smile, showing her perfect bright white teeth.

'Sorry to interrupt,' I say just as sweetly. Two can play at that game.

'Oh, it's fine, we were nearly finished anyway, weren't we, Benny?' she says as she puts her hand on Ben's arm. Benny, did she actually call him Benny? Wow.

'Err... yes, we are.' There is definitely no denying it this time, Ben looks very uncomfortable. Why didn't I just wait downstairs for him, this is so awkward.

'Right, well, Violet and I have a lunch date now,' Ben tells Zoe and I know it's silly and petty and fully down to my own insecurities but I take his wording of *date* as a victory over her.

'Of course. I will leave you both to it,' Zoe says with a false brightness, walking towards the door. 'It was lovely to meet you.' It's very subtle, but I can sense the displeasure in Zoe's voice.

'You too, bye.' As Zoe leaves, I see Ben visibly relax as his shoulders drop. I think this is the moment when perhaps alarm bells should be ringing. If there is nothing between them, why would he be so anxious in her company?

'I wasn't sure where I was going and ended up being early, I was going to wait downstairs, but the scary looking receptionist sent me up here.'

'Oh yes, she is quite scary. You don't need to apologise though, I'm glad you're here,' he says, slipping his arms around my waist. He's just about to kiss me when there's a knock on the door.

'Ben.' Whoever it is doesn't wait for a response and walks straight in. It's an older gentleman in a very suave grey suit that screams money. He stops when he sees me in Ben's arms. 'Oh sorry.'

'It's okay, Martin, this is Violet.'

'Ah, the girlfriend,' Martin says with a smile as he takes my hand in the firmest handshake I've ever felt. He has thick white hair and rosy red cheeks which reminds me of Santa Claus so I instantly like him. 'Lovely to finally meet you, Ben talks about you non-stop.'

Does he? A group of butterflies give a little dance, he talks about me at work – all good, I hope. It's the first time anyone as ever referred to me as Ben's girlfriend, and after a glance in Ben's direction I can see he's blushing. I do note he hasn't corrected Martin though. Considering it's a name I have been pretty adamant I didn't want I have to admit I do like the sound of it.

'This is Martin Greenwood, the managing director here at Nexus.'

'Lovely to meet you,' I say, startled to realise that Ben has spoken about me to his boss... *his boss*!

'Ben tells me you're opening your own shop. You design wedding dresses, don't you?'

'I do yes, should be opening in a couple of weeks. It's all quite exciting.'

'Good for you. My daughter's just got engaged, I will have to get the details from Ben and then send her in your direction.'

'That's so kind of you, thank you.'

'This one seems very proud,' Martin says as he pats Ben on his back. Ben is flushing redder by the second and I stifle a chuckle. 'You must both come around some time for dinner.'

'That sounds great, thank you.' What a lovely guy.

'I'll let you get on, Ben, but I've cleared my schedule for an hour later for us to talk about Zoe's account.'

Martin leaves and Ben seems to forget we're stood in a glass-fronted office.

'He likes you,' he says, placing his arms back around my waist.

'He seems like a nice boss,' I reply, moving my face

tantalisingly close to his. 'So... girlfriend, eh?' I tease, finally plucking up the courage to mention it, although technically he mentioned it first, just not to me.

Ben's eyes fall on my mouth. It's a look that suggests he's desperate to explore it with his own mouth and it sends a delicious surge around my body. 'Yep, is that okay with you?'

'More than okay.' It's official, Ben and I are no longer classed as casual bedroom romp buddies and are in an actual proper relationship.

Ben kisses me and playfully bites my lip which makes the tingle in my stomach spread. I really wish this wasn't a glass-fronted office.

'This is hardly very professional, Mr Matthews,' I tease, feeling like we're in a fishbowl with everyone watching us.

'Good point,' Ben says, letting go. He doesn't take his eyes away from me though and as always, they seem to be doing the talking for him. He looks like he is on the brink of saying something important but stops himself. The moment passes, and he seems to switch his train of thought. 'Lunch!'

He opens the door and we walk hand in hand towards the lift. I see Zoe stood at a desk in the centre of the office talking to someone. She gives me a look I can't quite put my finger on, but whatever it is, it isn't good. Trouble is brewing!

37

'Are you nervous, Mum?' I ask. It's the day of the art exhibition. Lilly's a whirlwind of excitement as Fred and I help her put the finishing touches to the corner of the village hall that's displaying her collection.

'I feel exhilarated, I've spent so long on them I can't wait for everyone to see them all.' The room's full of artwork from artists all around Lancashire. The local paper has arrived to take photos and Lilly is more than happy to oblige. Her bright wardrobe is back with a vengeance as she's wearing a multicoloured striped kaftan which reminds me of Joseph and his technicolour dreamcoat. She has large yellow dangly earrings which clash against the pink scarf in her hair. She looks every bit the eccentric artist as she poses joyously for photos in front of her canvases and I'm thrilled to see it. Bland Lilly doesn't look right. Fred is sneakily pilfering sausage rolls from the buffet on the other side of the hall, his strict diet has taken its toll on him and he's ready for some *hearty sustenance*, as he calls it.

'Don't let Mum catch you eating those.'

'She's far too busy stealing the show to worry about me,' Fred says with adoration as he watches Lilly chat animatedly to the photographer. She's in her element as people stop to view her paintings. I watch her make time for every single person who stops to have a look and I'm in awe of her magnetic warmth.

'Lilly looks like Lilly again,' Ben says happily. He's left work early to be here with us and he's right, Lilly's back to the woman we all know and love. She's been unrecognisable for the last few weeks. Quiet with no spark but here she is back to normal, filling the entire room with her effervescent personality.

'She sure does,' I say with a deeply grateful sigh.

All the Golden Girls have turned up to support Lilly too and are enjoying a glass of wine as they wander around the exhibition. Olivia Kimberley is in the corner flirting outrageously with a well-to-do-looking man who in turn seems to be quite enamoured with her. Winnie, Rosalind and Maggie are talking to a group of women I recognise from Hollymere. I can hear them explaining all about the village dance, asking if they want to buy tickets. Bonnie and Mary are taking it in turns to work the refreshments table and are shamelessly peddling a stash of tickets from under the table. I'm not entirely sure why they are being so secretive about it, it's not as if they're touting drugs!

The evening is a roaring success with Lilly selling a handful of her paintings.

'Mum, you've done brilliantly. I'm so proud of you,' I say as Ben and I join her at her corner of the room. 'And I would like to increase your sales, I'm buying this one.' It's the painting I fell in love with when I first visited Lilly in her studio of the three rabbits sat under a large oak tree.

'You don't have to pay, darling, you can have it.'

'No, I'm buying it. You've done loads for me, Mum. I really

want to do this. I'm going to hang it in my office.' Right above my desk so I can always be inspired by Lilly's work.

'If you're sure – sold!' Lilly sings. 'Here, I'll let you both in on a little secret, I've made another sale but not from this collection.' Lilly feels about for a box next to the table and pulls out a hidden canvas. She spins it around proudly to show us both. 'Ta-da, I finally finished it.'

'Is that Charlie Thompson?' Ben stutters. It's that bloody painting again of Mr Thompson in the buff.

'I brought it with me to show Charlie the finished piece. He was extremely pleased with it, as was his wife. She asked to buy it.'

'It's certainly showstopping, Lilly.' Ben glances at me, trying not to laugh.

'Ah here he is,' Lilly chimes as Charlie and Caroline Thompson walk over to us. We're all standing here looking at a naked portrait of him so this is mighty awkward. 'Here you go,' Lilly says, handing him the painting.

'Thanks, Lilly, it's great,' he says as his eyes twinkle approvingly at the painting.

'The likeness is uncanny,' Mrs Thompson states in awe. 'You have captured him perfectly, don't you think?' She looks to Ben and I as if we could verify this for her and I try not to grimace as I shrug. How the hell would I know? Why is everyone so blasé about the fact that we are all staring at a picture of Mr Thompson with no clothes on? I mean, I know it's art but still, you would think he would be a little shy about everyone basically discussing his manhood. Although maybe he's so impressed by the sheer size of it, he doesn't mind who sees. Ben's shoulders are shaking as he tries to hold in a laugh. I squeeze his hand tight and bite down on my cheek.

'It's brilliant, I'm seeing you in a whole new light, Charlie,' Ben manages to say without letting his face crack.

We leave them all to finalise the sale and rush off, Ben finally cracks and bursts out laughing once we're out of earshot.

'My God, I have seen that picture far too many times for my liking.'

'I can categorically say that wasn't something I thought I was going to see at your mother's art exhibition. I wonder where they're going to hang it?' Ben says, still laughing at the mortifying situation we found ourselves in.

'Not in the shop, I hope.'

We all make our way to the Chugging Bull at the end of the evening. Music is playing and the Golden Girls are all on top form as they dance around the pub. Fred and his friends are sitting in the corner talking rugby tactics and Ben and I have joined Hettie, Safiyah, Jack and Theo for a gin. Theo seems a little off though, he looks quite ashen and isn't really listening or taking part in the conversation.

'Are you all right, Theo?' I ask, leaning over to him. 'You look a little peaky.'

'Do I? I'm fine,' he snaps. He jumps up from his chair and disappears off into the crowd of dancers. That was weird, what's up with him?

Just then the music stops and a microphone makes an ear-piercing screech as someone talks into it.

'Erm... can I have your attention please,' a nervous voice calls. A voice we all recognise instantly.

'Is that Theo?' Safiyah asks, looking around trying to find him. The room goes quiet and everyone stands still. A crowd parts in front of us as Theo walks into the middle of the pub, looking over at Safiyah like he's about to throw up.

'Safiyah, could you come here, please?' Theo mutters into the microphone.

'Oh my God!' Hettie whispers as a huge grin explodes onto her face. I catch on a second later as it dawns on me what is happening. No wonder Theo looked so nervous.

'He's not?'

'He bloody is,' Hettie says, scrambling to get the camera on her phone on.

'Theo, what are you doing?' Safiyah says, standing up and walking into the middle of the floor. With all eyes on her she turns the colour of beetroot. Jane and Dave are stood to the side delightedly clutching each other as they watch their daughter, Jane is bouncing up and down like she's about to explode. Clearly Theo has already let them in on what he's about to do.

'Safiyah,' Theo says, shakily taking one of her hands in his, 'from the moment I met you, I was hooked. You're beautiful, funny, loving and I can't imagine my life without you in it. Every day you make me happy and every day I love you more. So I wondered if you would do me the greatest honour.' He nervously fumbles in his pocket and pulls out a little black velvet box. He opens it carefully and drops onto one knee, his hands shaking. 'Will you marry me?'

Without hesitation, Safiyah screams, 'YES!' Everyone cheers around them as he places the ring on her finger and kisses her. I grab Hettie and we jump up and down, hugging each other, both crying. Corks are popping as Norah comes out from behind the bar with bottles of champagne to toast the newly engaged couple.

'Congratulations!' Hettie and I scream as Safiyah bounds towards us.

'Show us the ring,' Hettie says, grasping Safiyah's arm. She holds her shaking hand out and a beautiful dazzling pear-cut diamond surrounded by a halo of smaller diamonds sparkles back at us. It's glamorous and eye-catching – just like Safiyah.

'Wow, it's beautiful,' I say.

Safiyah's glowing, I don't think I have ever seen her look so happy.

Hettie pulls Safiyah and me into a group hug and I'm beyond grateful that I'm here to be a part of this moment.

'Vi, I'm going to need a dress!'

There are quite a few sore heads around the village this morning. The party carried on late into the night and a lot of people are feeling rather delicate today including me. My head is banging, and I feel very queasy. I'm not entirely sure how much gin was consumed but with the parched feeling in my throat, and the little drummer boy pounding my brain, I think it's safe to say I packed quite a bit of it away myself – what a brilliant night though.

I fall out of bed and somehow drag myself along to the tearoom to meet Hettie and the new bride-to-be and we jump straight into discussing the wedding and more importantly the dress.

'The opening is just one week away so you can be my very first customer.' God, one week, is that all? So much has been done but I'm still waiting on the most important thing – the stock. The changing rooms and main shop are finished. Ben helped me prepare the rooms upstairs and my sewing machine and supplies are now in. I have a new desk as well as a large table for cutting material. The computer and card machine are installed, and it took me an entire evening to figure out how that worked. The vintage rails have been delivered and Ben, with a little help from Fred, installed them for me. I've been busy advertising the shop opening too. I placed an advertisement in the newspaper as well as pushing it as much as I can on social media. Hettie even gave me the name of a contact at *Brides* magazine and I was able to swing a last-minute advert albeit a small one in the back of the next issue.

After the much-needed coffee with the girls, I walk across the road to watch the very thing I have been looking forward to most since I was handed the keys – the shop sign going up. Jack being a graphic designer helped me design it. It has a sleek white background with the shop's new name Vintage Violets written in black scroll writing. A beautiful drawing of a violet borders the whole sign. It looks elegant, simple and classy, which is the exact tone I'm hopefully going to convey.

'Vintage Violets,' Fred says proudly as he walks up behind me, putting his arm around my shoulders. He must have walked into the village to watch the sign go up as well. 'Looks great.'

'It does, doesn't it.' I feel so overwhelmed by all the emotions that are revolving around me: excited, proud, anxious and shit scared of failing.

'Nervous?' Fred asks.

'So nervous,' I admit. 'But I've already had a couple of phone calls booking in appointments for next week so I'm feeling positive.'

'I'm so proud of you, Vi.'

'Thanks, Pops. I'm just glad you're here to see it.' I rest my head on Fred's shoulder as we stand, looking at my shop.

The stock finally arrives the following day and it takes two glorious days to price and hang all the dresses on the rails and place the vintage selection of beautiful jewellery and headpieces in a display cabinet. I channel some of Fred's meticulous traits and take my time, making sure everything looks perfect. I found a lovely light-grey sofa with a curved back and studded detail that now sits in the centre of the shop near a large mirror that was an absolute bargain find on eBay. So, with the fridge in the little kitchen stocked with Prosecco, my pretty little shop is ready for business. I stand behind the counter looking around at my little empire and I have this burning determination to make it work. I need to after all the money I've ploughed into it as my savings are well and truly depleted now. I've thrown everything into this venture but have to admit, the shop looks perfect. I have a feeling that this could be what I've been searching for... my new happy place.

'The sign is up, and this is your official invite to the opening,' I tell the Golden Girls at the end of another fun Zumba class later in the afternoon. 'I hope you can make it too, Roberto.'

'If there's free drinks, you can count me in,' he replies cheekily.

'After everything you have all done for me you can all have as many drinks as you like.'

'I'm looking forward to having a good old mooch around at the dresses,' Olivia says, smiling.

'Oh God, you're not in the market for another one, are you?' Jane asks, as tactless as ever.

'You never know; my new artist man could be a keeper.'

'Lucky number four eh, Liv?' Rosalind scoffs sceptically.

'Oh shut your face, you,' Olivia replies, giving her sister a playful shove.

38

Opening day has arrived and I'm stood on the shop step wondering how the hell I pulled it all together so fast. It's the first frosty morning of the season now we're in early October and I breathe in the crisp, cool air. I need to pinch myself. Who would have thought a few months ago that this is where I would be now? Hettie, Safiyah, my parents, Roberto and all the Golden Girls are here. Tessa has come over from the tea shop with a stand of cupcakes that she made for me to hand out for free. She says it's a thank you for the dress I gave her. Hettie surprised me with an amazing three-tier cake in red velvet. On top of the cake is a little model of me holding a wedding dress in front of a Vintage Violets sign. I love it, she is a cake-decorating master.

'That's amazing, Hettie. It looks too good to cut.'

Ivy has popped out of her shop to watch the proceedings as well as Linda, who's never one to miss an event. I'm under no illusion that she just wants to have a good nosey around my shop. Even Richard from the craft and ale shop has popped in with a large bottle of pale ale for me to wish me luck. A huge bouquet of flowers arrived this morning too from Imogen and Sarah which has spread the most gorgeous fresh aroma around the shop and is covering the light whiff of paint that has lingered. The publicity has worked a treat and a large group of brides have arrived to see the opening and arrange appointments. To say I'm chuffed to bits would be an understatement.

Ben is stood front and centre, giving me a reassuring wink so my nerves must be showing. Winnie is next to him with her thumbs up in the air and I start to feel choked. So many people here have made this dream of mine come true and I don't think I can find the right words to fully explain to them how much it all means. I did try to write a speech last night but it sounded corny and trite so I have decided to go with my heart and wing it.

'I just want to say a massive thank you to everyone here who has helped make this possible. I've dreamt of having my own shop for so many years but never thought it would actually happen. I will be forever grateful of your love and support,' I say, purposely looking over at Fred and Lilly. I'm teetering on the verge of tears so end my speech quickly – short and simple as I hate public speaking. 'So, without further ado, I declare Vintage Violets open!' I pop the cork of a bottle of champagne. Everybody cheers, and we all trail inside so everyone can have a good look around. A table is set up in the corner with glasses of bubbly and the cakes from Hettie and Tessa. The jewellery glistens in the display cabinets sending pools of rainbow light across the shop as everyone starts looking around, admiring the dresses. The whole room is literally sparkling as it welcomes its guests.

'So how does it feel being your own boss?' Ben says, sideling up beside me.

I wrap my arms around his neck. 'Unbelievable and I have you to thank.' I kiss him and the warm familiar trace of his lips leaves me feeling giddy with happiness.

'You can thank me later,' Ben whispers into my ear with a devilish smile.

A steady flow of visitors arrive throughout the day, making appointments.

'At this rate I may need to think about hiring someone to help,' I say with the pleasant exhaustion that you get after a thrillingly productive day. Lilly, Jane and Maggie have come back as I was closing up so I make us all a cup of tea.

'Have you enjoyed it?' Jane asks.

'I really have, it's so different working for yourself rather than someone else.'

'I think that Philip did you a favour, you know,' Maggie says thoughtfully.

'What, shagging Francesca?'

'Yeah, think about it. If he hadn't have done that you wouldn't be back here, you wouldn't have met Ben and you wouldn't have the shop.'

'You wouldn't have joined Zumba and cake club and got to know us lovely lot,' Jane adds. 'And you would have missed my Fiya's engagement.'

'Yeah, I guess so.' They're right, life is so much better now than it was when I was in London. I guess I have him to thank after all. I raise my mug in the air, 'Cheers, Philip, you may be a lying, cheating, conniving scumbag but you did me the biggest favour.'

'Cheers,' the other three ladies sing, holding their own mugs in the air before we erupt into laughter.

True to word, Safiyah is my first official customer. She has come in with Hettie and Jane and we have spent a very happy hour watching Safiyah try dresses on and dance around the room in all the different styles.

'Is it not a little early to be doing this? We haven't even set a date yet,' Safiyah asks as she looks at herself in a beautiful ivory strapless gown. She looks like a Disney princess.

'It's never too early to try dresses on,' Hettie says, thumbing through a bridal magazine. 'It's the fun part.'

'It is fun,' Safiyah agrees as she twirls around in the dress, making it spin out like a bell.

'That style really suits you,' I tell her as I make a note in my client book. Lilly bought me a huge leather-bound deep-purple book to write all my customers' information in, she even had my name engraved on the front in gold lettering.

'You look like a princess,' Jane sniffs.

'Mum, are you crying? What are you like?' she says, giving her mum a squeeze.

I pass Jane a tissue from the little table next to the sofa. Bridal boutiques always seem to make mothers and grandmothers emotional, so I'm prepared with lots of tissue boxes dotted about the place.

Safiyah gets dressed and when she returns, asks, 'Are you prepared for lots of appointments with me, Violet? You know how crap I am at making decisions.'

'That's the beauty of your bestie making your dress. You can take as long as you need.'

The next customer is Collette who has come in to try on her dress after the recent adjustments. She's thrilled with the finished product and has brought along her bridesmaids to try on some of the gowns that I have in stock. She picks three Grecian dresses in burgundy to match the ribbon on the wedding dress and a little cream flower girl dress.

I'm exhilarated after my first official sale in the shop, especially as I'm able to work the computer and card system without too much faffing – result! I have two more appointments for the rest of the day, leading to two sales, one of which being an order for a bespoke dress. Not bad for the first full day. My phone rings and I see Ben's name flash across the screen.

'Good afternoon, my sexy architect.'

'Someone sounds happy.'

'I've had a very productive day. Made some sales in the shop, got an order for one of my own wedding dresses and I've just checked my online Etsy shop. I have three orders for my pinafore dresses!'

'Get you.' He sounds impressed. 'I was calling to invite you for dinner, I better make it extra special now then.'

'Sounds perfect. I'm going to the dance committee HQ after work for our last meeting, but I'll be with you after that.'

'See you later then, I'll even treat you to your favourite pudding.'

Yum, chocolate cake and Ben, the most delicious combination. Heat floods my body and I hang up, hoping the meeting won't take too long. I'm about to take my cup into the kitchen when my phone rings again.

'Are you calling with more information to entice me round because you had me at "dinner"?'

'Violet?' I freeze, why didn't I check the name before I answered. Shit. 'Violet, are you there?'

My stomach lurches as if the floor has been swept from under me, making my legs go all wobbly. I end the call. It's been so long since I've heard his voice. How can a voice sound so familiar and yet like a stranger all at the same time? My phone rings again and Philip's name flashes across the screen. I let the call ring out and then place my phone in my bag. I have no desire to speak to him ever again so he can bugger off.

I've left my old life behind so what on earth does he want now?

I'm sat on the bench in the village hall with Safiyah and the Golden Girls. Bags of decorations and fairy lights are strewn over the floor in preparation for the dance tomorrow night.

'Right then.' Winnie stands up with a clipboard in her hand, looking ready for business. 'The marquee will be erected in the morning. I've spoken to Josh and he said his team should have it up by two o'clock. That will give us approximately five hours until the doors open. It will be tight, but it can be done.' Winnie sounds like she's worked out everything with military precision. She's in her element as she delegates everyone their jobs. A fire has been lit under her and she's thriving off the hustle and bustle of it all. I feel slightly nervous about what Winnie will do once the dance is over. Hopefully that won't be an issue now she is on the village council. 'Safiyah, the bar is your domain, so I will leave that for you to organise.'

'Yes, miss.' Safiyah salutes Winnie with a wicked grin.

'The rest of us can set up tables and chairs and hang the decorations. I've spoken to the DJ and he will be here at quarter past six to set up. The bands have been given their time slots which will give the DJ a break throughout the night. Do we have anyone willing to man the table to collect the tickets and money for anyone paying on arrival?'

'Yes, Norah has given us two of her staff to man the door. She said the pub will be fairly quiet anyway,' I tell Winnie.

'And we're using our events staff for the bar and hog roast,' Safiyah adds.

'Brilliant. Well, loads of tickets have been sold and I think there will be a few buying on the door, so I reckon we will raise lots for charity. All that's left to say now is see you tomorrow.'

'I'm going to close early tomorrow so I can help set up. You've done a great job, it's going to be a brilliant night,' I say to Winnie as we walk out together. If tomorrow night is a success, it will be all down to her.

'I have really loved it. I think I missed my calling in life. I should have been an events planner. I'm already thinking of the next village occasion to organise, something for Christmas perhaps.'

'Uh oh, I've created a party-planning monster,' I tease. Who knew quiet Winnie was such a party animal.

39

I'm closing the shop after my last appointment of the day. I made sure I didn't book any late appointments so I could help oversee arrangements at the marquee and still have time to get ready. The Kimberley sisters have been in to collect their dresses. Olivia's is a sparkly black cocktail dress – she's going all out to impress the artist. Rosalind's is a slightly more reserved yellow mid-length shift dress with three-quarter-length sleeves.

As I'm turning the open sign to closed, I look over at Hettie's bakery and see her holding a mug in the air waving at me with Maggie stood behind her. I assume that's code *for come over for a brew*, a benefit of working across the road from your best friend. I wave back, just as a woman passes Hettie's shop. Is that... it is, that's Zoe, Ben's client. What's she doing back here again? Has she come to see Ben? I watch her bump into Linda outside the Serenity Lounge and in typical fashion, Linda pulls her into conversation.

They talk for a few minutes and then Zoe follows Linda into the salon. She can't be having her hair done surely, it looks perfect already. I grab my keys and phone, noticing a missed call. I will deal with that later, it's probably Philip again as I've had a few more calls from him since last night. I'm hoping he gets the hint soon and gives up. I run across the road and dash into the bakery.

'Hello, neighbour,' Hettie sings happily. 'Tea?'

'Okay, tell me if I sound like I'm losing the plot a bit, but there's a woman who has just gone into the Serenity Lounge and it's Ben's client. I've seen Ben with her a few times now and each time she's all over him.'

'Erm... okay.' I can tell by Hettie's tone that she does think I'm losing the plot. 'Is she with him now?'

'Well no, but why is she here?'

'If you saw her going into Linda's then my guess is, she has an appointment.'

'But why here, don't you think it's a bit odd?' She lives in Lancaster, doesn't she? Plenty of salons there.

'When you say all over him, what do you mean?' Maggie asks from behind the counter as she puts her magazine down.

'Bending over in front of him, touching his arms, girly giggles and flicking her hair. You know the drill when women flirt,' I say, going over to the window to look back out onto the street. She must still be in the Serenity Lounge.

'Maybe she's here for Ben then,' Maggie says very conspiratorially.

Exactly what I was thinking.

'Mum, you're not helping,' Hettie snaps at Maggie. 'Maybe she just saw the salon and liked the look of it,' Hettie suggests optimistically, which I roll my eyes at.

'Oh come on, there's got to be more to it than that,' I say with my face scrunched up against the glass, trying to look down the street. 'Her hair looked perfect, big bouncy curls and you don't do your hair like that to then go and get it done professionally.'

'Do you think perhaps you're just a little sensitive about

things given what the shit pig did to you?' I can't help but laugh at the new name Philip has acquired.

'Maybe.'

'Come on, Vi. Ben adores you, and would he really play away in full view of all of us?'

'Philip did it in full view of everyone.'

'Yeah, well, as I said before he's a shit pig, but Ben isn't.'

'I agree with Hettie,' Maggie nods. 'He does really like you, look at what he did for you with the shop.'

'No, you're right.' I suddenly feel so guilty for thinking the worst of Ben but that doesn't mean Zoe has innocent motivations. 'You don't think she's coming to the dance tonight, do you?'

Images of Zoe turning up looking breathtaking in a showstopping dress and Ben pulling her into a leg-swooning kiss as everyone applauds fuzzes my thoughts and I feel a little sick. Dammit, my dress isn't showstopping!

'How would she even know about it?'

'There are flyers all around the village and the neighbouring villages too and Ben might have mentioned it at work.'

'So what if she does come, Ben's going with you,' Hettie says, trying to steer me onto a more rational thought process.

'Perhaps you should book a haircut,' Maggie suggests surreptitiously. 'Get it looking pretty for tonight...'

'Yes, good idea. It could do with a freshen up, I'll go make an appointment.' Linda will be more than happy to divulge any information she's currently learning about Zoe. 'Maggie, you are a genius.'

'Violet!' Hettie says forcefully.

'What? It's just an innocent catch-up with Linda. We haven't had a good chat in weeks,' I say, backing out of the shop. 'Rain check on the tea, I'm going back over to mine to wait for Zoe to leave.'

'No way, if you're doing this then I'm coming with you. Someone needs to talk sense into you,' Hettie says, pulling her apron off and following me out. 'Mum, you're in charge of the shop for a bit.'

'Hey, that's not fair,' Maggie whines.

'You shouldn't have put the idea in her head to begin with then,' Hettie says, throwing the apron at Maggie.

'Fine.' I concede to let Hettie come back with me and we sneak across the road and into Vintage Violets.

'We can watch from here,' I say, jumping behind the counter, keeping my eyes fixed on the salon.

'Is this not a little obvious, us both staring across the road?'

'We'll duck down behind the counter when she comes out.'

'Oh yes, because that will look better,' Hettie replies sarcastically. 'This is ridiculous, I'm at least making a brew.' She huffs then goes into the kitchen.

'Fine but be quick.'

I'll tell you what this situation needs right now – binoculars, that would give me a better view into the salon.

Hettie hurries back behind the counter a few minutes later with two piping hot cups of tea.

'You think I'm crazy, don't you?' I ask.

'A little. I get after what happened you have trust issues but we're hiding behind a counter waiting for a woman to have what could be a very innocent appointment.' It does sound a little crazy when you put it like that. Oh, I wasn't supposed to fall for the first guy I met. It was just meant to be fun and then we went past that so quickly and now there's Zoe and I'm afraid of it all falling apart. I don't want to get hurt again. I just need to find out what she's doing here and then maybe I can relax.

· · ·

After nearly an hour of drinking tea and munching our way through a pack of digestives that Hettie found in the kitchen, we see Zoe emerge from the salon. Her glamorous hair still looks the same, bouncy curls flowing perfectly down her back.

'There she is!' I shout. 'Duck.' We drop to the floor.

'Wow she's—'

'Hot, yeah I know.'

'Yeah, but like supermodel hot,' Hettie says, looking both dazzled and impressed. She quickly stops talking when she sees the scowl on my face. Damn, she does look good though. We peek out from behind the counter, Zoe stops and looks over towards the shop. For a heart-stopping moment I think she might come over, but she doesn't. Not sure I could explain why Hettie and I are sat on the floor with the lights off if she did.

'She was definitely looking at the shop then, wasn't she?'

'She's probably just wondering what the hell we are both doing hiding like two of the world's worst spies.' Hettie gets up and walks over to the window. 'She's going.'

We watch Zoe glide down the road away from us like some ethereal being.

'Gosh, even her walk is sexy,' Hettie says, a little disheartened. 'I don't have a sexy walk.'

'Oh don't you start, your walk is fine.' There's only room for one crazy lady around here and I've taken that spot. 'Come on.' I drag her out of the shop, lock the door and go over to the salon.

40

The smell of shampoo and hairspray hits me and there's a low buzz of hairdryers working away in the background.

'Violet, hello,' Linda chimes cheerfully, pulling me into a rather awkward hug. There are a few customers in having their hair and nails done, no doubt ready for the dance tonight.

'Hi, Linda, just wondering if you had any spare appointments. I could really do with a freshen up before tonight,' I say, pulling at the ends of my hair that I actually worked really hard on this morning.

'I can squeeze you in now if you like,' she says, taking a closer inspection of my hair. 'I think you need it.'

'Really that would be great. Thank you,' I say through gritted teeth – cheeky cow.

'What about you, Hettie?'

'Oh, nothing for me – just here with Vi.'

'So what are we having done?' Linda asks after she washes my hair and sits me down in front of the mirror, gently pulling her fingers through my wet hair.

'Oh, just a trim, please, and then maybe some waves ready for later. Are you coming to the dance?'

'Of course, looking forward to it actually. Winnie came in the other week selling tickets.'

We continue with some small talk about my shop and a few of the locals until the conversation moves on to Ben and Linda's whole demeanour changes. She's suddenly like a hawk circling for prey.

'So how are things with Ben?' Linda asks her eyes wide with interest. 'Will he be your date tonight?' I can see Hettie sat to the side reading a magazine through the reflection in the mirror, she puts it down at the sound of Ben's name.

'Oh, fine thanks, yes he will be.'

'We just had one of his clients in here.'

'Oh really?' I try to sound indifferent, pretending to be more interested in the magazine that's on my lap.

'I've just done her nails. I have to say you're a better woman than me,' she announces as she does the finishing touches to my hair. What is that supposed to mean? She clearly knows something that I don't and normally I wouldn't give her the satisfaction of asking but... I have to know.

'What do you mean?'

'Having my boyfriend working so closely with his ex, I would hate it.'

What! Oh my God, she's his ex. I forget to take a breath. It feels like someone has just thrown a bucket of ice-cold water over me.

'Didn't you know?' Linda asks inquisitively and I see the joy on her face that she has information I know nothing about.

'I, erm...' I'm struggling to form words, I look at Hettie for help, but she looks just as flabbergasted as me. 'Yeah, I think he mentioned it but it's no big deal, she's an ex for a reason, right?' I finally say, wanting to hide the shock that's stifling me.

Linda bends down low and grips hold of my shoulders. 'If you ask me, and you know me I'm no gossip, but I would say she still has a thing for Ben.'

'Why?' I don't even try to hide the fact that Linda has piqued my interest. I also let the comment about her not being a gossip slide because we all know that's utter bullshit.

'She didn't have an appointment, it seemed to be a last-minute decision while she was in the area to fish for information. She was asking a lot of questions about him and about you. She seemed to know he was in a relationship, asked if it was serious or not. She pretended she wasn't bothered but when I said he seemed happy she looked very uncomfortable,' Linda says with a very suggestive nod.

'Did she say if she was going to the dance?'

'I asked, and she said she was thinking about it. She asked if Ben was going or not. I said of course he was going and with you obviously.' She holds the mirror to show me the back of my hair which I couldn't care less about right now. 'All finished.'

'Thanks.' I jump up from the chair, delve into my purse and practically throw the money at Linda. 'Keep the change.'

I get out of the salon as quickly as I can with Hettie close behind me and take a deep breath. I'm stunned, I'm angry. How could he not tell me that he was working so closely with an ex? Unless there is something to hide. Was that the ex that wanted to move in with him? They only broke up a year ago.

'I knew there was more to it, Hettie. I should have trusted my instincts. I told myself to keep a distance between us and to not fall for him.'

'Okay, so it wasn't as innocent as I thought but he hasn't actually cheated,' Hettie says, imploring me to see sense.

'Not that I know of, no, but regardless of that he didn't tell me. That's his ex who he has history with. They looked so intense when I saw them in the tearoom together, she was clinging on to his arm. She clearly still has feelings for him. What if he still has feelings for her? There's no other reason to hide it if he didn't.'

Hettie stumbles for words, I know she wants to back Ben up, but she can't. He may not have lied but he has kept something pretty big from me and that's how it starts. A hidden truth here turns into a lie there and it builds and builds until before you know it, hearts are breaking.

'No wonder he looked so uncomfortable in his office. I'm not going through this again, Hettie, I can't. I was stupid to ignore things last time, I won't do it again.'

'Try not to jump to any conclusions, talk to him first.'

'Oh I will. I'll see you later.' He has some serious explaining to do. Anger fuels me away from Hettie as I march through the town towards Ben's house. I hoped the walk there would have given me time to calm myself but the more I think about it the more riled I get myself. If there is nothing to hide, why did he lie?

I arrive at Bracken Lodge but stop very suddenly as I open the gate because there he is, on his doorstep with his arms around her, his ex-girlfriend. My heart falls into my stomach. Not again. Somehow this actually seems to hurt more than when I caught Philip, and I fight to stay standing. Ben looks up over Zoe's shoulder.

'Violet!' His face has turned ashen. 'This isn't–'

But I interrupt him, pre-empting what he's about to say. 'This is exactly what it looks like, you with your arms around your ex-girlfriend.' He looks surprised that I know and the guilt is written all over his face, even Zoe has the decency to look ashamed. 'Or maybe not an ex at all.'

'I'll leave you both to talk,' Zoe says, stepping away from Ben. She looks at me with watery eyes. 'I'm sorry.' She doesn't look smug or happy to see my pain, she looks incredibly upset. Zoe rushes away out of view and I'm left wondering what she's apologising for. What have they done?

'Before you say anything, you've got it all wrong,' Ben says, walking towards me. His voice sounds fraught.

'So tell me she isn't your ex-girlfriend then,' I demand, daring him to lie to me.

'I can't.'

'So I haven't got it wrong then.'

'Okay, well, you haven't got everything wrong. She is my ex, yes, but there's nothing going on between us. What you just saw was me saying goodbye to her.'

'How very convenient,' I spit bitterly.

'It's the truth, please come inside and I will explain everything.' His eyes are crying out to me, but I can't fall for it.

'I don't want to come inside, I don't want to hear some bullshit excuse. I have things to do for the dance later. I came here to talk but I've seen all I needed to see.' I turn to walk away. I've been so excited all day to go and help set up and now it's the last place I want to be, but I promised I would and I'm late already.

'I was wrong, I should have told you who Zoe was and that we would be spending a lot of time together,' he says and something in his voice makes me turn back to him to listen. 'I didn't really know how to at first. I didn't want to scare you off knowing what happened with Philip and there was nothing between me and her plus I wasn't even sure we would win the contract,' he says ruefully. 'Then when we won it, I was going to explain but Fred got poorly and I didn't want to add to the stress.'

'Don't use my father as an excuse. You've had plenty of opportunities to tell me since then. I saw you both in the tearoom the other week, I walked past the window.'

'Why didn't you say anything?'

'I was trying not to read anything into it, hoping she was just a client, trying to have trust in you.' I wipe the tears away that have appeared without me even realising it. I feel so stupid for going against my better judgement at the time. Have I learnt nothing? 'You both looked very deep in conversation, I knew there was more to it.'

Ben hangs his head and takes a deep breath as if bracing himself. Shit, what is he going to say? I don't think my heart can take another blow.

'She told me that day that she wanted us to try again, that we had been foolish to give up and that she still loved me.' Oh God. See, I knew it. I should feel vindicated that I was right but I'm so wretched instead. 'I told her that it wasn't going to happen. That we could be friends and work colleagues but that's all.'

Why the hell would he pass Zoe over for me? He could at least try to make the story believable. 'I'm so sorry that I didn't tell you straight away but please understand why.'

'But she's a goddess,' I blurt out rather embarrassingly even though it's true. I pale in comparison to her. 'I mean, why would you pick me over her?'

'What?' Ben gives a hollow laugh. 'Are you being serious?'

'Yes, very, if I was a bloke... hell, I'm a straight woman and even I can appreciate her.'

'I happen to think you're incredible; beautiful inside and out.'

I honestly really want to believe him but how can I? I

promised myself that when I came back to Elmsbourne-Hollow I wouldn't let another man treat me how Philip had.

'Why was she here today?'

'I asked to be taken off her account a few weeks ago. She came to ask me to go back on it.' He asked to be taken off her account, why? For me? 'When you were in my office and Martin came in about the meeting, that's what it was about. I wanted him to give her account to someone else.'

'Why would you do that?'

'Because I didn't want to get her hopes up. I didn't want her to think that if we spent time together, I would change my mind. I can't do that to her because although I don't love her anymore, she is my friend and I don't want to hurt her. I also didn't want to ruin things with you. I was planning on telling you, I just didn't know how. I should have though because now it looks like I have something to hide but I promise I don't. I wouldn't cheat on you and I am truly sorry.'

Fuck, my head and my heart are screaming two different things and I'm so confused. In my heart I understand why he's kept this from me, we weren't even together properly when he had that first meeting with her. I can see by his face he regrets not telling me when things did get more serious, those eyes have always been so revealing about his feelings and thoughts. But my head is screaming at me not to fall for any more lies, to protect my heart. The pull in opposite directions is too much.

'I can't talk about this right now,' I say sadly, closing my eyes. 'I can't think straight and there's too much to do for tonight. I'm already late.'

'Violet, the bloody dance can wait, you can't walk away.'

'Actually, I can.'

'What about us?' he asks imploringly, desperate for some indication we're okay, but I don't know that we are. I don't know if I can trust him.

'I don't know. We'll talk later.'

41

I walk into the marquee that's been erected on the village green. Tables and chairs are set up and people are bustling about preparing for tonight. Winnie is busy putting lovely floral centrepieces in the middle of each table – beautiful autumnal decorations made from foliage she's foraged from the woods with berries and ribbons entwined in them and pine cones sprayed gold.

'Sorry I'm late, ladies.' I feel terrible. They have done so much already without me. 'The centrepieces look great.'

'Thank you,' Winnie says with a burst of excitement. 'I'm really pleased with them. There's still so much to do though. Do you think we will be ready in time?'

I check my watch, we have three hours until the doors open. 'It will be a squeeze but I'm sure we will be fine.' I leave Winnie and Mary to finish setting up the rest of the tables and go over to the bar which looks complete with twinkling fairy lights and lots of booze. Blimey, I could do with a tipple now after the last hour.

'Violet.' Hettie and Safiyah are rushing towards me.

'It looks great,' I say, avoiding eye contact. Yet again they're having to witness my crumbling love life.

'Gin is all stocked up, Norah came earlier and helped with the barrels and other spirits,' Safiyah says looking at Hettie hesitantly. I think they are both wondering how long I'm going to avoid the elephant in the room.

'So... did you see Ben?' Hettie finally asks.

'Yes, I turned up just in time to see them both having a lovely cuddle on his front step.'

'What?' Hettie says with a worried crease forming across her forehead.

'He said he was saying goodbye to her. I was right about her wanting him back, he admitted she had asked if they could give it another go.' My heart tightens as I think of them both. 'He said sorry for not telling me and that he told her no and asked to be taken off her account at work.'

'What did you say? Are you still together?' Safiyah asks.

'I don't know. I get why he didn't tell me, but I'm annoyed he kept the truth from me. It's how it starts isn't it, hiding truths here and there. How can I be sure nothing has happened?' Urgh, get me a gin. 'I can't worry about it now, we need to get this all done.'

I distract myself with fairy lights and pom-poms that Winnie and Co have made and before I know it all the decorations are up. The Kimberley sisters have made some lovely garlands out of the local foliage which are hung from the ceiling of the marquee. By the time we're all done, the place looks amazing, the tent twinkles like a lovely warm autumnal wonderland. As the DJ sets up in the corner, the ladies take it in turns to go over to the pub or pop home to get changed.

When it's my turn to get ready, I run over to my shop but as I shut the door behind me, the urge to hide out here for the night feels more appealing than getting dolled up and facing Ben. I want to stay here in my little shop, my own sanctuary and hide from it all. Why am I never enough for someone? What is it that is so wrong with me? Hold on, why am I blaming myself? This is silly. I've been looking forward to tonight for ages. I'm not going to sit here berating myself, filling my heart with self-loathing. I'm going to go out and have a bloody good time and see all the Golden Girls in their beautiful dresses.

I put on my make-up, fluff up my newly trimmed hair and slip into my dress. My mobile rings and I see it's Imogen. I haven't really got time for a chat, I need to get back over to the marquee for a final check of everything. I'll call her in the morning when we can have a proper talk. I step into my new sparkly heels and look back into the full-length mirror on the shop floor. In the middle of making everyone else's dresses, I've managed to squeeze one in for myself. A fitted mid-length off-the-shoulder dress in royal blue. I do feel good in it, even with being so glum about Ben. Ben fills my thoughts again so I try to shake him out of my mind. Come on, Violet, we're having a good night, remember. Head up, chest out. I give myself one last look and then after a deep sigh I walk out into the chilly evening and back across the green.

It seems busy already, music is vibrating from the tent and the aromas from the hog roast float deliciously across the air. I walk in to see everyone enjoying themselves. The Golden Girls are dotted about sampling the gin, giddy with excitement or perhaps just tipsy. Verity and Jenny are wearing the dresses I made them, Jane is floating around the tent gloriously in her emerald-green cocktail dress. Lilly is in a bright pink sixties-style prom dress that I whipped up for her and she's teamed it with a large fascinator that's balanced on the side of her head – typical Lilly style. You will be able to spot her a mile off all evening.

I see Ben by the bar and an involuntary troupe of butterflies break out in a dance across my stomach. He looks gorgeous in grey trousers and waistcoat, a crisp white shirt with the sleeves casually rolled up and a blue tie. With no jacket, he looks effortlessly charming and seriously hot. My heart gives a thud as he looks over at me with a hopeful little wave. I lift my hand slightly to wave back but the battle between my heart and head rages on. My heart is telling me to go over and pull him into the biggest snog, my head on the other hand is screaming at me to walk the other way, keep my distance and protect my seemingly fragile heart.

'Violet!' Winnie calls, hailing me over. 'This is Keira,' she says proudly, introducing me to her daughter.

I remember her beautiful smile and dimples from the photos. It's like I know her already and I'm saying hello to an old friend. 'So lovely to meet you, Winnie has told me so much about you.'

'You too.' She smiles back warmly.

'And you must be Daisy,' I say, kneeling down to a pretty little girl in a sequinned pink dress. 'I love your dress.'

'Thank you, I love yours too,' Daisy says as she admires mine. 'Did you make it? Grandma says you make dresses.'

'I did make it.'

'I think I would like to make clothes,' Daisy says in her small voice.

'I was about your age when I first learnt. Perhaps when you next visit your grandma you could come to my shop and we could make something together.'

'I think you have an apprentice in the making there,' Keira says, grinning at me.

'Sounds good to me, and you two must be James and Zach.' I look at the two little boys in matching navy-blue trousers and light-blue shirts, the younger of the two boys has Keira's dimples.

'Your grandma talks about you all so much.' They giggle and cling on to their mother tightly. We chat for a little while and it's so lovely to finally get to know them. I could chat to them all night but I don't want to monopolise their time so I leave them to enjoy themselves while I do the rounds, checking everything is going to plan. I find Fred loitering around the hog roast, he's still on his strict diet and desperate to indulge for the evening.

'Don't let Mum catch you,' I call as I swiftly walk past him. 'And just the one.'

42

We must have raised lots of money as so many people have turned up. The room is full, but I find myself constantly scanning around looking for Ben. A glowing Tessa is with Sam and I watch them twirl each other around on the dance floor. They seem so happy – love's young dream.

'It all seems to be a success,' I say, after making my way to Hettie and Safiyah.

'It really does. Maybe it could be an annual event,' Safiyah says happily. 'The whole village seems to be enjoying it.' She nods at Mr and Mrs Thompson who are heading towards the dance floor.

'Loads of people who don't even live in the village are here as well.'

'All in the name of charity. Right... drink!' I say, pulling them both to the bar. I get myself a large glass of wine – it's been a long day.

'Vi, the lads are coming over and Ben's with them,' Hettie whispers through the corner of her mouth. I look up to them approaching us, that's my cue to leave.

'I might just go and check on the front door.' I still can't face him, it's cowardly I know but I have no idea where our relationship can go from here. A couple of months in and I've ended up hurting already. I slip away before Hettie can convince me otherwise to check there aren't any problems with the staff manning the door. I know there won't be, but it's as good an excuse as any.

'You okay, Vi?' Fred says, stepping in front of me just as I get to the marquee door, looking very dapper in his suit.

'Hi, Dad. I'm fine, why?'

'Sit with me for a moment,' he says, walking to a nearby table and sitting down.

'Are you okay, do you feel ill?' I thought tonight might be too much for him. I'll get him water and a doctor.

'I'm fine,' he says, rolling his eyes at me. 'I want to talk to you about Ben. I haven't seen you with him all night and just watched you dodge him like a bullet.' Parents literally see everything. 'Your mother's told me what happened.'

'How does she know?'

'How does anyone know anything in this place.' Fred smirks. Hettie must have told Maggie. 'I'm going to say something, and I want you to listen. I know that you're hurt by what Philip did to you but punishing Ben for it isn't fair.'

'I'm not punishing him, he kept something from me,' I say defiantly. Why is Fred on Ben's side and not mine?

'I know what he did was wrong and believe me I am annoyed for you; I don't want anyone hurting my girl. But looking at it from his point of view, he did the right thing by trying to end his working relationship with this woman which could have put him in an awkward position professionally. He did that for you. He chose you over her, no matter what the consequence was for him at work. Should he have told you, yes, but no one is perfect, sometimes people make the wrong choice but for the right reasons. It's not all black and white.'

'I know.' Oh God, maybe he's right. Nothing like the stark reality from your father to put things into perspective.

'Don't be afraid to love someone again. There will always be a risk of heartbreak, of losing someone, but that is what comes with love. You will never be happy with anyone if you keep them at arm's-length. He made a mistake that's all, but he didn't cheat, and he feels terrible.'

'I know, you're right.' I sigh.

'If there is one thing that being with your mother has taught me, it is that you only live once. Sometimes you can't play it safe. You have to live a little and follow your heart.'

'So I should go and talk to him then?'

'Yes.' I kiss Fred on the cheek, as well as seeing everything, parents have another annoying habit of always being right. I need to find Ben.

Where the hell has he gone? I've spent all evening so far avoiding him and now I want to find him, I can't. Oh no, what if he's gone home. Dean passes me as he's being dragged to the dance floor by Olivia.

'Have you seen Ben anywhere?' I shout over the music. Dean doesn't answer but points behind me as he's pulled away. I turn to follow the line of direction he's pointing in, to find Ben standing there waiting for me, looking all sullen and brooding. Hell, he even does brooding well. Is there anything this man can't do?

'I thought you were avoiding me,' he says dolefully as he approaches me.

'I was.'

'I am sorry, Vi, I really am. I never meant to hurt you, it just never seemed the right time to bring it u–'

'I understand,' I say quickly, cutting him off.

'You do?' He looks quizzically at me and my sudden change in attitude.

'Look, I'm not saying I'm happy about it, but I get why you didn't tell me.'

'What you walked in on was just a hug goodbye. I told her I was happy with you. She was upset but accepted it and was leaving. I know you find it hard to trust after what happened before. I really hope I haven't ruined your faith in me.'

'My head and my heart are screaming very different things at me. I so want to believe you but I promised myself that I wouldn't fall for someone else's lies. I wouldn't go all in with my heart.' I know as I'm saying it though that the complete opposite has actually happened. I have gone in wholeheartedly, that's why it was so crushing when I saw them both together on his doorstep. 'Promise me, no more secrets.'

'No more secrets, I promise.' He gives me a look that reaches deep into my heart and I let go of all the barriers that have been holding me back. Seeing him with Zoe, I realised instantly that I've fallen in love with him. I've been denying it for so long, but Fred's right, there will always be a risk. I just have to take a leap of faith at some point. I step closer and lean up to kiss Ben. He cups my face with both hands and kisses me back.

'You look really beautiful,' he says.

'Not too bad yourself.'

As the music pumps around the marquee, Hettie, Safiyah and I are on the dance floor.

'I love a bit of cheesy pop,' Hettie bellows as we dance rather tipsily to old-school S Club 7. 'I feel like we're back at the school disco.'

'Me too.'

The Golden Girls come over and join in, except for Rosalind

who's pressed up against Paul, the butcher, at the bar. Olivia has ditched Dean (which he looks very pleased about) now that her artist boyfriend has arrived. They are slow dancing together in the middle of the floor which is quite a feat to such energetic pop music. He's very serious and intense, but Olivia seems to be enjoying that side of him, they are lost in their own little world together.

'That's it, ladies, shimmy,' Roberto shouts, stepping onto the dance floor. He's arrived wearing red tartan trousers and a matching bow tie. He looks fabulous dressed up; I've only ever seen him in very short shorts.

'Roberto, I'm so glad you made it!' I shout above the music.

'You couldn't have kept me away; I love a good party.'

'They're pretty spritely for a bunch of old girls,' Safiyah calls, impressed as she watches the Golden Girls spin around her.

'Hey, who are you calling old?' Jane says, clipping her daughter on the shoulder.

'Are you enjoying yourself, Winnie?' I ask as she waltzes past me with Daisy, her granddaughter.

'Oh, it's wonderful.'

'Everyone's been commenting on your table displays.'

'Someone asked if I would be interested in making some for Christmas,' she tells me, glowing with her flushed cheeks. 'I might even arrange a little wreath-making class before Christmas in the village hall.'

'Count me in. Right, I need a drink, all this dancing has worn me out.' I go over to the bar and as I pull my purse out I can see my phone lighting up inside my bag. Imogen is calling again. It's not like her to ring so late, I wonder what she wants. I really should have answered earlier, what if something is wrong? I quickly answer the phone as I run over to the marquee entrance so I can hear her better as the music is so loud.

'Hi, Imogen, sorry I meant to call you back!' I shout, stepping into the fresh cold air.

'Violet, thank God, I've been trying to get hold of you all day.' Imogen sounds distressed. Has she been calling me *all* day? Oh no, it must have been her earlier before I ran over to Hettie's. I didn't even check who it was.

'It's been a bit of a mad one today, sorry. Are you okay?'

'I'm fine but I need to warn you about something.'

But as I look up I know exactly what Imogen wants to warn me about and it's too late. I feel like I've just walked smack bang into a wall. Perhaps I've wandered out of the tent and into an alternate universe where everything is upside down.

'It's okay, I already know... listen, I'll call you later.' I hang up, my eyes are locked in front of me. I feel sick from the floor spinning all of sudden as my two worlds collide – the old from London and new one here in Elmsbourne-Hollow. I've spent the last few months separating the two; it looks so strange to see them both merging together.

How dare he turn up here... and why now?

43

Philip's standing on the village green near the entrance, although it isn't the Philip that I remember leaving back in the home we shared. It's the Philip that he was before, before the personality transplant. His hair isn't slicked back anymore, it's the slightly messy way it was when we first met. The sleek suit is gone too and in its place are jeans and the hoody I bought him last Christmas. The arrogant gleam and cold sharp edge that had crept over his face for the last year of our relationship, that I had never really noticed at the time because it happened so slowly, has gone, smoothed out. He's Philip again.

'Hi,' he says nervously, taking a step towards me.

'What are you doing here?' I ask, automatically stepping back away from him.

'I, err... wow, you look stunning.' He looks at my dress, ruffling his hands through his hair. His voice sounds gentle. No cutting undertone.

'What are you doing here, Philip?' I repeat, I can hear my anger building.

'I needed to see you, you wouldn't answer my calls. I went to the cottage but there was no answer. I saw the posters so thought you might be here.'

'You should have taken the hint when I didn't answer,' I say, strong and determined, and I think it shocks him because he's starting to look quite pallid. Did he honestly think I would be happy to see him? 'You can leave now.' I turn to go back inside. I've wondered why he did what he did for so long and always thought I would grill him for answers if I ever had the chance, but I see the reasons don't matter at all. He doesn't matter to me anymore.

'Violet, please wait,' he calls, desperately grabbing at my arm. I yank away from his grasp as I turn back to look at him, giving him the full force of my death glare. He winces at my recoil as if the action has pained him, he looks so wounded. I've never seen him like this before. He's pale and tired with dark circles under his eyes.

'Why are you here?' I ask, stony, void of emotion or affection.

'I came to tell you how sorry I am, I'm hoping we can talk... work things out.'

'Work things out!' I repeat aghast. 'You've got to be kidding me.' Is he mental, work things out? How much of a pushover does he truly think I am. All this time and he thinks I'd go back to him, just like that, forgetting everything he did! Fuck that, I'm going back inside.

'Wait, please talk to me, Vi. I messed up, I know I did. I made the biggest mistake of my life and I couldn't regret it more than I do in this moment.'

'Too little, far too late.'

Philip closes his eyes, backs away and slumps down onto the bench that's set to the side of the marquee and puts his head in his hands. I can't believe it, I actually feel sorry for him. In fact, no not sorry – I pity him, he looks so pathetic. What's happened to him? When I first came back home I would have done anything for him to have turned up on the doorstep, telling me what a mistake he had made, but now I thank my lucky stars he's no longer my problem.

'Christ, Philip, you look terrible!'

'I feel it.' He looks up at me so longingly. 'I want you back. Please take me back, Vi.'

'How can you turn up here and say that after what you did? You didn't just break my heart, Philip, you tore it out and stamped all over it.'

'I know, I look back and I have no idea what I was thinking.' Tears fill his eyes, he looks genuinely appalled at himself. 'I was just thinking with the wrong body part.'

'You said you loved her.'

'I was wrong, it was lust not love. It's you I love.' He wipes a tear away.

Love... I haven't heard him say those words in such a long time. I read them on messages that he sent and on the little notes he left me when he would leave the house early but not actually heard him say the words. 'I got so caught up in a lifestyle that wasn't me, trying to keep up with lads, the gym, the going out all the time. The competitiveness of work. I got cocky and arrogant, trying to impress everyone. It was so hard trying to keep the pretence up.'

'Cry me a river!' I say, looking up to the sky. Was he always this irritating?

'I have no right to ask this of you–'

'Then don't!' I interrupt, cutting him off before he can finish his sentence. We're both silent until in spite of myself I ask, 'Why her? Of all people why Francesca?'

I don't know why I need the answer to this. Perhaps because he chose her over me and my ego wants to know why. Is she a better person than me? Did I have her wrong all this time and she's actually a lovely person so of course why wouldn't he pick her? Was she easier to love than me?

'I don't know, really. I never intended for it to happen, I didn't go looking for anyone else, you have to believe me. It started about eighteen months before we split up.'

'Eighteen months?' A whole bloody year and a half. How could I have not seen it for so long? My heart gives a thump, not of anger but of sadness, that he could so easily do that to me for so long.

'I came to work to walk you home, but the tube was late and when I got to the shop everyone was gone and Francesca was locking up. It started to rain hard so she quickly opened back up and we jumped inside to take cover. I thought nothing of it at the time, I promise. She had always seemed so nice to me and I genuinely thought we were just waiting for the shower to pass. She opened a bottle of fizz while we waited, and one glass led to two and then more. Before I knew what was happening, we were kissing.'

'And you forgot all about me waiting for you at home,' I declare, feeling less sorry for him with each passing second.

'I'm ashamed to say yes.' He takes a deep breath. 'I hadn't intended to see her again. I felt awful about it but then I saw her out a few nights later – well, it led on from there really. It was fun and exciting, I took for granted what you and I had. She kept going on about how we were a perfect fit for each other, that we could help each other get to where we wanted to be. I feel like I was under some sort of spell. After you left things were okay, but I realised quickly that she was just so cut-throat about everything. She isn't warm and loving like you. It was a constant show. She's materialistic and cold. I started to see all the things you said she was and wondered how the hell I had let things get this far. I saw who I had become, and I got sick of pretending I was something I'm not.'

I don't know what to say. I feel vindicated in some way that I was right about Francesca all along, but looking at him, there's nothing left for us, it's too late. My heart has moved on.

'I'm so sorry for everything I did.'

'It wasn't just the affair, Philip, what about everything else? You constantly put me down and made me feel worthless. You manipulated me all the time, tried to control my life. You say you wanted to impress people and in doing so you had to knock me down in the process. I wasn't good enough for the little life you were trying to create. Why would I suddenly be good enough now?'

'I never meant to do those things. I can change. We were happy once, I wasn't always like this. I let things get out of hand, but I know now.'

'No, Philip, too much has happened. I'm starting to feel like myself again and I won't go back.'

Philip's quiet for a moment and then pensively asks, 'It can't really be over, can it?'

I sit down next to him on the bench. Five years ago I didn't think this was where we would be but here we are.

'What's done is done, but yes it's truly over,' I say forcefully because I want him to understand that it really is. 'I take it you're not with Francesca anymore?'

'No, we broke up a couple of weeks ago, when I came to my senses.'

'How did she take it, miserably I hope?' I sound bitter but I'm honestly not. I'm never going to like the woman.

'You know Francesca.'

'Unfortunately.'

'Did you really rugby tackle her to the ground?' he asks me doubtfully.

'Yes,' I say with a slight hint of a titter. 'I'm not sure what came over me, she said such awful things.'

'Do you know how much convincing it took to get her *not* to call the police?' Philip says, trying to force a smile.

'Really? The brazen witch, after what she did she was willing to report me.' Knowing her I'm actually surprised she didn't.

I can feel Philip watching me, he takes a deep sigh and looks wistfully into the distance as if accepting our fate.

'I wish we could go back to the day we met, when I helped you off the floor and you blew me away, I would do things so differently.'

'I wouldn't.' I sit up straighter and Philip looks confused. 'We had a lot of good times together and I wouldn't be where I am now otherwise.'

'Your shop?' He knows about Vintage Violets. 'Imogen told me about it. I had a look on Facebook, it looks amazing. She said you have some orders for wedding dresses already. I'm really proud of you, Vi, you did it.'

'You said it was just a pipe dream.'

'I did, didn't I? I really was a massive shit. Fuck, I'm so sorry. If I'm honest, I was worried that you would be more successful than me. The fire in your eyes always came so easily to you and I was jealous. I guess that's why I wasn't as supportive as I should have been. I'm so ashamed of myself... I am really proud of you though.'

'I couldn't have done it without everyone here,' I say as my heart warms thinking of all my friends in Elmsbourne-Hollow... and Ben. 'Imogen was calling me to warn me you were on your way. How did she know?'

'I was waiting for her before work this morning. I'd been thinking about you non-stop for the last couple of weeks. I went to see her to ask if she had heard from you. She told me you were happy and I needed to stay away. But I couldn't... What if I left London?' Philip says optimistically. He doesn't give up. 'You once told me that I was your happy place. It didn't matter where we were or what we were doing as long as we were together. I could get a job up here. You in your shop; we could buy a little house together, get married. Violet, we could be happy again,' he says, grabbing my hands and holding them in his. He genuinely believes we could be happy. He cups his hand on my face. 'I need you... I love you.'

I pull his hands from my face and hold them tightly in my own.

'No.' Even after all the pain he has caused I don't want to hurt him back, that's not who I am, but he does need to know the truth. 'I've... I've met someone else.'

'Oh... so you really don't love me anymore?'

'I wanted you to come after me when I left. I was lost without you, but you didn't, and then I found my way and Ben...'

'But we have so much history, Vi. How long have you known this guy for, five minutes? How well do you actually know him?'

I feel my nostrils flare with anger. 'History that a few months ago you were happy to throw away and you haven't been around, you have no idea how well I know him. How much he has been there for me.' And how much I love him. 'Philip, you will always mean something to me,' I say, still holding his hands. 'You don't just forget someone after five years and I can't believe I'm saying this, but I hope someday we can be friends – but that's all. It is over between us.'

'You loved me once, maybe you could fall in love with me again.' Before I know what's happening, he plants his lips on mine, they feel cold and strange.

'This looks cosy!' an angry voice booms in front of us. Ben is stood there with his face red and his fists clenched. Oh no, this looks bad... really bad.

44

'Ben, no,' I say, jumping up.

'What's this, payback for Zoe?'

'No, not at all,' I plead, my whole body runs cold as I see the look of betrayal in Ben's eyes.

'Philip, I assume?' Ben gestures to Philip and then looks back at me. 'After everything he did, after everything you said, and you would go back to him?'

'Hey, don't judge me, you don't even know me,' Philip says, getting to his feet, puffing his chest up to Ben childishly. 'I'm here because I love her.'

'Love!' Ben laughs scathingly as he looks from Philip to me. 'What you did was love, was it?' Ben turns around not waiting for an answer and walks away from the marquee and away from me.

'Ben, please come back, it's not like that.' I go to run after him, but Philip pulls me back.

'Leave him. Stay with me,' he pleads and my anger hits boiling point. He's still doing it; he's still trying to control me.

'Philip, I love him,' I say, shoving Philip away. There, I've said it out loud, albeit to the wrong person but it's out in the open. 'You haven't changed at all, you're still doing it. Putting yourself and what you want first, forgetting completely what I might want.' Philip lets go of me, looking defeated. 'Will you please just go and stay out of my life.' I run after Ben and I don't look back. He's already off the green when I catch up to him.

'Ben, wait,' I demand, stepping in front of him.

'Don't,' he says. He looks so angry. 'I don't want to hear it.'

'Tough, you're going to. He kissed me, I didn't kiss him back.'

'Violet, I saw you both. All cosy together on the bench, or did your hands accidentally fall on his? You weren't exactly pushing him away.' Ben's face is puce with anger but I can see the sadness emanating from his big beautiful eyes.

'It happened so fast. I was telling him about you.'

'About what a mug I am? I felt terrible over Zoe and all this time I thought we had something. I thought I was...'

'Thought you were what?' Please say it, please tell me you love me and this isn't just one-sided.

But he doesn't say it, instead he says, 'It doesn't matter.'

It does matter, it really fucking matters. My stomach lurches, the deep pang is back with a vengeance as I see how hurt he is. My heart is beating fast and my mouth runs dry, I feel fuzzy as panic explodes in my chest. He's slipping away from me. I need to make him understand but he starts talking again.

'I've never pushed you, even at first when you were distant, but I thought we were moving forward.'

'We are,' I plead as my voice wobbles.

'We're not. It's over, we're done.'

My world comes to a crashing halt as I hear those words. 'You're breaking up with me?' Ben stares at me but doesn't answer. He has to take that back, he just has to. How can he break-up with me over something I haven't done? Philip kissed me. 'I gave you the benefit of the doubt with Zoe,' I say angrily. I can't believe he's not giving me the same chance. I guess he doesn't love me if he can so easily walk away from us.

'I wasn't locking lips with her.'

'He kissed me,' I repeat angrily, clenching my fists. 'Well, you clearly had no intention of this being a serious relationship if you can end it so easily. I knew I should have kept it as just friends with benefits – no feelings.' It was a mistake to fall in love again.

'Friends with benefits?' he repeats, shocked. 'Jesus Christ, Violet, was that all I was to you?' He looks like he has just received another stab to the heart – but that isn't what I meant. My heart thunders in my chest as the conversation continues to spiral out of control.

'No, it was at first but–'

'Wow. If that's all I was then I guess you won't be disappointed that it's over. You can go back to *him* now you've got shagging me out of your system.'

'How dare you. That's not what I meant and you know damn well how much you mean to me.' I can't believe this is happening again. Philip turning up has ruined everything and I'm actually so angry with Ben for believing I could cheat on him. Does he not know me at all? He can't honestly believe that all I see us as is fuck buddies. This is getting ridiculous.

Ben lifts his hands behind his head and looks up to the dark night sky as he paces in front of me. I want to reach out to him and cuddle him. I want his arms around me and for this horrible nightmare to be over. I step towards him and reach out but he flinches away, his eyes filling with tears.

'Don't. I'm going. Don't follow me.' He turns and slowly walks away with his head down.

I crumple. My heart is broken all over again – this time I fear it's irreparable. Tears pour and my heart aches as I watch the man I love disappear out of view. I can hear Hettie calling my name, the night's cold, and the frost nips at the tears rolling down my cheeks. It's over. It's all over.

I walk back slowly in the direction of Hettie's voice. What the hell has happened in the last twenty minutes?

45

'No, Mum, it's over.' I blow my nose loudly. 'I've lost him for good.'

'Oh, Violet.' Lilly holds me close as I explain what happened last night. After Hettie had run out to me, I told her what happened and then left without saying goodbye to anyone. I sat on my bed, going over the conversation with Ben again and again, his voice telling me it was over. The pang of doom is back, mocking me for thinking I had defeated it in the first place. Every time I think of Ben's face it gives me a cold, hard thud.

'I didn't kiss Philip, I was telling him I had moved on with someone else.'

'Perhaps Ben just needs to cool down, it will all sort itself out in the end.'

'He looked so betrayed, Mum, the look on his face.' Bleugh, I feel like utter shit. 'I listened to him when it was the other way around.'

'But not straight away, you needed a bit of time, that's probably all he needs.'

'But I didn't end it. I'm so bloody angry that he did, without letting me explain. I thought he knew me better than that.'

'If Philip turns up again, send him my way,' she says, playfully boxing the air. If he turns up again, I won't need Lilly to box his ears in, I'll bloody do it myself.

'Please don't tell Dad. I don't want him worrying, not after being so ill.'

'I won't say anything yet but news spreads, Vi. He will hear it soon enough and it's better it comes from us than someone else. What are your plans today?'

'Going to go to the green to help pack away and then I have an appointment at the shop this afternoon.' I wasn't going to open on Sundays but a customer asked and I didn't want to say no, not while I'm trying to drum up business. I'm regretting agreeing to the appointment now though. I'm really not in the mood for feigning cheeriness with an excitable loved-up bride. Not while my heart is feeling the shattered effects of unrequited love. I'm back to square one again. Fuck!

'If Ben comes here...'

'I'll tell him where you are,' Lilly says with a sympathetic smile.

As I walk to the village green, I stop momentarily at the top of Ben's road. I want to go and bang on the door and scream at him for being a total knobhead for not believing me, for breaking us up so easily, but what's the point? He probably wouldn't answer the door to me anyway. I drag my feet into the village and as I get closer to the green there are a few people milling about already. Crap, what if everyone knows. I brace myself for fifty questions as I walk into the marquee. Hettie and Jack are taking down fairy lights. Winnie, Jenny and Jane are sweeping the floor, and Josh and Safiyah are busy packing up behind the bar.

'Hello, Violet.' Winnie bounces over to me, her normal jolly self. She can't know.

'Hi, Winnie. Did you have a good night?' I say, forcing my voice to sound bright. Perhaps I could get away with just making out I have a hangover.

'It was wonderful, the children thoroughly enjoyed themselves.'

'I'm so pleased.'

'Where did you sneak off to?' Jane says, sweeping past my feet. 'You and Ben make an early dart together, did you? Young love, eh?'

I could cry!

'Are you okay, love? You look a little peaky,' Jane asks.

'Err, yes, too much wine, I think.'

'Mum, could you stack some of those chairs over there,' Safiyah says, running over to rescue me and distract Jane. Hettie will have filled Fiya in on my sorry state of affairs I'm sure. 'Sorry,' Safiyah says, pulling me over to the bar. 'Are you okay?' Hettie, Jack and Josh come over to join us making me feel like the local circus freak as they all eye me with pity. *Roll up, roll up, come see the lonely spinster woman with three heads.*

'Not really, no.' I'm so embarrassed. I put my head down on the bar. It won't be long before my life is once again the centre of village gossip.

'I told Philip to piss off,' Jack tells me. 'He was loitering about, I wanted to smack the idiot in the face when Hettie told me.' His support is appreciated and sweet, even if a little violent.

'I didn't kiss him, guys, I promise.'

'Vi, you don't need to convince us,' Josh says, putting a reassuring hand on mine.

'Shame Ben isn't so trusting,' I say as my eyes prick. 'Has anyone seen him?'

'Not yet. He'll come around though, I'm sure,' Hettie says optimistically. 'Once he's calmed down and thought about it.'

'If there's no trust, then I'm not sure there is anything to sort out. I'm going to concentrate on the shop from now on.'

The majority of the marquee has been tidied away. All rubbish has been cleared, tables and chairs taken back to store at Winters Farm and the put-up bar has been disassembled and put away. The marquee will be taken down completely tomorrow.

'Are you sure you're okay, love? You don't seem yourself,' Winnie asks me. The Golden Girls are my friends, perhaps I should be honest and tell them. They will find out anyway.

'To be honest, things aren't great. Ben and I broke up last night.'

'What happened?' Winnie throws her arm around my shoulders.

'My ex showed up and Ben thought I was going back to him and we had an argument. It's just all a bit messy really.' I cry as I tell Winnie. Jenny and Jane overhear and gather round to listen too, and I find it strangely comforting.

'He will come to his senses,' Jane says forcefully.

'Of course he will,' Jenny agrees.

'I'm not sure he will but I'll be okay. I'm going to concentrate on the shop and making a success out of it.' I sniff. There are plenty of other ways to be happy besides being in love, Vintage Violets will be my new happy place. I knew it would be the moment I walked in the shop.

'If you need anything you only have to ask,' Jenny says, and the ladies nod in agreement.

'Thank you, I hope you don't mind but I'm going to get off. I have an appointment at the shop in a bit. I'll see you all at Zumba tomorrow. Thank you for your help with the dance. I'm really glad you enjoyed it.'

'Our pleasure, we seem to have raised a lot of money. We could count it up tomorrow and decide who we want to donate it to, if you like.'

'Sounds like a plan.' I raise a smile so I don't leave the wonderful Winnie worrying about me too much.

I leave the village green and make my way to the shop. I've checked my phone religiously throughout the day hoping to hear from Ben but nothing so far – complete radio silence. I open up and lean on the door as I close it behind me. In the safety of my beautiful little shop, the floodgates open and I burst into tears.

Shit. Shit. Shit.

I've come so far in the last few months just to balls it up all over again. At least I have my shop though, I should be grateful for that. My customer arrives on time and I somehow put on a brave face. The appointment is a success. A wedding dress and mother-of-the-bride dress are ordered and a further appointment booked to organise the bridesmaid dresses. I'm in the kitchen washing up the glasses when I hear the shop door ping. My heart jumps because I instantly hope it's Ben, perhaps he's calmed down and is thinking more reasonably now. My optimism is cut short though as I hear Hettie's voice.

'It's just me.'

'Hi. I was about to lock up,' I say, trying not to sound too disappointed.

'Good timing then,' Hettie says, holding up a bottle of wine.

46

I pull down three wine glasses as Hettie, Lilly and I sit at the trusty kitchen table. Fred has trotted off to the pub to watch the football under strict instructions to only consume soft drinks.

'Safiyah said she will join us after, she's just in the middle of something.'

'Have you heard from him?' Lilly asks.

'No. Hardly surprising is it?' I take a big gulp of wine.

'I thought I saw him in the village earlier. Over at the marquee,' Lilly says with a furrowed brow, looking at Hettie.

'You didn't say he was there.' I'm a little taken aback. Surely Hettie would have told me if she'd seen him. Lilly must be mistaken.

'Oh, erm, yes, he came to help move the last of the furniture,' Hettie replies quietly.

'Did he say anything?'

'Not much, kept himself to himself.' Now I know Hettie and Safiyah well enough to know that they both would have grilled him over last night. I can't imagine he would have had the option to keep himself to himself. Perhaps he didn't have anything nice to say and Hettie doesn't want to upset me – I didn't think it was possible but I feel even worse.

'Have you tried calling him?' Lilly asks me.

'No, I don't really know what to say. I told him it was Philip and not me. If Ben doesn't want to hear it then I'm not going to beg.'

We polish off the bottle of wine far too easily when Hettie's phone buzzes.

'It's Fiya, she wants us to meet her at the farm, she has gin,' Hettie says, smiling, hoping that the offer of gin will coax me out.

'I'm not in the mood.' I want to crawl into bed and wallow with old films and chocolate and then vent my energy into a good workout tomorrow. Wow, never did I think I would be the type of person who wanted to exercise through her problems. I've changed!

'Oh, come on. We can drown your sorrows,' Hettie says playfully. With the amount of sorrow drowning I inevitably do I should really buy shares in Winters Gin.

'Go on, love. If Ben shows up, I will tell him where you are.'

Hettie pulls out the puppy dog eyes and pouts her bottom lip. 'Please come.'

'Oh all right.' I sigh, getting up from the table and grabbing my coat. A night with my friends can't hurt, I guess. I give Lilly a kiss on the cheek and set out on the brisk evening walk towards Safiyah's.

It's dark already, just the glow of the street lamps casting little pools of light as we walk towards Winters Farm. I draw in the chilly air which fills my lungs with a crisp cold freshness and pulls me from my lethargic melancholy like a slap in the face. My feet crunch across the leaves that have fallen.

'How come you didn't mention you had seen Ben?' I finally ask. I find it so strange she didn't tell me.

'He didn't say much, there wasn't much to tell.'

We make it to the high street, and I can see my little shop on the other side of the road, a pretty wedding gown display glistening in the window. A swell of pride bubbles within like a tonic warming my insides, making me realise that my life isn't all in tatters. I still have some remnants of a happy place so not all is lost. At the end of the road the marquee is still up.

'Why are there lights on in the tent?'

'Safiyah said to meet her in there, might as well use it while it's up,' Hettie says as we get nearer. 'I'll run and grab a couple of blankets for us in case it's cold in there. I'll only be five mins.'

'I'll come with you.'

'No, I won't be long and Fiya's waiting for us. Just let her know where I've gone.' Hettie scuttles off, leaving me alone. I head towards the marquee, the large door is open, and I can see fairy lights twinkling around the room. I could have sworn they were taken down earlier. Wow, Safiyah really has made an effort to make it look atmospheric.

'Safiyah!' I call as I look around the large empty tent. My voice echoes, there is only a table with two chairs in the whole marquee, and a red blanket sat folded on the back of one of the chairs. Hettie didn't need to go and get one after all although we might need another chair. The table is lit with candles. Quite romantic for the three of us. Where is everyone? I walk towards the table only now noticing little rose petals scattered on the floor guiding my way. My heart beats faster. I approach the table and see a familiar piece of chocolate cake sat on the table with two spoons. Suddenly it all makes sense. Hettie disappearing off like that, Safiyah nowhere to be seen. I spin around and my heart explodes with joy. Ben's here, standing in the doorway, doing that brooding thing again that I find so annoyingly sexy.

'Hi.' I've never been so happy to see his face.

'Hi,' he replies quietly. He looks so handsome in jeans and a grey knitted jumper.

'You did all this?'

'I had a little help.'

So Safiyah and Hettie were in on it then. Hettie the distraction while Safiyah helped set it all up.

'Look, I need to explain. I get that what you saw was bad and I'm really sorry, but I didn't kiss him back. It was all just a shock and happened so quickly and–'

'I know,' he says, stopping me before I can go off on a tangent. He walks towards me. 'I had a visitor today.'

'Who?'

'Philip.'

'What!' Shit, what did he say? 'Where? Why? Because if he said he and I are getting back together then he's lying, we are categorically not.' I'm defensive and sound a little manic which is probably doing nothing to help the plausibility of my side of things.

'He didn't say that.' I'm so confused, what did he say then? 'He didn't need to tell me, I had already figured it out but still, he said that I shouldn't make the same mistake he did and let you walk out of his life. He admitted it was all him, hoping to win you back but that it didn't work.'

'Oh... wow.' I'm stunned he did that for me. Perhaps the Philip that I first met is still in there somewhere. There is hope for him yet. Just not with me.

'I should have let you explain. I'm sorry I walked away from you. I saw you both together and I thought you were going back to him. I thought it was over. Punishment for not being honest with you about who Zoe was. As soon as I got up this morning, I knew I should have let you explain, fought for you at least, made my feelings clear. You listened to me, I should have done the same. I went to yours to talk, but no one was in. I got back home, and Philip was waiting for me on the doorstep, he'd asked a few locals where I lived. After that I went looking for you in the village to tell you, but Hettie said you had left so I asked for a bit of help.'

'What did you want to tell me?'

'How I feel.' He steps closer, he's only inches away from my face. His comforting scent sweeping my nose, his warm breath brushing my face.

'Which is?' I say breathlessly, desperately hoping it's the words I want to hear.

'That I'm hopelessly and completely in love with you, Violet Brown,' he says, pulling me into the warmth of his body.

'You are?' He loves me, he bloody loves me.

'From the moment you threw cake all over me, I haven't been able to stop thinking about you. You have turned my life on its head in the most wonderful way. Last night, thinking I had lost you made me realise that I don't want to spend another night without you.'

I can't wait any longer. My lips find his.

'I love you too, Ben Matthews.'

47

I'm in the kitchen at Vintage Violets, making a quick brew between appointments. I've sent Lola, my shop apprentice, across the road to pick us up a little cake each that we can scoff between customers. The shop door pings, she's back already.

'That was quick–' I stop still though because it isn't who I was expecting to see. In the middle of my shop, in an oversized faux fur lavender coat and large dark sunglasses is Anna Pemberton, as if she's just stepped out of a Hollywood film set with a dark mane of perfectly blow-dried hair framing her immaculate (slightly botoxed) face. From her stationary position, she's scanning the shop with a look of pleasant appreciation.

'Anna.' I never expected to see Anna again, let alone here – in Vintage Violets.

'I was in the area so thought I would pop in and see the place. Imogen's told me all about it,' Anna says, taking off her sunglasses and revealing her bright sparkling blue eyes. 'I hear you're doing very well.'

'Yes, it's really taken off.' I must look pretty gormless stood here with my mouth wide open, but I'm stunned. What is Anna

307

doing here? When I last saw her, my life was an utter shamble of a mess. That seems like a lifetime ago. Anna walks over to a dress that's hung on a mannequin near the window, she lifts the Vintage Violets label and reads it.

'One of your own designs?' She sounds impressed.

'Yes.'

'It's beautiful.' Anna turns to me like a proud mother, her eyes full of intrigue. 'Not that I'm surprised by any of this,' she says, opening her arms, gesturing to the entire shop before her. 'I always knew you had it in you.' A smile escapes her lips, but it is quickly replaced with a more solemn gaze. 'I owe you an apology. I should have fired Francesca that day not you. I'm sorry about what she did to you.'

'It's okay, I always understood why you had to let me go. I hardly acted in the most dignified way, hitting her like that and it worked out for the best. I was just so sorry that I let you down.'

Anna looks around at the shop again. 'Oh, Violet, you have not let me down. You will be pleased to know that Francesca no longer works for me.'

'Really?' What happened there, I wonder?

'She tried to convince me that she had only got with Philip after you left. Shoulder to cry on turning into something more but I never really trusted her after that, couldn't prove anything of course. After Philip dumped her, she got her claws into another poor unsuspecting soul, the fiancé of one of my very important clients who we make a lot of red-carpet gowns for. She soon handed her notice in once she realised I knew.' That woman! Can she not find a single man to grasp hold of? 'I'm promoting Imogen.'

'That's wonderful, she most certainly won't disappoint you.' I'm so delighted for Imogen, she really deserves it. She's always been the slightly unsung hero of the boutique.

'That's all I really wanted to say.'

'Thank you for coming, Anna. You taught me so much. I don't think this would be half the success it has become without the time I spent working for you.'

Anna smiles as she takes one last look around. 'If you want to send me any of your dress designs for us to stock, I would be more than happy to have them.'

'Thank you.'

OH. MY. GOD – Anna wants my dresses… *my dresses*!

'I will keep a look out for the Vintage Violets by Violet Brown name in the bridal world. I'm sure it will go far, unless it's soon to be a different surname,' she says, pointing to the sparkler on my ring finger. That woman does not miss a beat.

'Soon to be Violet Matthews actually,' I gush.

'I'll be excited to see what you design for yourself.'

'I'll make sure you get an invite.' This seems to be acceptable to Anna because she smiles, nodding.

'Goodbye, Violet.' And with that, Anna Pemberton sweeps out of the shop. I stand there for a moment, stunned. Did that really just happen? The door pings again, and Lola walks in chatting away to Hettie and Safiyah. Normal order is restored.

'I know we're early but I'm too excited,' Safiyah says, jumping up and down. 'Can I see it, please?'

With her wedding just three months away, she's like an excitable puppy. Safiyah has come for her first fitting since the dress was finalised and is yet to see the finished product.

'It's hung up in the changing room,' I say nervously. I hope she loves it as much as I do. 'Lola, do you want to help Fiya get into it.' Safiyah and Lola bounce off to the changing rooms, both as giddy as each other.

'Right, you, sit down,' I say, steering Hettie towards the sofa. 'Can I get you anything?' I know I'm fussing but I want to. 'A pillow or a drink?'

'God, anyone would think I was ill not pregnant,' Hettie huffs as she awkwardly sits herself down with her humongous bump.

'You only have two weeks left, I'm concerned your waters might break over my lovely floor,' I say with a laugh. 'There's a mop bucket on standby.'

'Charming.' Hettie smiles and lovingly strokes her bump.

My phone beeps with a message from Ben. *See you at home. I'll cook, chocolate cake for pudding xx* Ah, life is good.

If someone was to ask me where my happy place is, the answer would be easy. It's where my little shop of happiness is. It's where all my loved ones are, where my heart is – it's home in Elmsbourne-Hollow. That's my happy place.

ACKNOWLEDGMENTS

I'm so excited to be writing an acknowledgments page, I never thought I would get the chance to write one. Someone has chosen to publish my book - crack open the wine, sound the klaxons... it's so exciting. A dream come true for me. There are so many wonderful people who I want to say thank you to, so here it goes...

Firstly, to Betsy Reavley for taking a chance on me and giving me this opportunity. I will be forever grateful to you for letting me be a part of the Bloodhound gang. A huge thank you to my lovely editors, Morgen Bailey and Heather Fitt who have answered all my questions, worked so hard on my manuscript and helped make this whole experience a joy.

To my very patient and loving husband Matthew. When I told you I wanted to pursue my writing, you didn't laugh or tell me I was crazy, you simply handed me a computer and told me to write and for that I will be forever grateful. You are my biggest support and I love you and our boys so very much. Noah and Seth, I wanted to show you both that if you have an ambition in life, you should never give up on it. I hope I have made you proud and you know how much I love you both.

To my mum Helen, and sister Alexandria. You are my biggest cheerleaders. Your faith in me has never faltered and I appreciate that more than you know. You are both strong, wonderful woman who have encouraged me every step of the way, I couldn't ask for better role models. Thank you.

Dad, I so wish you were here to see this. You may not be with me anymore but I hope where ever you are, you're proud. I love you.

To my three gin drinking besties Julia, Feebee and Stacy. Thank you for the laughs, love and cocktail fuelled nights.

To my Lennie family, thank you for the love and giggles in our family chat.

Whilst this book went through the editing phase, we were hit with a pandemic, the world stopped. Covid 19 impacted us all, my family included. We lost my brother-in-law to the virus. Because of this, he has become such a huge part of the book for me, it didn't feel right to let the acknowledgments pass without including him in it.

Alex Lennie, you are loved. You are missed. xx

Finally, to anyone who has taken the time to read this book, thank you from the bottom of my heart and I hope where ever you are reading this, you're in your happy place.

Much love

Ruth xxx

Printed in Great Britain
by Amazon